"I'm still the same man you fell in love with."

She looked into his eyes. "I don't think so."

"Like hell." He dragged her to him with one arm around her waist. His mouth dropped to hers in a demanding kiss that stole her breath. She could feel the thunder of his heart against hers. Wrapped in his strong arms, she lost herself in the kiss. She felt the passion, the chemistry that had always made her pulse pound. The kiss fired that old aching need for this man she couldn't have.

It swept her up, made her forget for a moment the gulf that lay between them. He drew her closer, pressing his body to hers, deepening the kiss. With desire burning through her, all she wanted was for him to sweep her up in his arms and carry her upstairs to her bed.

B.J. DANIELS

UNFORGIVEN

entertain, enrich, inspire™

Recycling programs
for this product may
not exist in your area.

ISBN-13: 978-0-373-77673-3

UNFORGIVEN

Copyright © 2012 by Barbara Heinlein

www.Harlequin.com

Printed in U.S.A.

I had only sold four books
when my former newspaper managing editor
convinced me to quit a job I loved to follow my
dream. That day, I promised to dedicate
my first single-title book to him.
So this book is for you, Bill Wilke.
Neither of us could know back then
what a huge favor you did for me.

UNFORGIVEN

CHAPTER ONE

THE WIND HOWLED DOWN the Crazy Mountains, rocking the pickup as Sheriff Frank Curry pulled to the side of the narrow dirt road. He hadn't been to this desolate spot in years. Like a lot of other residents of Beartooth, he avoided coming this way.

The afternoon sun slanted down through the dense pines, casting a long shadow over the barrow pit and the small cross nearly hidden among the weeds. The cross, though weathered from eleven years of harsh Montana weather, stood unyielding against the merciless wind that whipped the summer-dried weeds around it.

After a moment, Frank climbed out of the truck, fighting the gusts as he waded into the ditch. Someone had erected the wooden cross, though no one knew who. Back then the cross had been white. Years of blistering hot summers and fierce, long snow-laden winters had peeled away the paint, leaving the wood withered and gray.

The brisk fall wind kicked up a dust devil in the road. Frank shut his eyes as it whirled past him, pelting him with dirt. The image he'd spent years trying to banish flashed before him. He saw it again, the young woman's broken body lying in the barrow pit where it had been discarded like so much garbage.

The lonesome moan of the wind in the tops of the

thick wall of pines was the only sound on this remote rural road. That night, standing here as the coroner loaded the body, he'd sworn he would find Ginny West's killer if it was the last thing he ever did.

Now, he looked again at the cross that marked this lonely place where Ginny had died. The wind had plastered a dirty plastic grocery bag against its base.

Feeling the crippling weight of that vow and his failure, Frank crouched down and jerked the bag free. As he rose to leave, he heard the sound of a motor and looked up to see a small plane fly over.

RYLAN WEST LAY DAZED in the dirt. He'd lost his hat, gotten the air knocked clean out of him and was about to be trampled by a horse if he didn't move—and quickly.

To add insult to injury, as he lay on the ground staring up at all that blue sky, he saw Destry Grant's red-and-white Cessna 182 fly over. He didn't have to see the woman behind the controls to know it was *her* plane. Hell, he could call up Destry Grant's face from memory with no trouble at all and did so with frustrating regularity even though he hadn't laid eyes on her in more than ten years.

In the past few weeks that he'd been home, he'd made a point of staying out of Destry's way. He told himself he wasn't ready to see her. But a part of him knew that was pure bull. He felt guilty and he should have. The last time they'd seen each other, he'd made her a promise he hadn't kept.

Not that anyone could blame him under the circumstances. Eleven years ago he'd left Beartooth, Montana, joined the rodeo and hadn't looked back. That is, until a few weeks ago when he'd grown tired of being on the road, riding one rodeo after another until they'd become a blur of all-night drives across country.

He had awakened one morning and realized there was only one place he wanted to be. Home. He'd loaded up his horse and saddle, hooked on to his horse trailer and headed for Montana. He'd yearned for familiar country, for the scent of pine coming off the fresh snow on top of the Crazy Mountains, for his family. And maybe for Destry, as foolish as that was.

He swore now as he listened to the plane circle the W Bar G, hating that Destry was so close and yet as beyond his reach as if she were on the moon. That hadn't been the case when they were kids, he thought with a groan. Back then he couldn't have been happier about the two of them growing up on neighboring ranches. They'd been best friends until they were seventeen and then they'd been a whole lot more.

"What the hell is wrong with you?"

Rylan blinked as he looked over on the corral fence to see his younger brother Jarrett glaring down at him. To his relief, he noticed that Jarrett had hold of the unbroken stallion's halter rope. The horse was snorting and stomping, kicking up dust, angry as an old wet hen. His brother looked just as mad.

"Nothin's wrong with me," Rylan said with a groan as he got to his feet. At least physically, that was.

"If Dad finds out that you tried to ride that horse…" Jarrett shook his head and glanced toward the sky and Destry's plane. His brother let out a curse as if everything was now suddenly crystal clear.

Rylan grabbed the reins from his brother, hoping Jarrett had the good sense not to say anything about him trying to ride one of the wild horses their father had

brought home from the Wyoming auction—or about
Destry. If he and Jarrett had that particular discussion,
more than likely one or both of them would end up
with a black eye.

He knew how his family felt about the Grants. Hell,
he felt the same way. Even after all these years, just
thinking about what had happened still hurt too badly.
Just as thinking about Destry did. But as hard as he tried
to put her out of his mind, he couldn't do it.

"I just heard the news. It's all over town," his brother
said as her plane disappeared from view.

DESTRY GRANT BANKED the small plane along the east
edge of the towering snow-capped Crazy Mountains
and then leveled it out to fly low over the ranch.

It never failed to amaze her that everything from
the mountains to the Yellowstone River was W Bar G
Ranch. Say what you want about Waylon "WT" Grant—
and God knew people did, she thought—but her father
had built this ranch from nothing into what it was today.

She'd spent the past few days in Denver at a cattle-
man's association conference and was now anxious to
get home. She was never truly comfortable until she
felt Montana soil beneath her boots.

The ranch spread below her, a quilt of fall colors.
Thousands of Black Angus cattle dotted the pastures
now dried to the color of buckskin. Hay fields lay
strewn with large golden bales stretching as far as the
eye could see. At the edge of it all, the emerald green
of the Yellowstone River wound its way through cottonwoods with leaves burnished copper in the late October air.

Destry took in the country as if breathing in pure

oxygen—until she spotted the barns and corrals of the West Ranch in the distance. But not even the thought of Rylan West could spoil this beautiful day.

The big sky was wind-scoured pale blue with wisps of clouds coming off the jagged peaks of the Crazies, as the locals called the mountain range. Behind the rugged peaks, a dark bank of clouds boiled up with the promise of a storm before the day was over.

Just past a creek tangled with dogwood, chokecherry and willows, the huge, rambling Grant ranch house came into view. Her father had built it on the top of a hill so he'd have a three-hundred-and-sixty-degree view of his land. Like the ranch, the house was large, sprawling and had cost a small fortune. WT scoffed at the ridicule the place had generated among the locals.

"What did WT think was going to happen?" one rancher had joked before he'd noticed Destry coming into the Branding Iron Café for a cup of coffee last spring. "You build on top of a knob without a windbreak, and every storm that comes in is going to nail you good."

She hadn't been surprised that word had spread about what happened up at WT's big house in January. During one of the worst storms last winter, several of the doors in the new house had blown open, piling snowdrifts in the house.

Even early settlers had known better than to build on a hilltop. They always set their houses down in a hollow and planted trees to form a windbreak to protect the house from Montana's unforgiving weather.

That was another reason she'd opted to stay in the hundred-year-old homestead house down the road from WT's "folly," as it'd become known.

She was about to buzz the house to let her father know she was back, when she spotted something odd. An open gate wouldn't have normally caught her attention. But this one wasn't used anymore. Which made it strange that the barbed-wire-and-post gate lay on the ground, and there were fresh tire tracks that led to the grove of dense trees directly behind the homestead house where she lived alone.

She frowned as she headed for the ranch airstrip, wondering why anyone would have reason to drive back there. As she prepared to land, she spotted a bright red sports car heading toward the ranch in the direction of WT's folly. In this part of the state, most everyone drove a truck. Or at least a four-wheel-drive SUV. The person driving the sports car had to be lost.

AFTER LEAVING THE PLANE at the hangar, Destry drove straight up to the main house in the ranch pickup. She pulled in as the dust was settling around the red sports car she'd seen from the air. As the driver shut off his engine, she saw her father roll his wheelchair down the ramp toward them.

WT had been a handsome, physically imposing man before his accident. Not even the wheelchair could diminish his formidable strength of will, even though he was now grayer and thinner. The accident hadn't improved his disposition, either, not that it had been all that great before the plane crash.

WT was a complicated man. That was the nice way people in the county explained her father. The rest didn't mince words. Nettie Benton at the Beartooth General Store called him the meanest man in Sweetgrass County.

Right now, though, WT looked more anxious than Destry had ever seen him. As he wheeled toward the car, Destry shifted her gaze to the man who had climbed out. For a moment she didn't recognize her own brother.

"Carson?" For eleven years, she'd wondered if she would ever see her big brother again. She ran to him, throwing herself into his arms. He chuckled as he hugged her tightly, then held her at arm's length to look at her.

"Wow, little sis, have you grown up," he said, making her laugh. She'd been seventeen when he'd left, newly graduated from high school and on her way to college that coming fall. She hated to think how young she'd been in so many ways. Or how much that tragic year was to change their lives. Seeing Carson on the ranch again brought it all back with sharp, breath-stealing pain for everything they'd lost.

Carson had filled out from the twenty-year-old college boy he'd been. His hair was still a lighter chestnut from her own. They both had gotten their hair color from their mother, she'd heard, although she'd never seen as much as a snapshot of Lila Gray Grant. Unable to bear looking at photographs of Lila, her father had destroyed them all after his wife's death.

Her brother's eyes were their father's clear blue, while her own were more faded like worn denim. It had always annoyed her that her brother had been spared the sprinkling of freckles that were scattered across her cheeks and nose. He used to tease her about them. She wondered if he remembered.

Around his blue eyes was a network of small wrinkles that hadn't been there eleven years ago and a sadness in his gaze she didn't recall. Like their father, he was strikingly handsome and always had been. But now he was tanned, muscled and looked like a man who'd been on a long vacation.

"What are you doing here? I mean—" She heard the crunch of her father's wheelchair tires on the concrete beside her and saw Carson brace himself to face their father. Some things hadn't changed.

"Carson," WT said and extended his hand.

Her brother gave a slight nod, his face expressionless as he reached down to shake his father's hand. WT pulled him closer and awkwardly put an arm around the son he hadn't seen in years.

For the first time in her life, Destry saw tears in their father's eyes. He hadn't cried at her mother's funeral, at least that's what she'd heard through the county grapevine.

"It's good to have you home, Carson," their father said, his voice hoarse with emotion.

Carson said nothing as his gaze shifted to Destry. In that instant, she saw that his coming back to Montana hadn't been voluntary.

Her heart dropped at what she saw in her brother's face. Fear.

CHAPTER TWO

CARSON COULDN'T TAKE his eyes off his sister. When he'd left she'd been a tomboy, wild as the country WT couldn't keep her out of. Eleven years later, she'd turned into a beautiful woman. Her long hair, plaited to hang over one shoulder, was now the color of rust-red fall leaves, her eyes a paler blue than his own. A sprinkling of freckles graced her cheeks and nose. Even after all these years she never tried to conceal them with makeup.

He smiled. "You have no idea how much I've missed you." Or how badly he felt about the pain he'd caused her. "Little sis," he said, pulling her into his arms again.

She hugged him tightly, making him wonder what their father had told her about his return. Given her surprised reaction, he'd guess the old man hadn't told her anything.

"Why are we standing out here? Let's go inside," WT demanded impatiently. "Don't worry about your luggage. I'll have one of the ranch hands unload it for you. You haven't even seen the house yet."

Carson released Destry and glanced behind him at the looming structure. How could he miss it? He'd seen the massive house perched like a huge boulder on the hill from way down the road. He didn't need to ask why his father had built such a house. Apparently WT still hadn't shed that chip on his shoulder after growing up poor in the old homestead house down the mountain. Back then, the house and a few acres of chicken-scratch earth were all he'd had.

But WT had changed that after inheriting the place when he was only a teen. He'd worked hard and had done well by the time he'd married. Carson had never known poverty, nothing even close to it.

But WT couldn't seem to shake off the dust of his earlier life. He just kept buying, building, yearning for more. The manor on the mountain, planes, a private airstrip, and he'd even mentioned that he'd built a swimming pool behind the house. A swimming pool in this part of Montana so close to the mountains? How impractical was that?

As his son, Carson had certainly benefited from his father's hard work. But it came at a price, one he'd grown damned tired of paying.

"Wait a minute, WT," he said as his father began to wheel himself back toward the house. He hadn't called him Dad since the fourth grade. "There's someone I want you to meet."

DESTRY WATCHED THE passenger side of the sports car open and one long slim leg slide out.

She hadn't noticed anyone else in the car, not with the sun glinting off the windshield, and neither she nor her father had apparently considered that Carson might bring someone home with him. That now seemed shortsighted. Carson was thirty-one. It was conceivable he'd have a girlfriend or possibly even a wife.

Destry glanced at her father and saw his surprised

expression. She cringed. WT hated surprises—and Carson had to know that.

"I want you to meet Cherry," her brother said, going to the car to help the woman out.

Destry felt her mouth drop open. Cherry was tall, almost as tall as Carson who stood six-two. She was a bleached blonde with a dark tan, slim with large breasts.

Cherry gave WT a hundred-watt smile with her perfectly capped ultrawhite teeth, which were almost a distraction from the skimpy dress she wore.

Carson was looking at their father expectantly, as if awaiting his reaction. There was a hard glint in her brother's eyes. He had to know what WT's reaction was going to be. It was almost as if he was daring their father to say something about the woman he'd brought home.

Beside her, their father let out an oath under his breath. Destry didn't need to see WT's expression to know this wasn't the way he'd envisioned his son's homecoming.

Cherry stepped over to WT's wheelchair and put out her hand.

He gave her a limp handshake and looked to Carson. "I think it would be best if your…friend stayed in a motel in Big Timber." Big Timber was the closest town of any size and twenty miles away. "Of course I'll pick up the tab." Only then did he turn his gaze to Cherry again. "I thought Carson would have told you. We have business to discuss. You'd be bored to tears way out here on the ranch."

"WT," Carson said in the awkward silence that followed, "Cherry is my *fiancée*."

"Destry, show Cherry the swimming pool," her father ordered. "Carson and I need to talk. In *private*."

WT ROLLED HIMSELF INTO his den and straight to the bar. His son had brought home a Vegas showgirl and thought he was going to marry her? Over his dead body. As he shakily poured himself a drink, he realized that might be a possibility if he didn't calm down.

"I'll take one of those," Carson said as he came into the room behind him. "I have the feeling I'm going to need it."

Unable to look at his son right now, he downed his drink, then poured them both one. His hands were shaking, his heart jackhammering in his chest.

"Close the door," he ordered and listened until he heard the door shut. "You aren't going to marry that woman," he stated between gritted teeth as he turned his wheelchair around to face his son.

Carson took the drink WT held out to him and leaned against the long built-in bar. His son had grown into a fine-looking man. WT felt a surge of pride. Until he noticed the way his son was dressed. Loafers, a polo shirt and chinos, for God's sake. Who the hell did he think he was? He was the son of a *rancher*.

WT hated to think what that sports car parked out front had cost or about how much money he'd spent keeping Carson away from Beartooth.

"You aren't going to marry that woman," he repeated.

Carson met his gaze and held it with a challenge that surprised WT. With an inward shudder, he realized this wasn't the son he'd sent away more than a decade ago. That scared twenty-year-old boy had just been grateful to get out of town alive.

"I'm in love with Cherry," Carson said, as if daring him to argue the point.

WT shook his head. "Doesn't matter. It's not happening. And I don't want to talk about that right now," he said with a wave of his hand. "We need to talk about the W Bar G. You're my son. This is where you belong. When I'm gone, I want to know you're here, keeping the ranch and the Grant name alive."

"I think I have more pressing matters to concern myself with right now, don't you?"

WT fought to control his temper. "You let me worry about the sheriff and that other matter."

"That other matter?" Carson demanded. "Is that what you call Ginny West's murder?"

WT refused to get into the past with his son. He'd looked forward to this day from the moment Carson was born. No one was going to take that away from him.

"As I was saying," WT continued, "I'm not going to turn the W Bar G over to you until I know you can handle running it. You're going to have to learn the ranching business."

Carson took a long gulp of his drink and pushed himself off the edge of the bar to walk around the room. WT tried to still the anger roiling inside him. He knew Carson was upset about being summoned home. Just as he'd been upset about being sent away eleven years ago.

He watched his son take in the den he'd had built so it looked out over the ranch with a view that ran from the mountains to the river. WT joined him at the bank of windows.

The valley was aglow with golden afternoon light. WT loved the way his land swept down from the base of the mountains in a pale swatch of rich pasture, hay and alfalfa fields to the river. Much of the land had dried to the color of corn silk. It was broken only by rocky outcroppings, hilly slopes of pine and the rust hues of the foliage along the creeks that snaked through the property.

It was an awe-inspiring sight that he feared was wasted on his son.

Carson finally spoke. "Even if everything turns out the way you think it will, I don't understand why I have to learn the business. Destry's doing a great job running the ranch, isn't she?"

"She has only been filling in until you returned."

"Does she know that?" his son asked, his tone rimmed with sarcasm.

WT took a swallow of his drink, giving himself time to rope in his anger. "I want *you* to run the ranch."

"What about my sister? She isn't some horse you can put out to pasture."

WT let out a curse. "She needs to find a man and get married before it's too late for her."

He thought of the times she'd come home from a branding or calving filthy dirty as if she thought she was one of the ranch hands.

"It's unseemly for a woman to be working with ranch hands," he said, repeating what he'd told Destry more times than he cared to recall. Like her mother had been, she wasn't one to take advice. Especially from him. "She needs to start acting respectable."

"Maybe you haven't heard, but women can vote now."

"Biggest mistake this country ever made," he said, only half joking. He thought of Lila and the trouble he'd had with her. Women were too headstrong and independent. He still believed a woman's place was in the home and said as much to his son.

Carson didn't seem to be listening. He stood staring down into his drink. WT wondered what he hoped to find there. Carson had always been moody as a boy. His mother's doing when he was young, WT thought with a curse. Why couldn't Carson have been more like Destry?

That thought made his stomach churn. People said Destry was too much like him. They had no idea.

When Carson looked up at him again, his expression was both angry and guilty. "You take this ranch away from my sister and you'll kill her. Hasn't she lost enough because of me?"

"You talking about that no-count rodeo cowboy Rylan West?"

"She loved him and would have married him if—"

"She's not marrying him any more than you're marrying that whor—"

"Careful, that's my fiancée."

WT looked at him hard, then laughed. "You're not fooling me with this halfhearted protest about not wanting to take the ranch away from your sister any more than you are with this ridiculous engagement. You have no intention of marrying that woman."

"Don't I?"

"Well, let me put it to you this way. You marry that woman and I'll leave this whole place and every dime I have to some goddamned charity."

Carson cocked his head at him and smiled. "Now who's bluffing?"

WT smiled back. "The difference is I can *afford* to call your bluff. I suspect *you* don't have that luxury." He narrowed his gaze, feeling his ire rise even higher. "You have no choice if you want my help with the sheriff. You'll stay here and take over the ranch. Or you can go it alone without another dime from me. There is no third option and, from what I've heard, you might be in need of a damned good lawyer soon. I hope I've made myself clear," he said as his cook and housekeeper, Margaret, rang the dinner bell.

"Perfectly," Carson said and drained his glass.

NETTIE BENTON AT THE Beartooth General Store was the first person to see Carson Grant driving by in that fancy red sports car.

It wasn't blind luck that she'd been standing at the front window of the store when Carson drove past. The once natural redhead, now dyed Sunset Sienna to cover the gray, spent most of her days watching the world pass by her window at a snail's pace. It was why, as the storeowner, she often knew more of what was going on than anyone else in these parts.

"Bob," she called to her husband. No answer. "Must have already gone home," she muttered to herself. The two of them lived behind the store on the side of the mountain. Bob didn't spend much time in the store his parents had turned over to them when they'd gotten married thirty years ago. He didn't have to.

"Nettie loves minding the store—and everyone's business," he was fond of saying.

Nettie hurriedly grabbed the phone and began calling everyone she knew to tell them about Carson Grant.

"Nettie?" Bob called from the office in the back. "What's all the commotion out there?"

Not only was Bob getting hard of hearing—at least hard of hearing her—he wouldn't appreciate her news.

Though he might have enjoyed seeing the bleached blonde with Carson.

"It's Carson Grant," she said as she stepped to the office doorway.

Bob didn't look up from the bills he'd been sorting through. "What about him?" he asked distractedly.

"He's back in Beartooth."

Her husband's head jerked up in surprise. *"What?"*

"I saw him drive past not thirty minutes ago." She'd recognized Carson right off, even though it had been years since she'd laid eyes on him.

"Why would he come back *now?*" Bob asked, clearly upset. But then most of the county would be upset, as well.

"I would imagine it has something to do with the rumor circulating about new evidence in Ginny West's murder."

"What new evidence?"

"I heard it was some kind of fancy hair clip one of the kids found over at the old theater. Now they're speculating that she might have actually been killed there and not out on the road." She frowned. "Are you all right?"

Bob was holding his stomach as if something he ate hadn't agreed with him. "You give me indigestion," he said angrily as he shoved the bills away and pushed himself to his feet. "I wouldn't be surprised if you weren't making all of this up."

"It was Carson Grant, sure as I'm standing here."

"What I want to know is why he wasn't arrested years ago?" Bob demanded. "Everyone knows he killed that poor girl. If your sheriff can't figure that out, then there's something wrong with him."

Her sheriff? "Well, I, for one, am not convinced Carson did it," she said as he pushed past her and headed for the back door and home.

"The fact that you're the only one who believes that should tell you something, Nettie." He didn't give her a chance to respond as he slammed out the back door.

Surprised, since that was the most passion she'd seen in her husband in years, maybe ever, she wandered back to the front store window to entertain herself until she was forced to wait on a customer, should one come by.

The narrow two-lane paved road was empty—just as it was most days. The town of Beartooth was like a lot of small Montana towns. It had died down to a smattering of families and businesses. Not that it hadn't been something in its heyday. With the discovery of gold in the Crazy Mountains back in the late 1800s, Beartooth had been a boomtown. Early residents had built substantial stone and log buildings in the shadow of the mountains where Big Timber Creek wound through the pines.

By the early 1900s, though, the gold was playing out and a drought had people leaving in droves. They left behind a dozen empty boarded-up buildings that still stood today. There was an old gas station with two pumps under a leaning tin roof at one end of town and a classic auto garage from a time when it didn't take a computer to work on a car engine at the other.

In between stood the Range Rider bar, the post office, hotel and theater. There'd been talk of tearing down the old buildings to keep kids out of them. Nettie was glad they hadn't. She thought fondly of the hidden room under the stage at the Royale theater where she'd lost her virginity. Unfortunately, that made her think of the sheriff, something she did her best not to do. *Her* sheriff, indeed.

Directly across the street from Nettie's store was the Branding Iron Café where ranchers gathered each morning. Right now a handful of pickups were parked out front—and another half dozen down the street in front of the bar.

Nettie knew the topic of conversation among the ranchers must have Carson Grant's ears burning. She wondered if the West family had heard yet and how long it would be before one of them either ran Carson out of town again—or strung him up for Ginny West's murder.

But it was her husband's reaction that had her scratching her head.

"WHERE'S YOUR SISTER?" WT asked Carson as he looked up from his meal and apparently realized for the first time that Destry wasn't at the table.

"She got a call that some cattle had gotten out and were on the road," Carson said.

His father grunted in answer, the sound echoing in the huge dining hall. Carson idly wondered how often this dining room was ever used. Not much, he'd bet, since everything looked brand-new, and it wasn't as if WT had friends or family over. He'd never been good at making or keeping friends.

"Why didn't she call one of the ranch hands to take care of it? Or our ranch foreman? This is what I pay Russell to do," WT said irritably after a few bites.

Carson tamped down his own irritation. "I would imagine she didn't want to bother them in the middle of their dinners, especially when she's probably more than capable of taking care of it herself." Knowing his sister, that would be exactly her reasoning.

"You see what I mean about your sister?" WT asked with a curse. "She doesn't know her place."

"*This* is her place," Carson said defiantly in the hopes that an argument would end this meal faster. It couldn't end soon enough for him.

WT continued to eat, refusing to rise to the bait. He hadn't even acknowledged Cherry's presence since she'd sat down. Did he really think that by ignoring her she would leave? Under other circumstances, Carson might have found all of this amusing.

He'd done his best to convince his father to give him enough money so he could leave the country. Coming back here only reminded him of everything he'd spent eleven years trying to forget.

But WT had been adamant. There would be no money, not even any inheritance, if he didn't return.

"What about the sheriff?" he'd asked.

"He has a few questions, that's all."

A few questions about Ginny's murder after all these years?

Clearly WT didn't realize how dangerous it was for him being back here, he thought, recalling the look on Nettie Benton's face when he'd driven by her store earlier today. There had been no reason to try to sneak back here. In a community this small, there were few secrets.

This was Montana where there was still a large portion of the rural population that believed in taking the law into their own hands—just as they had in the old days. That could mean a rope and a stout tree.

He mentioned that now to his father.

"I told you not to worry about any of that," WT said without looking up.

"Don't worry about it? Do I have to remind you that

the last time I saw Rylan West he swore he'd kill me if he ever saw me again?"

His father finally looked up from his plate, his expression one of mild amusement. "I guess you'd better not let him see you then."

DESTRY FOUND THREE W Bar G cows standing in the middle of the county road, just as a neighboring rancher had described over the phone. She slowed the truck, all three cows glancing at her but not moving. They mooed loudly, though, associating the sound of a truck with the delivery of hay.

"You girls are out of luck," Destry said as she began to herd them with the pickup back up the road toward W Bar G property. She regretted missing her brother's first dinner at home, but hoped he would understand. He and his fiancée needed time alone with WT so they could work out whatever was going on. Her being there would have only made things more strained, she told herself.

As it was, her conversation with Cherry by the pool earlier had left her even more concerned about her brother. Apparently the two had met at the Las Vegas casino where they both worked, Cherry as a dancer and Carson in the office.

Destry couldn't imagine her brother living in Vegas, let alone working in a casino; neither could she see him settling down on the ranch. But then again, she didn't know him anymore.

She wondered how much Carson had told his fiancée about what had happened eleven years ago. Did Cherry know about Ginny's murder? Or that Carson was still the number one suspect?

She lowered her pickup window to feel the air, driving slowly as she moved the cattle at a lazy pace down the road. They were in no hurry, and neither was she.

This far north, it wouldn't get dark for hours yet. Even with the possibility of an approaching storm, it was one of those rare warm fall afternoons in Montana. The rolling hills had faded to mustard in contrast to the deep green of the pines climbing the mountains. As always, the Crazy Mountains loomed over the scene, a bank of dark clouds shrouding the peaks.

She loved living out here away from everything. In this part of Montana, you could leave the keys in your pickup overnight, and your truck would still be there in the morning. The rural area's low crime rate was one reason Ginny West's murder had come as such a shock. It rattled everyone's belief that Beartooth was safe because you knew your neighbors. Now, like a rock thrown into Saddlestring Lake, Carson's return would create wide ripples.

Ginny West's murder—and her breakup with Carson right before it—would be rehashed in booths and at tables in the Branding Iron Café and on the bar stools at the Range Rider bar.

There were still plenty of people around who believed Carson had killed her. Rylan West among them, she reminded herself with a sinking heart.

What would he do when he heard that Carson was back?

The cows mooed loudly as she brought the pickup to a stop and got out to open the barbed-wire gate. She'd seen a broken fence post where she figured the cows had gotten out. She'd let Russell know. Overhead, a hawk soared on an updraft.

As she waded through the tall golden grass, grass-hoppers buzzed and bobbed around her. She lifted the metal handle to loosen the loop attached to the gate and, slipping the post out, walked the gate back to allow the cows into their pasture.

At the sound of a vehicle on the wind, she looked up the road. Dust churned up in the distance.

"Come on girls," she said to the cows, swatting one on the backside with her hat to finally get them moving. She could hear the growing sound of the vehicle's engine and was thankful she'd managed to get the cows off the road in time. Once she had them inside the fence, she dragged the barbed-wire gate back over to the post.

Destry had just cranked down the lever that kept the gate taut and closed when she heard the truck slow. She turned, squinting in the cloud of dust, as the pickup stopped only feet from her.

When she saw who was behind the wheel, her heart took off at a gallop.

CHAPTER THREE

RYLAN SWORE AS HE SAW Destry standing at the edge of the road. Had he really thought he could come storming out to the ranch and not run into her? One look at her and he'd known he wasn't ready for this.

Destry looked the same and yet completely grown up. Her hair was longer, that same rich russet color that reminded him of fall in Montana. It was plaited down her slim back except for a few strands that the wind lifted around her face under the shade of her straw hat. She wore a yellow-checked Western shirt and jeans, both accenting her more mature, rounded figure.

Her eyes were still that faded blue that often matched Montana's big sky. As he looked into them, he felt that old spark. It burned into him, hotter than a Montana summer day.

One look at her and he realized all the running he'd done the past eleven years had been for nothing. He couldn't escape the way he felt about this woman any more than he could forgive her brother for what he knew he'd done.

His sister's murder was like a line drawn in the dirt. Neither of them could step over it. Destry was convinced her brother was innocent of Ginny's murder. Rylan would never believe that. Nothing had changed.

"Destry," he said through his open window. The

word felt alien on his lips, and he realized how long it had been since he'd uttered it aloud. It brought with it an ache that made him grit his teeth.

DESTRY HAD WATCHED FROZEN to the spot as the pickup came to a dust-boiling stop next to her. The early evening light ricocheted off the windshield, blinding her for a moment before the driver's side window came down.

The shock of coming face-to-face with Rylan after all these years sent a tremor through her. She stared into those familiar brown eyes, seeing the Rylan West she'd fallen in love with as a girl. For a moment, lost in his gaze, she had the overpowering feeling that if he would just get out of that pickup and take her in his arms they could find their way back to each other.

"Destry?" The sound of her name on his lips made her heart pound with the familiarity of it.

She found her voice. "I wondered when I'd see you. I should have known what it would take. I guess I shouldn't be surprised."

He shoved back his Stetson. "I reckon not. I need to see your brother."

She shook her head. Before he'd left town, she'd tried to convince Rylan that her brother couldn't have killed Ginny. "If you just knew him the way I do…"

But his mind had been made up. Just as it was today. She could see it in the clenched muscles of his strong jaw, in the set of his broad shoulders. He'd looked the same way the day of his sister's funeral when he'd gone after Carson, the two of them getting into a fistfight at the cemetery until Rylan's father had broken it up.

"I was hoping…" She couldn't even bear to say the words, her hopes like daggers through her heart. She'd dreamed about the day she would see Rylan again. Her dream crumbled like the dried leaves on the cotton-woods nearby, turning to dust in the wind.

The man she'd known was gone. It was high time she let go of the past. Let go of Rylan West.

RYLAN NEARLY BUCKLED under the pain he saw in her eyes. "Don't make this any harder than it already is."

She sighed, cloaking the hurt with a smile, a smile with an edge to it. Anger fired her blue eyes. It burned hot as a flame. She knew what he planned to do.

For weeks after Ginny's murder, he'd tried to find proof that would put Carson Grant behind bars. What he kept running into was the same thing that had kept Carson free all these years—a lack of evidence.

"I have to get my sister justice since the law isn't going to. As Ginny's oldest brother, I owe her that."

"And you think this is the way?" she said, sounding sad and disappointed in him.

"Stay out of this, please."

"Carson's my *brother*."

"And Ginny was my sister. At least you still have your brother."

"Not if you have your way."

He had no intention of killing Carson—just getting the truth out of him, one way or the other. He snatched off his hat and raked his fingers through his hair in frustration. Now that he and Carson were both back, Rylan intended to see his sister's murderer behind bars. He said as much to Destry.

"He didn't do it, Rylan," she said. "He never left the ranch that night."

"According to his alibi. *You*. But we both know that

was a lie." He fought back the image of her naked in his arms the night they'd made love for the first time at the old abandoned ski lodge high on the mountain. Little did they know what was happening in the valley below them.

Her hands went to her hips, her gaze blazing. "Carson didn't know I'd left the ranch to meet you. It was an honest mistake since you and I were both sneaking around back then."

"I notice that even you didn't bring up Carson's other alibi."

"What would be the point? My brother could have a half dozen alibis and you still wouldn't believe him."

Rylan swore because she was right. "You have to admit his best friend isn't the most reliable alibi, not to mention that Jack French would say the moon was made of cheese if your brother asked him to. Destry, when are you going to stop covering for your brother and see him for what he really is?"

She took a step toward the pickup, her fists balled at her sides. "When are you going to realize that you might be wrong?"

Rylan looked away, his jaw tensing in frustration. "This isn't getting us anywhere." He'd never believe Carson wasn't Ginny's killer, and Destry would defend her brother until hell froze over. "We both know why your brother is back in town. The county attorney threatened to bring Carson back in handcuffs if he didn't return for questioning about the new evidence."

"New evidence? Is that true?"

He saw her surprise. "Your father didn't tell you? I thought you would have heard." But then again, Destry hardly ever left the ranch, from what he'd heard.

"I just assumed WT forced Carson to come back," she said.

Rylan shook his head. "A gold hair clip with my sister's name on it was found under the stage at the Royale. We're pretty sure Ginny was wearing it the last time we saw her."

"So she was at the old theater that night?"

"The sheriff thinks she might have met someone there, probably her killer, then was taken by car to where her body was left." He looked away, fighting the roiling emotions boiling inside him.

"Maybe now the real killer will be found," Destry said.

He hated the hopefulness he heard in her voice. She would be devastated when the truth came out.

"Destry," he said, as kindly as he could, "the county attorney wouldn't have forced your brother to come back here unless the evidence pointed to him."

Her blue eyes narrowed to slits. "If you're so sure this so-called new evidence will prove my brother guilty, then why are you out here ready to take the law into your own hands?"

"Because the *law* in this county is Sheriff Frank Curry. Everyone knows that he does whatever your father tells him to."

Destry shook her head angrily. "Or because you know a hair clip isn't going to prove that my brother had anything to do with her death."

"Not unless someone can place your brother in the old theater that night."

"Don't you think if my brother had been there, someone would have mentioned it by now?" she demanded.

She had always been strong and determined. It was

one of the reasons he'd loved her more than life. If his sister hadn't been murdered that night, he didn't doubt they'd be married now, probably have a couple of kids.

Did Destry ever think about what might have been? She'd made a life for herself on the W Bar G. He'd heard how she had taken over after her father's plane crash. She was born to ranch, that's what people said. They also said how lucky WT was to have such a daughter. Everyone liked Destry and with good reason.

Carson, though, was another story.

"I warned your brother that if I ever saw him again… Destry, I can't live with myself unless I do something. Can't you understand that?" He hated the pleading he heard in his voice. It upset him that it mattered what she thought of him, even after all these years.

Her gaze softened. "I *can* understand. But not this way. Find out who your sister was meeting in town that night."

He flinched at the mental picture of the coroner and EMTs bringing his sister's body out of the shallow ditch beside the road a few miles outside of town. The killer had thrown her into the ditch, leaving her for dead, leaving her to die alone beside the road.

"She ran into *your* brother," he snapped.

She made an impatient sound. "How can you be so sure that Ginny wasn't seeing someone else that she kept not only from Carson, but also from your parents and even from you?" she demanded.

He swore under his breath as he slapped his hat back on to his head. "Some *mystery* man? That's just some story your brother cooked up to shift suspicion onto someone else. This isn't getting us anywhere. It's the same old argument. It's why I left eleven years ago. Your brother killed her."

"Are you willing to stake everything on it? If so, then there is nothing more I can say, is there?" She turned toward her truck.

"What if you're the one who's wrong, Destry?" he called after her. "Ginny said your brother had been following her. How can you be so sure your brother didn't leave the ranch that night? It wouldn't be the first time he lied. Or the first time he hurt Ginny, would it?"

CARSON KNEW BETTER THAN to try to reason with his father, but he had to give it a shot. As he looked down the table, he wondered if WT believed he'd killed Ginny West. Or if it mattered to him. Apparently being Waylon Thomas Grant's male heir trumped everything—even murder.

"Tomorrow morning, I'll show you the new grazing land I've picked up since you've been gone," WT was saying.

"Aren't you worried about this new evidence that's turned up?"

WT scoffed. "The state attorney general has been putting pressure on local law enforcement to clear up their cold cases. The sheriff is just going through the motions. I doubt there's any new evidence. I wouldn't worry about it."

"I'd feel a whole lot better if I knew what it was."

"Doesn't matter. We'll get you the best lawyer money can buy." He looked up from his meal. "But it won't come to that. You never left the ranch that night. Stick to that story. Jack will back you up, right?"

Carson said nothing for a moment, shocked by his father's cavalier response. "You can't really think I could get a fair trial in this county." When WT didn't respond, he tried again, "With enough money, I could leave the country. There are still foreign countries that the U.S. can't extradite from."

WT looked up at him and frowned. "I built this ranch for my son to take over. So I'm certainly not paying to send him out of the country."

"I can't very well take over the ranch if I'm on death row," Carson snapped.

"You're not going to prison. If the sheriff had anything on you, I'd know."

Carson shook his head in disbelief. "Frank Curry might owe you his life, but not even his gratitude is going to save me if this new evidence makes me look guilty."

WT let out an exasperated sigh. "Stop worrying. No one is fool enough to cross me. Not even the damned state's attorney general."

"If you're so powerful, why did you insist on me leaving eleven years ago? Why didn't you let me stay and fight the allegations? If that's all you thought they were?"

WT shook his head and angrily shoved away his plate.

For a few minutes, the only sound in the huge dining room was the click of Cherry's silverware as she kept eating.

Carson wished he could walk away right now and not look back. But that was no longer an option. He would need a lot of money to leave the country. If WT wouldn't pony it up, then he needed the ranch and the money he could get for it. He thought of his sister. He had to convince WT to give him the money so he could disappear.

"Dad?" The word came at a cost after refusing to call WT that for so many years. *"Dad?"*

His father turned on the only other person in the room. "Cherry. That your real name? It sounds like a stage name."

Carson swore under his breath as he watched WT take off the gloves. WT would fight as dirty as he had to get what he wanted.

His father threw him a challenging look. But he was no longer that scared kid who'd been sneaked out of Beartooth in the cover of darkness. Ginny's murder and a target on his back had changed him. Nor did he need to come to Cherry's defense. She could take care of herself.

Cherry slowly licked her painted lips and turned her full attention to WT. She'd chosen a hot-pink low-cut top that barely covered her nipples and white capris that cupped her toned bottom. Her dyed blond hair was piled haphazardly on top of her head with stray tendrils curling down around her face. The fake eyelashes gave her a sleepy, half-soused look, but then again, it could have been the wine she'd consumed with abandon since they'd sat down to supper.

"I'm a *dancer*," she said proudly, daring him to dispute it.

"A *dancer?*" WT repeated and added, "And I'm a high flier on the trapeze."

Cherry smiled. "Carson told me that his great grandfather used to be in the circus but I didn't know you—"

"He's making fun, Cherry," Carson said dryly.

She narrowed her eyes at WT. "Making fun of *me?*"

"No," WT said. "My *son*. And by the way, my grandfather rode in a Wild West Show. Not a *circus*."

Carson laughed and shot a wink to his fiancée.

At the head of the table, WT bellowed for Margaret to serve dessert.

CHAPTER FOUR

RYLAN TOOK OFF IN A dust devil of anger as Destry climbed into her pickup, her legs weak, her heart aching. Seeing Rylan again had sent her already spinning-out-of-control world even further into orbit. She couldn't look as he drove on down the road toward the W Bar G. There was no stopping him, no way to call the ranch to warn her father and brother since she hadn't grabbed her cell phone—not that she could get service often this close to the mountains. Nor could she beat him to the ranch.

She feared not only for Carson. Her father wouldn't hesitate to shoot a trespasser. Especially a West toting a gun.

Running into Rylan like that had been a shock, one that still reverberated through her. She couldn't tell if the trembling in her hands as she started her truck had more to do with anger—or fear. Or those old feelings that still lingered when it came to that tall, lanky cowboy.

There'd been other men in the years since Rylan had left, even one she'd been fairly serious about, but she'd always measured them against her first love and they'd always come up short.

But did she even know this Rylan? This man so full of rage and set on vengeance at any cost?

Unable to resist it any longer, she glanced in her rearview mirror.

To her surprise, she saw Rylan hit his brake lights up the road. She watched him in the mirror, waiting and praying he'd changed his mind about confronting her brother.

It wasn't as if she didn't understand what was driving him. But he was wrong about Carson. Her brother had loved Ginny.

For long minutes, they sat like that, both pulled off the road fifty yards apart. Both apparently debating what to do next.

"Please, Rylan," she said under her breath, half plea, half prayer.

She let out the breath she'd unconsciously been holding as she watched him turn his pickup around and head back in her direction. She thought he might stop again, but he didn't.

He didn't even look at her as he roared past in a cloud of dust headed away from the W Bar G. He'd said everything he had to say, she thought as she watched him go, her heart in her throat.

What had changed his mind? Hopefully he'd realized after he'd calmed down that the stupidest thing he could do was go to the ranch gunning for Carson.

Whatever had changed his mind, she was thankful. Not that it took care of the problem. She knew Rylan was right. He wouldn't be the only one riled up about Carson's return. If Carson stayed here, he wouldn't be safe.

She sat for a moment, then leaned over the steering wheel letting all the emotions she'd bottled up the past eleven years spill out. She cried for all that had been lost to her, to both their families. Finally, drained, weak with relief and regret, she sat up and wiped her eyes. She'd been strong for so long.

For years she'd told herself she could live without Rylan. She'd moved on with her life. She was happy. At least content. But seeing him, coming face-to-face with him, hearing his voice, looking into his eyes...

He'd always been handsome, but now his body had filled out. He was broader in the shoulders, his arms sinewy with muscle, his face tanned from working outside. There were tiny lines around his eyes that hadn't been there before, but if anything, they only made him more handsome.

His hair was still thick and the color of sunshine, his eyes that honey-warm brown that she'd gotten lost in from the first time she'd looked in them. Her heart had always swelled at the sight of him. She'd never stopped loving him—just as she'd promised. Today proved what her heart already knew. She never would.

Pulling herself together, she turned the pickup around and headed back toward the ranch. Thoughts of Rylan aside, she just prayed that this new evidence would prove that Carson was innocent.

As RYLAN HEADED home, he thought about the first time he'd laid eyes on Destry Grant. She'd come riding up with the W Bar G's ranch foreman at a neighbor's branding on a horse way too big for her. She would have been five at the time to his six. He recalled how serious she'd looked.

What stuck in his mind was that she'd stayed at the branding all day, cutting calves into the chute as if she was ten times her age, and later, when one of the cow-

boys' hats had blown off and spooked her horse, she'd
gotten bucked off and hit the ground hard. Her face had
scrunched up, but she hadn't shed a tear. She'd climbed
the fence to get back on her horse and ridden off.

He'd never seen anyone so determined.

What chapped his behind now, though, was that she
hadn't changed one iota when it came to that stubborn
determination and pride. He hated that, when it came
to her brother, she just refused to see the truth.

He'd left eleven years ago because he couldn't bear
being around her with his sister's death standing between them. He'd always rodeoed, but after college,
he'd joined the pro circuit. It had been exactly what he'd
needed—traveling from town to town across the country, never staying in one place too long. If he needed
company, there were bronco and bull riders to hang out
with, and if he felt in need of female attention, there
were always buckle bunnies and rodeo groupies who
were up for a good time.

The rodeo had helped him heal. He'd felt badly about
bailing on his family, but his mother and father had two
sons at home and he'd kept in touch. The only people he
hadn't wanted to hear anything about were the Grants.
Especially Destry.

His family had welcomed him back with open arms
and the ranch was large enough that there was plenty
of room as well as work. Not that he'd have moved back
into his childhood room at the ranch, even if his mother
hadn't turned it into her quilting room.

He'd moved into an old cabin on a stretch of land
adjacent to the W Bar G until he could decide what he
wanted to do next. The cabin had a roof he could see
daylight through and that required a bucket or two when

it rained, and often at night he heard mice gnawing on something under the floorboards.

Still, it was better than most of the places he'd slept in while on the rodeo circuit, and he was home.

If only he didn't feel in such limbo. He'd saved nearly every dime he'd made rodeoing so he had options. But he feared moving ahead meant dealing with the past, something he'd put off all these years.

He swore under his breath, as frustrated with the situation between him and Destry as he'd been eleven years ago. He'd known seeing her again would be difficult. *Difficult?* He laughed to himself at how that word didn't come close to adequately describing their encounter.

It hurt like hell. Like being bucked off a horse and hitting the ground with such force that it stole his breath for what seemed like forever. After that initial impact with the ground came the pain in his chest, an ache that radiated through his entire body, and for long moments, he was unable to move or breathe. A small death. Just like seeing Destry after all this time, a moment he would never forget.

And just like getting bucked off a wild horse and being anxious to ride another time, he couldn't wait to see her again.

As he pulled up to his cabin, he saw his father's pickup parked out front. Taylor West climbed out of the truck as Rylan cut his engine. One look at his father's face and he knew he'd heard that Carson Grant was back.

"Where have you been, son?" he asked as Rylan got out. Taylor West was a large man, his blond hair graying around the temples. Years ago he'd been asked to do some modeling. A cowboy through and through, he'd turned down the offer, married his high school sweetheart, Ellie, and settled down to bring a daughter and three sons into the world. Rylan couldn't have asked for better parents or a more stable family—until his sister, Ginny, was murdered.

His parents were both strong and, with the help of his brothers, had somehow managed to survive the tragedy. Probably better than Rylan the past eleven years.

"Son?" Taylor asked again.

"Just went for a ride," Rylan said, a half-truth at best.

His father studied him for a long moment. "I know you heard the news."

He nodded and shifted on his boots as he felt that old aching anger settle in his belly. "If there's new evidence, then why isn't Carson Grant already behind bars?"

His father shook his head. "These things take time. The sheriff—"

"The *sheriff?* Frank Curry isn't going to—"

"Frank told me he's just waiting for the new evidence to be run through the crime lab."

His father was often too trusting. "And how long is that going to take?" Rylan demanded.

"We have to give Frank a chance. The sheriff mentioned that they have more resources than they did eleven years ago and that a lot of cold cases are being solved now because of it. All the evidence is being reviewed. They need enough to convict."

Rylan grasped on to hope. "It has to be enough that they can nail the son of a bitch." He hated to think, though, what Carson's arrest would do to Destry. Her brother could be facing the death penalty.

"Frank Curry is hoping he can keep a lid on this

community until then," Taylor said. "Son, I need your word that you won't do anything to make this any worse."

Rylan thought about earlier, sitting on the narrow track of dirt road, the wind whistling in his side window, his heart pounding after coming face-to-face with Destry again. He didn't have to tell his father that he'd been running for years from the past. Or that he didn't think he could live with himself if he let his sister's murderer remain free.

Taylor West knew his son. He'd been the one to pull Rylan off Carson the day of Ginny's funeral when the Grants had had the audacity to show up.

"You've got to let the law handle this," his father said now.

"And if the law doesn't?" Rylan asked.

"Then we'll cross that bridge when we get to it."

Rylan studied his father for a long moment. "I'll wait to see what the sheriff comes up with."

His father laid a big hand on his shoulder. "Thank you, son. I can't lose another one of you."

SHERIFF FRANK CURRY dragged the evidence box marked Ginny Sue West over to his desk and lifted the top. Until recently, it had been years since he'd reviewed the material. He'd had to force himself to put it away. The case had kept him awake at night.

He'd read through the report dozens of times. Everything had been pretty straightforward. Local girl Ginny West had been struck in the head with a blunt object before her body had been dumped beside the road a couple of miles from town.

She'd still been alive at the time. In the shallow ditch

where she was found, there was evidence of where she'd tried to crawl out. But her injuries had been significant. She'd died of the blows she'd sustained before her body had been found.

There were no defensive wounds, which led him to believe she'd known her killer, and that's why she'd gotten into a vehicle with him. That didn't narrow down the suspects since Ginny West would have felt safe getting into a vehicle with most anyone in the county.

The ranch pickup Ginny had driven into town had been found behind the Range Rider bar. Originally, Frank had thought she might have met with foul play because of something that had happened in the bar earlier that night.

However, no one remembered seeing her. Which had led him to believe she'd never gone inside the bar. Whoever she'd run into in the parking lot behind the bar had made sure of that. Which could explain why her purse was found in the pickup.

The main suspect had been Ginny's boyfriend who'd she'd broken up with about a week prior to her murder. Several locals had seen Carson Grant arguing with Ginny in public. It hadn't helped either that Carson was WT Grant's son or that Carson had been in some minor scrapes growing up. People in this community never forgot.

Carson, who'd sworn he'd been on the ranch all night, also had an alibi. And there was no evidence to prove he'd had a hand in Ginny's murder. The town was convinced, though, and Frank thought it had been smart of WT to send Carson away.

Now, with the new evidence and Carson back in Beartooth, if there was any chance of closing this cold case, then Frank was taking it. But the last thing he needed was another murder on his hands, though.

He had asked the lab to put a rush on the tests. It was a long shot, but if he could get some DNA evidence, they could all move on with their lives. And if there was nothing on the barrette... At the very least it had gotten Carson back to town. Now he just had to hope talk of new evidence would force the killer to make a mistake and out himself.

His instincts told him that even with his suspicions about Carson Grant, this case wasn't as cut-and-dried as everyone thought.

CHAPTER FIVE

CARSON LEFT THE HOUSE after dinner on the pretense of going for a walk. Cherry had turned in early. He couldn't help smiling when he thought about her and WT at dinner. He wished he was more like her. She could handle WT with one hand tied behind her.

Margaret, the housekeeper and cook, had put a box of his old clothes in the bedroom he and Cherry shared. He'd found a pair of his Western boots and put them on, along with some worn jeans and a flannel shirt. When he looked in the mirror, it gave him a shock. He'd expected to see the twenty-year-old he'd been, but his face gave away an unmistakable regret.

He'd left the house, unable to bear another moment with his father. He hadn't gone far down the road when he saw Destry go roaring past in one of the ranch pickups.

The fact that she was just now coming back didn't bode well. Something told him the cows she'd gone to rescue from the road weren't the only problem she'd run into. Did it have something to do with him?

He'd known his being back here would be trouble for her. He loved his sister and hated what he'd put her through already. Now it was about to get worse. Destry would be collateral damage, but he had little choice.

All of this had been set in motion long before she was even born.

It wasn't far to the homestead house as the crow flies, but over a mile by road. After he started down the mountain, he spotted the barn and corrals on the mountain just out of sight from the house. Nearby was the airstrip and hangar where the plane was kept.

Not far into the walk, he regretted not driving. The wind felt cold. Either that or his blood had thinned. It wouldn't be long before snow would blanket the ground, and stay there through April, even May.

Down the road in the fading light of day, he caught sight of the old house where he and Destry had grown up.

"So you were born…poor?" Cherry had asked.

"My father had been dirt poor, as WT called it. He was doing okay by the time I came along and even better when Destry was born. We weren't rich, by any means. We lived in the old homestead. He hadn't built the new place yet or had his plane accident." Funny, but Carson recalled those years more fondly than he'd expected he would.

"WT made some good investments, bought up any land that came available—and usually cheaply since this was before Montana property went sky high. As they say, the rest is history," he'd told her.

Cherry had been impressed. "Well, that's good for you," she'd said.

Was it? If WT still lived in the old homestead house and the ranch was small as it had been when he started, would he be so dead set on his son taking the place over? Carson doubted it.

And wouldn't things have been different when Ginny

West was murdered? WT couldn't have afforded to send his son away for eleven years. Carson would have had to stay—no matter the consequences.

Cherry had been surprised that his sister preferred living in the two-story log house instead of the mansion their father had built. Carson understood only too well. But he would have made the old man build him his own house, something new and modern and even farther away. Clearly, he wasn't his sister.

The twilight cast a soft silver sheen over the land, making the dark pines shimmer as he crossed the cattleguard and approached the house. This far north, the sun didn't set in the summer months until almost eleven. Now, though, it was getting dark by eight-thirty. Soon it would be dark by five.

The wind had picked up even more, he noticed distractedly. Something was definitely blowing in. The wind was so strong in this part of Montana that it had blown over semis on the interstate and knocked train cars off their tracks.

It was worse in the winter when wind howled across the eaves and whipped snow into huge sculpted drifts. He remembered waking to find he couldn't get out to help feed the animals because the snow had blown in against the door. Often he'd had to plow the road out so he and Destry could get to the county road to catch the school bus.

It had become a state joke that while other states closed their schools when they got a skiff of snow or the thermometer dropped below zero, Montana schools remained open in blinding blizzards and fifty-below-zero temperatures. Carson remembered too many days when the ice was so thick on the inside of the school bus windows that he couldn't see outside. He hadn't missed the cold, especially enjoying winters in Las Vegas.

He reminded himself that, with luck, he and Cherry would be back there before their vacations were up.

Carson found his sister unloading firewood from the back of a flatbed truck and stacking it along the rear of the house. As a kid, she'd always turned to hard work or horseback when she was upset. He watched her for a moment. She was working off something, that was for sure.

"I thought we had hired hands for that?" he asked, only half joking.

She grinned and tossed a sawn chunk of log in his direction. He had to step out of the way to keep it from hitting him.

"Think you got enough wood there?" he asked as he fell in to help stack the truckload of logs along the back of the house. Firewood had been stacked in that spot for as long as he could remember.

"Takes quite a few cords to get through the winter with this latest weather pattern," Destry said.

"I can't imagine what it must take up at the Big House." He'd heard her call it that and thought how appropriate it was to compare WT's mansion with prison.

"Dad doesn't heat with wood," she said. "Went with a gas furnace. The wood fireplaces are just for show."

He stopped, already winded from the exertion of trying to keep up with his sister. "Why do you stay here?"

"You know I've always loved this old house."

"I'm not talking about this house. I'm talking about this ranch, Montana. I gave you some good advice before I left." He'd told her to go away to college and not come back. To run as far away from WT as she could get. She should have listened. "You obviously didn't take it."

"But I appreciated the advice." Destry stopped throwing down wood long enough to smile at him. "I was able to get my degree in business and ranch management and still stay around here, so it all worked out for the best."

"Destry, what's here for you but work?"

"I love this work." She looked out at the darkening land beyond the grove of trees for a moment, her expression softening. "I couldn't breathe without open spaces."

He wondered what had happened either before she'd left to see about the cows—or while she was gone. Maybe it was just his return that had her upset. "Destry, you know I can't stay here."

She jumped down to stack logs, making short order out of the pile she'd thrown from the truck bed. "What does Dad say about that?"

"What do you think he says?" He felt his blood pressure rise. "I don't know how you can put up with him. I can't."

"What will you do?"

He shook his head. He didn't have a clue. The old man definitely had him between a rock and a hard place. Destry was in an even worse corner, but he didn't have the heart to tell her.

She stacked more of the wood for a moment. "I'll pick you up early in the morning," she said, stopping to study him. "Be ready."

"Where are we going?"

"You'll see."

He smiled at his sister. "I've missed you."

"Yeah, I've missed you, too."

Rylan had just thrown a couple of elk steaks into a cast-iron skillet sizzling with melted butter. A large baked potato wrapped in foil sat on the counter since the steaks wouldn't take long.

The secret with wild meat was not to overcook it. He'd learned that at hunting camp when he was a boy. At least today he wasn't cooking over an open campfire. The wonderful scent of the steaks filled the cabin, and for the first time in weeks, he felt as if he was finally home.

The knock at the door made him curse under his breath. He really wasn't in the mood for company.

When he went to the door, he was shocked to find Destry standing outside on the wooden step. He tried to hide his surprise as well as his pleasure in seeing her again. Leaning his hip against the door frame, he studied her for a moment as he waited for her to speak—that was until he remembered his steaks and swore as he hurried back to the stove.

When he looked up from flipping the beautifully browned steaks, she had come in and closed the door behind her. The cabin immediately felt smaller. Too small and too warm.

"I assume you're not here for supper," he said, wondering what she *was* here for. Being this close to her jolted his heart, reminding him of things he'd spent years trying to forget. "I'm a pretty good cook if you're interested."

"No, thanks." She appeared as uncomfortable as he felt in the tight quarters, which surprised him. He'd only seen her lose control of her emotions once. The reminder of their night together did nothing to ease his tension. He pulled the steaks off the stove, his mouth no longer watering for them, though, and gave her all his attention.

Destry was the only woman he knew who could make a pair of jeans and a flannel work shirt sexy. Her chestnut plaited hair hung over one shoulder, the end falling over her breast. He remembered the weight of her breasts in his hands, the feel of her nipple in his mouth. His fingers itched to unbraid her hair and let it float around her bare shoulders.

"I'll make this quick since I don't want your steaks to get cold," she said. "Thank you for changing your mind about going to the W Bar G earlier."

He shook his head. "Don't. You don't know how close I came."

"You stopped before it was too late," she said quietly.

"Yeah, but that was today. I can't make any promises about tomorrow."

Her blue eyes shone like banked flames. Even in the dull light of the cabin, he could see the sprinkling of freckles that arced across her cheeks and nose. She looked as young as she had in high school. The girl next door, he used to joke. And that was still what she was.

Only now she was all woman, a strong, independent, resilient woman who made his pulse quicken and heart ache at the sight of her. Pain and pleasure, both killers when your heart was as invested as much as his was.

He wanted to reach for her, to pull her into his arms, to kiss that full mouth....

"Enjoy your steaks," she said, turning toward the door.

He couldn't think of anything to say, certainly not something that would make her stay. He listened to her get into her pickup, the engine cranking over, the tires crunching on the gravel as she drove away.

He dumped his steaks onto a plate, but he'd lost his appetite. Destry was determined to make him a saint when he was far from it. Now he wished he'd kicked Carson's butt.

But he figured Destry would have still ended up on his doorstep tonight—only she wouldn't have been thanking him. She would probably have come with a loaded shotgun and blood in her eye.

THE STORM BLEW IN WITH a vengeance just after midnight. Destry woke to rain and the banging of one of the shutters downstairs. She rose and padded down the steps wearing nothing but the long worn T-shirt she'd gone to bed in.

As she stepped off the bottom stair, she slowed, surprised to feel the chilled wind on her face. Had she left one of the windows open?

The air had a bite to it, another indication that winter wasn't far off. This time of year the days could be hot as summer, but by night the temperature would drop like a stone. Soon the water in the shallow eddies of the creek would have a skim of ice on them in the morning and the peaks in the Crazies would gleam with fresh snow.

She thought about her brother's earlier visit. What had he walked all the way down here for? She'd been too worked up over seeing Rylan at the time to question him. Later she'd had the feeling he wanted to tell her something. Whatever it was, he'd apparently changed his mind.

After they'd finished stacking the wood, she'd invited him in, but he'd declined. Just as he had when she'd offered to give him a ride back up to their father's house.

"I need the exercise," he'd said and had taken off before it became completely dark.

Her thoughts turned to her visit with Rylan earlier that night. Just the memory of him cooking steaks in that small cabin, warmed her still. It had seemed so normal, so welcoming, like the Rylan she once knew. He might come after Carson again when she wouldn't be there to talk him out of it. But at least it wouldn't be tonight.

Destry hugged herself from the chill as she started across the open living room. The worn wood floor beneath her bare feet felt freezing cold. The shutter banged a monotonous beat against the side of the house. The wind curled the edge of the living room rug and flapped the pages of a livestock grower's magazine left on an end table.

It wasn't until she reached the back of the house that she realized it wasn't a window that had been left open—it was the back door.

A chill rattled through her that had nothing to do with the wind or the cold. Through the open doorway, the pines appeared black against the dark night. They whipped in the wind and rain below a cloud-shrouded sky.

Destry reached to close the door but stopped as she caught movement out beyond the creek. Something at the edge of the trees. Without taking her eyes off the spot, she reached for the shotgun she kept by the back door to chase away bears. She didn't have to break it down to know it was loaded. There were two shells, one in each barrel.

She stared through the darkness at the spot in the pines and cottonwoods where she would have sworn she saw something move just moments before.

As she stood in the doorway, large droplets of rain pinged off the overhang, splattering her with cool mist. The wind blew her hair back from her face and molded the worn T-shirt to her body.

What had she seen? Or had she just imagined the movement?

Another chill raced across her bare flesh. She hated the way her heart pounded. Worse, that whatever had been out there had the ability to spook her.

The door must not have been latched and had blown open. But as she started to close the door, she recalled the downed fence and the tracks leading into the trees behind her house that she'd seen from the air. With everything that had happened, she'd forgotten about them.

Few people who lived out in the country locked their doors, especially around Beartooth. Destry never had. But tonight she closed the door, locked it and, leaving the shotgun by the back door, took her pistol up to her bedroom.

CHAPTER SIX

NETTIE BENTON DIDN'T notice the broken window when she opened the Beartooth General Store early the next morning. She hadn't gotten much sleep, thanks to Bob and the bad dreams he'd had during the night. She'd awakened to find him screaming in terror—as if his snoring wasn't bad enough.

He'd finally moved in to the guest room, or she wouldn't have slept a wink. When she'd gone to open the store's front door, she'd looked across the street and seen the new owner of the café chatting with a handful of customers. Just the sight of Kate LaFond threatened to ruin an already bad day.

The woman had purchased the Branding Iron after the former owner had dropped dead this spring. Just days after the funeral, Kate LaFond had appeared out of nowhere. No one knew anything about her or why she'd decided to buy a café in Beartooth.

The community had been so grateful that she had kept the café open, they hadn't cared who she was or where she'd come from. Or what the devil she was doing here.

Everyone but Nettie. "I still say it's odd," she said to herself now as she stood at the window watching Kate smiling and laughing with a bunch of ranchers as she refilled their coffee cups.

An attractive thirtysomething brunette, Kate had apparently taken to the town like a duck to water. It annoyed Nettie that, after only a few months, most people seemed fine with her. They didn't care, they said, that they didn't know a single relative fact about the woman's past.

"It's just nice to have the café open," local contractor Grayson Brooks had told her. Nettie had noticed how often Grayson stopped by the café mornings now. Grayson owned Brooks Construction and was semiretired at forty-five because of his invalid wife, Anna. He had a crew that did most of the physical work, allowing him, apparently, to spend long hours at the Branding Iron every morning.

"Kate's nice and friendly and she makes a pretty good cup of coffee," Grayson had said when Nettie had asked him what he thought of the woman. "I think she makes a fine addition to the town."

"Doesn't hurt that she's young and pretty, I suppose," Nettie had said.

Grayson had merely smiled as if she wasn't going to get an argument out of him on that subject, although everyone knew, as good-looking as he was, he was devoted to his wife.

"Did you ever consider it's none of our business?" her husband, Bob, had asked when Nettie had complained about Kate LaFond to him. He'd been sitting in his office adding up the day's receipts.

"What if she has some dark past? A woman like that, she could have been married, killed several husbands by the age of thirty-five, even drowned a few of her children."

Bob had looked up at her, squinting. After forty years

of marriage, he no longer seemed shocked by anything she said.

"Why on earth would you even think such a thing?" he'd asked wearily.

"There's something about her. Why won't she tell anyone about her past if she has nothing to hide? I'm warning you, Bob Benton, there is something off about that woman. Why else would she buy a café in a near ghost town, far away from everything? She's running from something. Mark my words."

"Sometimes, Nettie" was all Bob had said with one of his big sighs, before leaving to walk up the steep path to their house.

Now, Kate LaFond looked up. Their gazes met across the narrow stretch of blacktop that made up the main drag of Beartooth. The look Kate gave her made a shudder run the length of Nettie's spine.

"That woman's dangerous," she said to herself. It didn't matter that there was no one around to hear. No one listened to her anyway.

Nettie moved from the window and went about opening the store as she did every morning. Lost in thought, she barely heard something crunch under her boots. She blinked, stumbling to a stop to look down. That's when she saw the glass from the broken window.

DESTRY DROVE UP TO THE big house, anxious to spend some time with her brother. She hadn't slept well last night after discovering the open door, so she'd had a lot of time to think.

She was worried about her brother. Even more worried about what he might have come down to the house to tell her last night.

This afternoon she would be rounding up the last of the cattle from the mountains. After a season on the summer range, they would be bringing down the last of the fattened-up calves, and all but the breeding stock would be loaded into semis and taken to market.

Destry always went on the last roundup in the high country before winter set in. The air earlier this morning had been crisp and cold, the ground frosty after last night's rain. But while clouds still shrouded the peaks of the Crazies, the sun was out down here in the valley, the day warming fast.

As she pulled up to the house and honked, she was surprised when her brother came right out. He'd never been an early riser even as a boy. He must really be desperate to get away from their father. Or was it his fiancée?

"Okay, where are we going?" Carson asked as he climbed into the pickup.

Destry nodded her head toward the bed of the truck and the fishing tackle she'd loaded this morning.

"Fishing?" He shook his head as she threw the pickup into gear. "Did you forget I don't have a fishing license?"

"With all your problems, you're worried about getting caught without a fishing license?"

He laughed. "Good point." He leaned back in the seat as she tore down the road, and for a moment, she could pretend they were kids again heading for the reservoir to go fishing after doing their chores.

Destry barreled forward, having driven more dirt roads in her life than paved ones. The pickup rumbled across one cattle guard after another, then across the pasture, dropping down to the creek.

Because it was late in the year, the creek was low. She slowed as the pickup forded the stream, tires plunged over the rocks and through a half foot of crystal clear water before roaring up the other side.

Tall weeds between the two-track road brushed the bottom of the pickup, and rocks kicked up, pinging off the undercarriage. Out of the corner of her eye, she saw Carson grab the handle over the door as she took the first turn.

"Sorry to see your driving hasn't improved," he said.

She laughed. "You've been gone too long."

"Not long enough."

"Come on, haven't you missed this?" She found that hard to believe. Didn't he notice how beautiful it was here? The air was so clear and clean. The land so pleasing to the eye. And there was plenty of elbow room for when you just wanted to stretch out some.

The road cut through the fertile valley, stubble fields a pale yellow, the freshly plowed acres in fallow dark with the turned soil.

"Apparently you haven't been listening to me any more than WT has," her brother said. "This is just land to me. I feel no need to take root in it."

They fell silent, the only sound the roar of the engine and the spray of dirt clods and rocks kicked up by the tires. The land dropped toward the river, falling away in rolling hills that had turned golden under the bright sun of autumn.

Ahead she saw the brilliant blue of pooled water and smiled, feeling like a kid again. Over the next rise, she swung the pickup onto a rutted track that ended at the water's edge. Summer had burned all the color out of the grass around the small lake. Only a few trees stood on the other side, their leaves rust red, many of the branches already bared off.

Destry parked the truck next to an old rowboat that lay upside down beside the water like a turtle in the sun. Getting out, together they flipped the boat over and carried it to the water before going back for the poles, tackle box and the cooler she'd packed.

"When was the last time you went fishing?" she asked as they loaded everything into the boat.

"Probably with you. As I recall I caught more fish than you, bigger ones, too."

She laughed. "Apparently your memory hasn't improved any more than my driving."

Their gazes held for a long moment. Carson was the first to look away. "Hop in. If you're determined to do this…" He pushed the rowboat off the shore and climbed in.

Destry breathed in the day, relaxing for the first time since her brother's return. She dipped her fingers into the deep green water. It felt cold even with the October sun beating down on its surface.

"I assume you brought worms," Carson said, reaching into the cooler. He opened the Styrofoam container and tossed her a wriggling night crawler, chuckling when she caught it without even making a face.

"You never were like other girls," he said.

"I'm going to take that as a compliment." The water rippled in the slight breeze as the boat drifted for a few moments before Carson took the oars. He rowed the boat out to the center of the reservoir, then let the tips of the oars skim the glistening surface as they drifted again.

Destry watched her red-and-white bobber float along

on top of the water in the breeze. From the horizon came the loud honking of a large flock of geese. The eerie sound seemed to echo across the lake as the geese carved a dark V through the clear, cloudless blue.

Nothing signaled the change of season like the migration of the ducks and geese. She thought of all the seasons she'd seen come and go, so many of them without her brother, the lonesome call of the geese making her sad.

"I don't want you to leave again," she said without looking at him.

Water lapped softly at the side of the boat. The breeze lifted the loose tendrils of hair around her face. A half dozen ducks splashed in the shallows near the shore, taking flight suddenly in a spasm of wings. Beads of water hung in the air for an instant as iridescent as gleaming pearls.

"I'll bet there aren't any fish in this reservoir anymore," Carson said. He was lying back on the seat, eyes closed, his pole tucked under one arm, the other arm over his face. He wore a T-shirt and an old pair of worn jeans, the legs rolled up, and a pair of equally old sneakers. The Western straw hat he'd been wearing rested on the floor of the boat.

"Doesn't really matter if there are fish, does it?"

Carson moved the arm from his face enough to open one eye and look at her. "Only if you hope to catch something."

"I'm happy just being here," she said.

"*You* would be. Some people actually like to catch fish when they go fishing." He went back to half dozing on the seat.

"Are you really going to marry Cherry?" Destry asked after a few minutes had passed.

"Why else would I have asked her?"

"Because at the time it seemed like a good idea?"

Her brother snickered. "It did seem like a better idea in Vegas than in Beartooth, Montana. She doesn't exactly fit in here, does she?"

"Is she bored to tears?"

"Yep, and worried about grizzly bears coming down and eating her in the middle of the night. She can't believe the closest big-box store is over an hour away." Carson laughed. "I hate to think what will happen if she breaks a nail."

The sound of her brother's laughter filled Destry with such love for him. She leaned back, letting the warm morning and the gentle slap of the water on the side of the boat lull her. Overhead, a red hawk circled on a warm thermal.

"You haven't asked me if I killed Ginny," Carson said, and she felt the boat rock as he leaned up on one elbow to look at her.

She thought she could see the hawk circling overhead reflected in his gaze. "You didn't. You couldn't."

He scoffed and lay back again, the arm back over his face. "If there's one thing I've learned, it's that we're all capable of despicable acts when we're backed into a corner. But thanks for believing in me, sis. It means a lot."

NETTIE FELT SICK TO HER stomach as she stared at the shattered window, the shards of glass glittering on the floor. Who had done such a thing?

She took a step back, her heart pounding as she realized whoever had broken the window could still be somewhere in the store.

Rushing to the phone, she dialed the sheriff with trembling fingers. "I've been burglarized!" she screamed into the phone the moment the dispatcher put her through.

"Who is this?" Sheriff Frank Curry asked in a voice so calm it set Nettie's already frayed nerves on edge.

She'd known Frank Curry since she was a girl. "Who the devil do you think it is?" she snapped. "My store was burglarized." She dropped her voice. "He might still be here."

"Lynette," the sheriff said. He was the only person who called her by her given name. The way he said it spoke volumes about their past. In just one word, he could make her feel like that lovestruck, teenage girl again. "Perhaps you should wait for me at your house. Where's your *husband?*"

She knew only too well what Frank thought of her husband. "Just get up here and don't you dare send that worthless Deputy Billy Westfall instead." She slammed down the phone, shaking even harder than she'd been before. She was fairly certain whoever had broken in wasn't still here. At least not on the lower floor.

The upper level was used for storage. Moving to the second-floor door, she eased it open and peered up the dark steps. She listened, didn't hear a sound and closed the door and bolted it.

If the burglar was up there, he wouldn't be going anywhere. She checked her watch and, leaving the closed sign on the front door, settled in to wait. As she glanced across the street to the café again, she realized she'd never had a break-in before Kate LaFond came to town.

"WHERE'S CARSON?"

Margaret turned from the stove, eyes narrowed. "Good morning to you, too, Waylon."

WT cursed under his breath. He hated it when she called him Waylon. She only did it because she knew it annoyed him. Or to remind him where he'd come from. As if he needed reminding.

"Don't act as if you didn't hear me," he snapped.

"Why? *You* do."

He didn't know how many times he'd come close to firing her. But they both knew he'd pay hell getting anyone else to cook and clean for him—let alone put up with him.

The real reason he hadn't sent her packing was that she knew him in a way that no one else did, not that he would ever admit it to her. Like him, she also knew the pain of poverty. Of wearing the same boots until even the cardboard you'd pasted inside couldn't keep the rocks from making your feet bleed. She knew about hand-me-down clothes and eating wild meat because there wasn't anything else.

Christmases had been the worst. That empty feeling that settled in the pit of the stomach as the day approached and you knew there would be no presents under the tree. It was hell when even Santa Claus didn't think you deserved better.

A couple of do-gooders in the area had left presents for him one year. WT had been too young to know what it had cost his parents to accept them. He'd greedily opened each one. A football. A pair of skates. A BB gun.

He remembered the feeling of having something that no one had ever worn or used before him. He'd run his fingers along the shiny BB gun, seeing his reflection in the blade of the skates and holding the warm leather of the football thinking it the happiest day of his life.

The next Christmas, though, he'd seen the look on his father's face and realized his mother's tears weren't those of joy. There was no Santa Claus, only people who felt sorry for him and his family. He'd made sure the do-gooders skipped his house from then on and swore he'd never need or take charity again.

No one knew about any of that—except for Margaret. Yes, that shared past was one reason he didn't fire Margaret—and that she put up with him. Also, they knew each other's secrets. That alone was a bond that neither of them seemed able to break. Margaret knew him right down to his black, unforgiving soul.

"I was looking for Carson," WT said, tempering his words now as he wheeled deeper into the kitchen. "Have you seen him?"

"He left with his sister. I believe they've gone fishing."

"Fishing?"

"Yes, fishing. They haven't seen each other in more than a decade. I would imagine they want to spend some time together." She didn't add, "Away from you," but he heard it in her tone.

He grunted and spun his wheelchair around to leave.

"Even if you can get him cleared of a murder charge, you can't keep him here against his will," she said to his retreating back.

"We'll see," he said, gritting his teeth.

CARSON SURREPTITIOUSLY studied his sister as he pretended to sleep in the gently rocking boat. Everything about this grown-up Destry impressed him. There didn't seem to be anything she couldn't handle on the ranch. This afternoon he'd heard that she was planning to ride up into the high country to finish rounding up the cattle. He'd never been able to ride as well as her. Nor did he have her knack for dealing with the day-to-day running of a ranch. The ranch hands had always respected her because she'd never been afraid to get her hands dirty, working right alongside them if needed.

He felt a wave of envy, wishing he were more like her. There was a rare beauty about her, a tranquility and contentment that he'd have given anything for. Was she really that at peace with her life? Or was she just better at hiding her feelings than he was?

Stirring from his dark thoughts, he sat up. "So who are you dating?"

"Dating?" She let out a laugh. "I don't have time to date. Oh, don't give me that look. I've dated. Don't you be like Dad and try to marry me off to someone with good pasture or grazing land."

Carson remembered how WT had been about him and Ginny West.

"Why can't you be interested in one of the Hamilton girls? Now that's some nice ranch land those girls are going to inherit, a whole section of irrigated pasture along Little Timber Creek."

Carson laughed now at the memory and shared it with Destry.

She chuckled. "He's been pushing me to go out with Hitch McCray in hopes of someday getting that strip of land between ours and the forest service land to the north."

"He'd even marry you off to Hitch?" Carson let out a curse. "I wouldn't let Hitch have a mean stray dog. Anyway, he's too old for you."

She smiled at that. "He's only forty."

"Seriously, you've put in your time taking care of WT. Isn't it time for you to have some fun?"

Destry shook her head, smiling. "I haven't been holed up here. There's just nowhere I want to be but here or nothing else I want to do with my life. I could never leave Montana, no matter what." She studied him. "What about you? What do you want to do with your life?"

He shrugged. He truly didn't know. He'd thought he was happy in Las Vegas working at the casino, had seen himself married to Cherry and living the rest of his life in the desert.

But some bad luck, WT and this new evidence had changed that.

Destry was studying him openly. "Isn't there someone you'd like to spend your life with?"

"How can you ask that?" Carson said with a laugh. "I'm engaged to be married."

"Do you love her?"

He sobered. "Not like I loved Ginny."

"I'm sorry."

"Don't be. I'm like you. I'm fine." He almost told her everything then, but he couldn't bring himself to spoil this beautiful morning with her. Soon enough he would be responsible for breaking her heart. Again.

"What if you could clear your name?" Destry asked.

"After all these years?" he asked with a shake of his head. But her words conjured a future he'd thought lost to him. As he looked out across the land, he told himself not to, but for the first time in years, he felt a sense of hope he hadn't since Ginny was killed.

CHAPTER SEVEN

BETHANY REYNOLDS FINGERED the locket at her neck and tried not to think about her husband as she reached for her hastily discarded clothing.

Her husband, Clete, would have never thought to give her a silver heart-shaped locket. Clete didn't have a romantic bone in his body. What had the man gotten her for their first Valentine's Day together? A set of snow tires.

The only reason he'd married her was to get her elk hunting tag. Only a few tags were given out each year in the area he loved to hunt. She'd lucked out and gotten one.

It had taken a moose even to get Clete to notice her. She'd been mooning over him for years. But it wasn't until she'd come into the Range Rider where he'd worked as a bartender and started showing her moose photos that he finally came around.

She'd drawn a moose tag—and bagged one. That was big news since moose tags were more rare than elk. Of course Clete had been jealous as all get out.

"*You* got a tag?" Clete had said.

She'd grinned, enjoying his jealousy—until he'd asked, "Who shot it for you?"

Bethany hadn't even bothered to answer him as she'd turned to show off her moose. It was three times bigger than she was and would feed herself and her family all year.

"What's moose meat taste like?" one of her "city" friends had asked.

"A little sweet, a darker meat than elk or deer. I'll get you a package of steaks to try," Bethany had promised. Behind her, she'd heard Clete banging around behind the bar, louder than usual.

It wasn't until the bar had cleared out some that he'd called her over. "So you shot it yourself," he'd said and offered her a drink.

She'd never been one to hold a grudge or turn down a free drink. Not to mention the fact that she'd had a crush on Clete since junior high. He'd been Beartooth's claim to fame, a football player who'd played for the Grizzlies at the University of Montana. That is until he got hurt.

Bethany had always known she was going to marry him. She even did that silly thing all lovesick girls do, she wrote Mrs. Clete Reynolds and Bethany Reynolds so many times that she believed it.

When he'd gotten injured his sophomore year at U of M, he'd dropped out, come home and gotten a job bartending at the Range Rider.

"Just until the leg heals," he would say. Everyone knew better. When the bar came up for sale, the owner sold it to Clete and carried the loan.

"So tell me about this moose," Clete had said that day at the bar as he'd glanced up from one of the photos to look at her. There'd been only one other time that he'd looked at her like that, years ago at the Fall Harvest Festival when she was sixteen. She'd told him that day she was going to marry him and that he'd better wait for her to grow up.

But it had taken the moose to bring them together years later.

"You gutted it yourself?" he'd said.

It was so big that she'd had to crawl inside it.

The moose had gotten them dating. But it had taken the *elk* permit to get Clete to pop the question. It was almost an accepted thing, women giving up their tags so their men could hunt more, even though it was illegal. If you got caught.

Most things came down to simply that, she'd learned. Like affairs, she thought as she slipped into her Western shirt.

"That was amazing," said the man on the bed.

She felt warm fingertips brush along the top of her bare butt and smiled to herself. Some men were breast men, others leg men. This one was all about her large, round butt and she loved it.

Clete had never appreciated her backside. Hell, he wasn't all that wild about her other parts, either. Love-making with Clete had become so mechanical that Bethany could just lie there and think about anything else she wanted until it was over. At just barely thirty-two, she was in her prime and was glad at least there was one man around who appreciated that fact. This man had never thought she was too young for him.

"I'm glad you were able to get away today," he said.

She finished snapping her Western shirt and stood. This was when she usually told him that she couldn't do this anymore. If they got caught, they both had too much to lose, not to mention it was wrong.

Bethany always left him, swearing she wouldn't go back. But after a day or two, she'd weaken. He made her feel as if she was the most beautiful woman in the world. He also was smart enough to know a woman didn't want snow tires on Valentine's Day, she thought as she again touched the tiny heart-shaped silver locket he'd given her. It felt cold against her bare skin.

"I have to work a double shift at the café tomorrow," she said and groaned at the thought. She'd worked at the café through high school and thought those days were behind her once she married Clete. She'd been wrong about that, too.

"I'm sorry, Sweetie, but I'm going to be busy for a few days myself."

She turned to look at him, a little surprised by his words. He always had more free time than she did. Lately, she'd felt as if he was losing interest in her and that scared her.

"Oh, and don't forget to take that off before you go home, will you," he told her, motioning to the locket resting against her skin.

The locket, like their affair, was their secret. "I won't forget."

DESTRY COULDN'T WAIT to ride horseback up in the high country above the ranch. She did her best thinking on the back of a horse. Or no thinking at all, which would have been fine with her this afternoon.

When she stopped by the house on her way to the barn, Cherry was lying by the pool.

"Is it always this quiet here?" Cherry asked.

"Always," Destry said, looking toward the spectacular Crazy Mountains.

"Where do you shop?" Cherry asked.

"Nettie at the Beartooth General Store sells the essentials, food, supplies, even some clothing and muck boots."

"Muck boots. You have a lot of use for those?" Cherry smiled up at her.

"Actually we do, especially in the spring and during a winter thaw when you're out feeding the animals."

"I can't imagine," Cherry said with a shake of her head. "Carson said there are grizzlies and they sometimes come down in the yard?"

Destry could tell that the thought had been worrying her. "Occasionally." She didn't add that this time of year bears were fattening up for the winter and stuffing themselves before going into hibernation.

Cherry sighed. "I have to tell you, this place gives me the creeps. It's too…isolated."

Destry thought about what her brother's fiancée had said as she prepared for her trip up into the mountains. She'd noticed that Carson had spent little time with Cherry and suspected he was seeing her differently against the Montana backdrop. Cherry was like a fish out of water—and clearly unhappy being here.

Inside the big house, Destry followed a familiar, alluring scent as she walked down to the kitchen to find Margaret making fried pies. A dozen of the small crescent shaped pies were cooling on a rack next to the stove. Against the golden brown of the crusts, the white frosting drizzled over them now dripped onto a sheet of aluminum foil.

"You're just in time," Margaret said, smiling, as she lifted two more pies from the hot grease and put them beside the others.

"They smell wonderful." Destry picked up a still warm pie and took a bite. The crust was flaky and but-

tery and delicious. She licked her lips, closing her eyes
as her taste buds took in the warm cinnamon apple filling and sweet icing.

"Do they meet your satisfaction?" Margaret asked
with a smile as Destry groaned in approval.

"I swear they're the best you've ever made," she said
between bites.

Margaret laughed. "You always say that."

Even with fried pies cooling nearby, Carson sat at the
counter in the kitchen with nothing but a cup of coffee
in front of him, looking miserable.

"Why aren't you out by the pool?" she asked.

"I'm showing Carson around the ranch," their father
said as he wheeled into the kitchen. "He's been gone
so long he doesn't know anything about the operation.
I planned to take him out first thing this morning, but
apparently he went fishing."

Carson grunted as he stared down into his cup. "And
didn't catch a darned thing."

WT ignored him, shifting his gaze to Destry instead.
"Where are you going dressed like that?"

"Riding up to collect the rest of the cattle from summer pasture," Destry said as she poured herself a half
cup of coffee.

"I thought we had ranch hands for that," her father
said.

She merely smiled. It was an old battle between
them. He made little secret of the fact that he didn't
like her actually working the ranch. But she'd always
loved calving on those freezing cold nights in January
when she could see her breath inside the barn. There
was nothing like witnessing the birth of a new calf,
branding to the sound of bawling calves, the feel of

baking sun on your back or riding through cool, dark pines gathering cattle in the fall.

He had the idea that marriage would change her. It often amazed her that her own father didn't know her at all.

"On your way out you might tell your brother's fiancée that at this altitude she's going to get burned to a crisp out there," WT said to her.

"Don't bother," Carson said. "Cherry likes to find out things on her own. Anyway, she can take care of herself."

As her father and brother left, Destry grabbed a couple of Margaret's famous fried pies, wrapped up a couple for Russell Murdock, their ranch foreman, and finished her coffee. She was on her way out when the phone rang.

She picked it up to save Margaret the effort. "W Bar G, Destry speaking."

The voice on the other end of the line was low and hoarse. It could have been a man or a woman's. "You tell that brother of yours we don't want the likes of him around here."

"Who is this?" she demanded, but the caller had already hung up. As she returned the receiver, she saw Margaret looking at her and knew it wasn't the first time someone had called threatening Carson.

"People who call making threats hardly ever do anything more," Margaret said, turning back to her fried pies. "I'd be more afraid for anyone who tries to come on this ranch. Your father's been carrying his .357 magnum since your brother came home."

So he'd been expecting trouble. That made her all the more worried for her brother. She scooped up the pies, said goodbye to Margaret and headed for the barn. Since his accident, her father had put in a paved path down to the barn, even though he no longer rode.

As she saddled up, she promised herself that for a few hours, she was going to put all of her worries aside. She loved the ride up into the high mountain meadows and the feel of the horse beneath her. So many ranches now used everything from four-wheelers to helicopters to round up their cattle, leaving the horses to be nothing more than pasture ornaments.

She much preferred a horse than a noisy four-wheeler. Her horse Hay Burner, a name her father tagged the mare, was one she'd rescued along with another half dozen wild horses from Wyoming.

Destry had fallen helplessly in love with the mare at first sight. She was a deep chocolate color with a wild mane and a gentle manner. She'd taken well to cattle and cutting calves out of the herd.

As Destry rode out to join the ranch foreman and the ranch hands for the ride up into the Crazies, she breathed in the scent of towering pines and the smell of saddle leather.

Meadowlarks sang from the thick groves of aspens as white cumulous clouds bobbed along in a sea of clear blue. The air felt cool and crisp with the sharp scent of the pines and the promise of fall in the changing colors of the leaves. Overhead, a bald eagle circled looking for prey. Nearby a squirrel chattered at them from a pine bough.

"Everything all right at the house?" the ranch foreman asked as Destry rode beside him.

Russell Murdock had let the others ride on ahead of them. He'd been a ranch hand when she was young and had worked his way up to foreman. He'd been with the W Bar G longer than anyone except Margaret. Destry considered them both family.

In his late fifties, Russell was a kind, good-natured man with infinite patience with both the ranch hands and WT. He'd been the one who'd dried her tears when he'd found her crying in the barn when she was a girl. He'd picked her up from the dirt when she'd tried to ride one of the ranch animals she shouldn't have. He'd also been there for her when Carson had left and Rylan had broken her heart.

"It's an adjustment for Carson," she said.

Russell smiled over at her. "He's staying?"

She met the older man's gaze. They'd been too close over the years for her to lie to him. "WT thinks he is. I guess it will depend on this new evidence in Ginny West's murder investigation."

Russell nodded knowingly. "You know there's talk around town…"

"I've heard. I'm hoping as long as Carson stays on the ranch there won't be any trouble."

Russell looked worried but said no more as the trail rose up through a mountain pass and the sound of lowing cattle filled the air. Once they reached the ridge, the foreman rode on ahead to catch up with the others.

Destry lagged behind to stop and look at the view of the ranch. She heard someone ride up beside her.

"Quite the spread, wouldn't you say?" Lucky leaned over his saddle horn and looked to the valley below. "I heard your brother is back. Does that mean he's going to be running the place now?"

Pete "Lucky" Larson had been with the W Bar G

since he and Carson graduated from high school together.

"You'd have to ask him," Destry said, hoping that
would be the end of it.

"Kind of hard to ask him since I haven't seen him.
Wouldn't you think he'd at least ask me in for a drink?
After all, we go way back."

She glanced over at the cowboy. Pockmarked with a
narrow ferretlike face, Lucky made her a little uneasy
lately. It was the way he looked at her, as if he thought
she needed being brought down a peg or two.

"I figure if Carson is running the place, he'll want
to give me a nice raise, don't you think? I know I'll
never get to live like your old man, but I'd like to live
better than I do."

Ranch hands on the W Bar G were well paid. Lucky
was probably overpaid, if the truth were known. "Carson's been pretty busy," Destry said. "But if you think
you're due for a raise, you should take it up with Russell. He's the ranch foreman."

"Is that right?" His gaze brushed over her like a
spider web, making her want to brush it off. "Carson's
busy, huh? Not too busy to be asking around about a
poker game, though. You should tag along to the next
game. Maybe you'll get lucky," he said with a wink.
"From what I've seen, you don't get out much."

"But *you're* going to have more time to get out," Russell said, startling them both since they hadn't heard
him approach. "You can collect your pay, Lucky. I've
put up with your lip as long as I'm going to."

"I was just visiting with the boss lady," Lucky said
and looked to Destry. "Isn't that right?"

Destry looked at him and felt a shudder. Was it possible Lucky had been in the woods behind her house watching her? "Like Russell said, collect your pay. I think you'd be happier on some other ranch."

"You're making a big mistake, Boss Lady," Lucky said as he reined his horse around and shot her a furious look.

NETTIE WATCHED AS Sheriff Frank Curry pushed back his Stetson and kneaded his forehead for a moment before glancing up. Hands on her hips, she scowled down at him from the back doorway of the store. He'd taken his sweet time getting out here, and for a good ten minutes, he'd been stumbling around in the pine trees behind the store. What was the fool doing? Certainly not figuring out who'd broken into her store.

Frank had weathered well for his age, sixty-one, only three years older than herself. He even still had his hair, a thatch of thick blond flecked with gray. He no longer wore it in a long ponytail like he had when he'd roared up to her house on his motorcycle and asked her out all those years ago.

While his hair was shorter, he now wore one of those thick drooping mustaches like in all the old Westerns. His shoulders were still broad, and he looked great in the jeans he wore with his uniform shirt and cowboy boots.

"You're not going to catch whoever broke into my store by wandering around out there in the woods."

He grinned. "Wanna bet?"

She reached for the broom she kept by the door, wanting to wipe that grin off his face.

He held up both hands in surrender and took a step back.

"Settle down. Anyone who knows you would have more sense than to break into *your* store, Lynette."

"Bet it was those Thompson brothers' kids. Young whelps. Those kids don't have the sense of a rock. I chased a few out of my store the other day. Wild as stray cats."

Frank shook his head. "Weren't kids. Come out here and I'll show you. And put down that damned broom. I don't want to have to arrest you for assaulting an officer of the law."

She came down the back steps and followed him a few feet into the pines.

"Look here. That's what broke into your store," he said.

Nettie stared down at the tracks in the soft earth. "A bear?"

"A fair-sized grizzly."

Nettie shook her head. "That is the craziest thing I've ever heard, Frank Curry. He just broke the window and left?"

"Must have gotten scared away." He shrugged, dusted off his hands and started to leave.

"That's it?" she demanded of his retreating back. "That's all you're going to do?"

He turned. "You want me to go after the grizzly and put him in jail for breaking your window? You're lucky that's all he did. If he'd gotten in, you'd have had one heck of a mess to clean up. I'd suggest you get that window boarded up until you can get it fixed. I'm sure your husband can do *that*."

She ignored the dig about Bob. "You're assuming the bear will be back."

"Aren't you? I'll call FWP to set out a trap."

She doubted the Fish, Wildlife and Parks department would get someone out with a trap today, she thought, glancing into the dark pines. A cool breeze stirred the lush boughs, making a sound like that of a grizzly moving through them. Her skin prickled. A hunter had been mauled by a grizzly just last year back up a canyon near here.

"In the meantime, I'd keep an eye out if I were you. The pines are pretty thick here by your back door. I'd hate for a grizzly to tangle with you. Grizzlies are still protected by law, so don't hurt him." He laughed at his own joke.

She mugged a face at him and stepped back into the store. From the front window, she watched the sheriff cross the street to Kate LaFond's café. She hoped his ears were burning as she cussed him to Hades and back.

CHAPTER EIGHT

NETTIE THOUGHT ABOUT having her husband tack up a piece of plywood over the broken window. But it would be less trouble just to call the contractor who lived down the road. Bob would make a big deal out of it, while Grayson Brooks would be quick and efficient and not complain.

Grayson answered on the first ring.

She quickly apologized for calling and asked how his wife, Anna, was.

"She's fine, Nettie. What can I do for you?" He was soft-spoken, always polite and agreeable.

"A darned grizzly broke the back window at the store," Nettie said. "I can't get it fixed until next week at the soonest according to the glass shop in Big Timber. I was hoping—"

"You want me to board it up for you?"

"Would you mind? I know you're busy with your work and Anna."

"No problem. I have a lovely woman who stays with Anna when I'm at work. The bear didn't get into the store and do any damage?"

"Luckily not. But I wouldn't be surprised if he comes back."

"I'll drive up to Beartooth now," Grayson said. "Don't you worry about a thing."

AFTER A DAY on horseback in the mountains, Destry was anxious to get back to the ranch. She'd gone home first, showered and changed, and then driven up to the big house. She felt badly about missing dinner her brother's first night at home. She could well imagine what that meal had been like with just their father and Carson and Cherry.

As Destry stepped into the living room, she saw Cherry thumbing through a magazine beside the fire.

"Where's Carson?"

"He left just a few minutes ago. I'm surprised you didn't see him."

"Where did he go?" Destry asked, wondering why he hadn't taken his fiancée with him. She'd seen their father's pickup out front, so the two of them hadn't left together and Carson's fancy sports car had been parked in the four-car garage and hadn't moved since he'd arrived.

"He said he had some business to take care of in town."

Destry felt her panic rise. "Beartooth?"

Cherry nodded. "He told me not to wait up for him, so I would imagine he found himself a poker game. Why are you—"

But Destry was already out the door. She ran to her pickup and took off toward town.

As she tore down the road, she saw dust ahead, and if Cherry was right, that must be Carson in one of the ranch trucks. He was headed toward Beartooth all right.

Had he lost his mind? Given the way some people in the community felt about him, he needed to stay close to the ranch.

Unfortunately, he not only wasn't on the ranch, he

seemed to be heading right into the badger's lair. She watched the ranch pickup drive past the post office, café and general store to turn into the parking lot behind the Range Rider bar.

Destry followed but had to park down the road a ways because the back lot was now full. Carson had picked the busiest night of the week to come here. What was he doing? Was he looking for trouble?

She'd hoped to find him still outside the bar, but he'd already gone in by the time she pushed open the back door. The smell of stale beer filled her nostrils as she walked into the packed room.

The band broke into a slow country-western song. She didn't see Carson anywhere around. She started to turn back when she spotted him.

He was standing at the end of the bar, back in the corner. If anyone had seen him come in, they hadn't reacted yet.

"What are you doing here?" she demanded under her breath as she stepped to his side.

"What would you like to drink?" he asked. She smelled alcohol on his breath. Clearly he'd had more than a few already. "I was just about to get a beer."

"Have you lost your mind?" she whispered, keeping her back to the crowd as she grabbed hold of her brother's arm. "Let's get out of here."

"Come on, little sis. Have a drink with me. I was going crazy at the ranch and I figured I might as well get it over with," Carson said.

"Dying? Is that what you're planning to get over with? Because if you stay in this bar—"

"I can't hide at the ranch like I'm some kind of fugitive." The pain in his voice made her let go of his arm.

From behind her she heard the name Grant and the scrape of a bar stool. Someone had recognized Carson and was no doubt making his way toward them.

"It would be better, little sis, if you left now," Carson said, looking past her.

"I'm not leaving without you."

He gave her a pleading look. "I know what I'm doing."

She shook her head and braced herself as she felt a hand drop on her shoulder. Turning, she came face-to-face with Hitch McCray. Hitch ranched on his mother's place to the north and had never made a secret of his interest in Destry or any other woman, for that matter.

At forty, he was still a bachelor. Word on the Beartooth grapevine was that no woman would ever be good enough for his mother. And since Ruth Mc-Cray ran the ranch—and her son—with an iron fist, there wasn't much chance of McCray getting married until his mother was dead, if he hoped to get the ranch.

"Mind if I dance with your sister?" Hitch asked Carson.

"I'd appreciate it if you did. Destry doesn't have enough fun," her brother said as several cowboys at the bar turned to glare at him.

Destry was shaking her head, but Hitch had hold of her arm and she felt her brother give her a push toward the dance floor. "Hitch, no, I can't—" The rest of her words died on her lips as she spotted Rylan leaning against a pool table in the far back. His gaze practically burned her skin.

All the fight went out of her. Hitch pulled her onto the dance floor. She didn't want to dance, but neither did she want to make a scene and call even more attention to herself or her brother.

Her heart was pounding from the heat of Rylan's gaze on her. That and fear for her brother. The effect was making her both heavy on her feet and light in the head. She stumbled, stepping on Hitch's boot toe.

"I'm sorry," she said as she tried to pull away from him. "I don't want to dance. I need to get my brother and…" Past him, she saw Kimberly Lane try to drag Rylan out on the dance floor, and the rest of the words died on her lips. Kimberly was saying something to Rylan, leaning into him, smiling, her glossy lips next to his ear.

"I've had my eye on you, you know," Hitch said.

The words didn't register at first. Destry was distracted, worried about her brother and sick at heart to see Rylan with another woman. She looked back to the spot where Carson had been standing, fearing a fight was about to break out. To her relief, she saw her brother check his watch, then pick up his beer and head for the door. She watched, but no one followed him out.

She realized Hitch had said something she'd missed as the song ended and the band broke into another slow one. She watched Rylan glance in her direction as Kimberly stepped into his arms and began moving to the music.

Destry looked away, willing herself not to care. She just wanted to get out of the bar. She started to step away, but Hitch drew her back.

"Did you hear what I said? I've been watching you," Hitch repeated, lowering his voice as if he wanted to make sure he wasn't heard.

She drew back to look into his face. *"What?"*

He grinned. "I've been watching you for years."

Destry thought of the downed gate, the tracks into the property, the feeling that someone had been in the trees behind her house.

"You've turned into quite the woman," he said, eyeing her up and down.

"You've been watching my *house?*" She tried to pull away, but he had a tight grip on her.

"I've been watching more than your house," Hitch said with a laugh. "You and I need to get together sometime and—"

Suddenly Hitch stopped talking—and dancing. Destiny blinked, startled to see Rylan standing next to them. Hitch seemed to hesitate before he let go of her and stepped back. It took her a moment to realize what was happening.

Rylan had cut in?

Her heart beat so hard that her chest ached. She tried to swallow the lump in her throat as he took her hand and drew her to him. It had been so long since she'd been this close to him, let alone in his arms. She caught the familiar scent of him. It kick-started her pulse. Just his touch sent goose bumps skittering over her skin.

She looked into his eyes. All that warm brown blazed with something so strong she felt it quake through her. He drew her closer, his lips going to her ear.

"What the hell are you and your brother doing here?" he whispered. "I'm trying really hard to ignore the fact that he is still walking around free, but he's pushing it, coming here tonight."

She drew back to look at him again and saw that his gaze was hard and still hot with a mixture of emotions that seemed about to boil over. "I know, that's why I came in to get him."

Rylan shook his head as he gazed down at her. "You can't save your brother from himself. He'll only take you down with him, Destry."

"Thanks for the advice." She tried to pull away, but he held on to her.

"Ginny didn't take my advice about your brother and look where it got *her*." With that, Rylan released her, turned and walked off the dance floor, leaving her standing alone in the middle of a song.

Anger welled in her, but nothing compared to the hurt as she watched Rylan go back to Kimberly.

Destry turned and, pushing her way through the crowd, hurried out the back door of the bar. She stopped short under one of the pine trees in the parking lot when she saw her brother standing with a man talking. Even from where she stood, she could tell that the man was threatening him.

"Carson," she called, making them both turn as she started toward them.

The man stepped back from her brother. She couldn't hear what he said as he climbed into a large dark SUV, but it was clear her brother knew him.

"Who was that?" she asked as Carson sauntered toward her. He came into the dim light from the back of the bar, and she saw that his lip was bleeding. "You're hurt." She started to reach for him, but he pushed her hand away.

"I'm fine."

"You're not fine. Why was that man threatening you?" she demanded as he moved past her toward the ranch pickup he'd driven into town.

"Stay out of it," Carson said as he retrieved his open bottle of beer from where he'd left it on a pine stump. He took a long drink.

"That's why you came here tonight. You were meeting him." Her voice sounded strained even to her. "What kind of trouble are you in?"

"You're a bigger fool than I am, you know that?" he said, ignoring her question as he leaned back against the pickup, fished a package of cigarettes from his pocket and lit one. "I saw the way you were looking at Rylan West. How many times are you going to let him break your heart?" He took a drag, releasing the smoke in a ghostlike cloud that rose up into the cold night air.

She said nothing. He sounded drunk and angry, a side of her brother she'd never seen before.

"I thought you had more sense," he said, sounding disgusted with her.

She couldn't bear to see him like this. Her heart ached because, under the anger and the alcohol, she could see his pain. "Let me help you."

His laugh held no humor. "There is no help for me. Hasn't been for years."

"I heard you'd been looking for a poker game."

He swore. "So Cherry blabbed. Great. Bringing her here sure was a mistake."

"Carson, what are you doing?"

He smiled at that. "You mean, do I have a plan? Sis, I haven't had a plan since I was nineteen. What about you? What's your plan now that Rylan seems to have moved on?"

She flinched at his words. "I'm not letting it destroy my life," she snapped back.

"Aren't you?" He cocked a brow at her. "Your life is

the ranch, and the old man is going to kick you off and give it to me while you're mooning over Rylan West, who is chasing that Lane girl. Is that what you want?"

She'd suspected that was exactly what their father had planned, but hearing it still hurt. "What I want doesn't matter. Haven't you figured that out yet?"

"Now look who's feeling sorry for herself," he said as he dropped the cigarette and crushed it under his boot.

She felt her chin go up. "I know Dad wants you to take over the ranch. He's always wanted that. Have you tried being honest with him? Told him what *you* want. Or do you even know?"

Carson lowered his head, his gaze on the ground. "What I want is to be rid of the whole damned place."

"What do you mean?" Her heart dropped. "You wouldn't sell the ranch."

"That's what the old man thinks," he said. "I could give a damn about the place. I know how you feel about the ranch and I'm sorry."

She doubted that. He didn't know how she felt about the ranch any more than he understood how she felt about Rylan. She couldn't let go. Not of the ranch. Not of Rylan. The land held her soul. Rylan her heart. Even if her father hadn't needed her after his accident, she couldn't have stayed away. This country was in her blood. It filled her with every breath she took.

"That man who was threatening you," she said, realizing that whatever the trouble was, it had followed him from Nevada. "You owe him money, don't you?"

"Yes, okay? I owe him a whole lot of money for some gambling debts. That's right, little sis. I need money."

"Have you asked Dad?"

He scoffed at that. "Even if he'd give me some, it wouldn't be enough. I need the *ranch*."

"You can't, Carson. It's his legacy. If he even suspected, it would kill him."

"What do you care about *his* legacy? It isn't like he's ever given a damn about you."

There it was, finally out in the open. *"Why?"* Her voice broke. She'd asked herself this for as long as she could remember. Why was their father the way he was with her?

"Whatever the reason, he wasn't going to leave you the ranch even if I hadn't come home." He opened the truck door to leave.

"Tell me the truth. There has to be a reason he feels the way he does other than you being the male heir."

"Don't you know, Destry?" he asked, his back to her. "Haven't you always known?"

"No." The word came out on a breath. Her heart thundered in her chest, the suspected truth crushing it with the weight of a draft horse.

"Why don't you ask him then?" He slid behind the wheel and looked at her. "Some things are just the way they are. I'm sorry. We can't change them. Give up. I have." He started the truck engine.

The back door of the bar opened, filling the night with the blare of music and the dull roar of voices. She turned, startled. Rylan stood silhouetted in the doorway. His gaze seemed to soften when he spotted her in the shaft of light coming from the open door, fingering its way through the pines.

He stood for a moment, the country music spilling from the bar kicking up a beat as the band broke into a cowboy jitterbug.

She swallowed, knowing that what her brother had said about Rylan breaking her heart again was nothing more than the truth, but it hurt more than he could know.

Had Rylan come out looking for her brother? Or for her?

He seemed to hesitate before he stepped back into the bar, the door closing behind him, muting the music again. In the cold shadow of the pines, her heart seemed to throw itself against her rib cage as if to prove that it could be broken over and over again.

Destry turned but wasn't surprised to find her brother and the ranch truck he'd driven to town in gone. Carson always had a way of disappearing when things got tough.

RYLAN WALKED BACK INTO the bar and picked up his pool stick, his emotions a tight knot in his belly. Why had he gone after Destry? There was nothing more he could say. Worse, no way to protect her.

"What's going on?" Kimberly asked, hands on her hips, alcohol firing her anger, as she stepped in front of him to block his shot.

"I'm going to play some pool and then I'm heading home."

She cocked a brow at him. Kimberly had been two years behind him and Destry in school. Pretty, but not his type. Not that his type mattered when he was looking for nothing more than a diversion. Tonight, though, nothing was going to distract him from thoughts of Destry.

"You went outside to check on her, didn't you? So, was she gone?" Kimberly demanded.

"I'm not talking to you about this, okay?" By the look on her face, clearly it wasn't. He dropped the pool stick on the table and, with the tip of his hat, said good-night and left the bar through the front door. He wasn't up to a fight with Kimberly. Nor was he looking to run into Destry again tonight.

Once in his pickup he'd left parked down the road from the bar in the pines, he headed out of town. Warring emotions roiled inside him. Seeing Destry had knocked the wind out of him. The Range Rider was the last place he'd expected to see her.

Now as he drove toward the ranch, he mentally kicked himself for going to the bar tonight. He hadn't wanted to be alone with his thoughts. Since his talk with Destry on the road yesterday, he kept going over their conversation in his head.

"How can you be so sure that Ginny wasn't involved with someone else who she kept not only from Carson, but also from your parents and even from you?"

Destry's words had stirred up things he didn't want to be digging around in. But he couldn't keep going the way he was, doing nothing, pretending he could let it go, he told himself now. Just as he kept pretending he could let Destry go.

He thought of his beautiful, sweet sister. Ginny had been the light of his family's life. The only girl in a family of three boys. He and Ginny had been only a year and a half apart in age, which had made them close. She wouldn't have kept secrets from him, he told himself as he drove toward the West Ranch.

Hadn't he been the one she'd confided in when she and Carson had gotten into a fight and he'd sprained her wrist?

"It isn't what you think," she'd cried when she'd come into his room holding her wrist. But he'd seen the hurt in her eyes. Just as he had seen Destry's pain tonight behind the bar.

He shoved that image away, letting his anger at Carson Grant replace it.

"What did that bastard do to you?" he'd demanded of his sister. He'd been ready to go after Carson Grant even then. It had been coming for a while, the trouble between Carson and Ginny, and, as her oldest brother, Rylan had tried to get her to break up with him.

"It was my fault," Ginny had said, blocking the door to keep him from heading for the W Bar G. He'd often wondered in the years since her death if things would have been different if he had gone that night and had it out with Carson then.

"Carson was holding me, I pulled away and tripped and fell," she'd claimed.

"You were fighting, don't even try to deny it."

It had taken a while, but he'd gotten the story out of her. She and Carson had quarreled, though she wouldn't say about what, but it had been her own clumsiness. "Carson was so sweet and so sorry that I'd hurt myself. Rylan, he wouldn't hurt me. I'm the one who's hurting him," Ginny had tried to convince him. Or had she been trying to convince herself?

Rylan had kept her secret and his parents never found out. A mistake, he'd thought a thousand times since and again now, as he pulled up to the house.

The lights were off. His brothers were at a community dance in Big Timber with their girlfriends they'd had since high school. All of the West kids had gone to the Beartooth one-room schoolhouse until ninth grade when they'd had to go the twenty miles across the Yellowstone River to school in Big Timber, or Big Twig, as they'd all called it.

His parents had said earlier that they were going to Bozeman for dinner and a movie. Which meant he had the house to himself.

As he killed the engine and started to get out of the pickup, he hesitated. All of Ginny's belongings had been packed up and stored in a corner of the basement. He'd seen the boxes marked with her name when he'd returned and had been looking for some of his own belongings his mother had stowed away for him.

He knew his mother hadn't gone through Ginny's things. In fact, it had been his father who'd boxed up everything in the weeks after the funeral. He doubted his father had looked through them, either. It would have been too painful. Taylor West would instead have done the job with quiet efficiency, the same way he ranched.

Opening the pickup door, Rylan walked toward the dark house. It was a pale yellow two-story structure with white trim and a wide railed porch across the front. The large yard light cast long shadows as he climbed the porch steps and entered the unlocked front door.

Out of habit, he didn't turn on a light, didn't have to. He knew this house by heart. As a teen, he'd sneaked through it in the dark more times than he could count. His mother wasn't one to move the furniture around, so the place had changed little in eleven years.

At the basement stairs, he opened the door and turned on the light. It was an old-fashioned basement with small windows, lots of concrete and steep wooden steps. The old, damp smell was almost pleasant in its familiarity.

He closed the door behind him as he descended the stairs. There were a half dozen large boxes piled in the far corner. Ginny's white bed frame and mattress stood against a far wall where it would never be used again. Her empty matching white chest of drawers and vanity were next to it.

The sheriff had taken her computer. Rylan didn't know if it had been returned or not. Her fifteen-year-old computer would be almost an antique by now. The only other item of clothing that had been missing was the letterman jacket Ginny had been wearing that night. She'd seldom gone anywhere without it after lettering in cheerleading, basketball and track.

Rylan made his way to the boxes. Each had only one word printed on it. *Ginny.* The first box he opened held nothing but a frilly pink, white and mint green comforter and matching pillow shams in a modern art design.

The second box was filled with her clothing just as the third and fourth were. No sign of the jacket, though. There was still the faint smell of the perfume she used to wear. Or maybe he'd only imagined it. Either way, it hurt so much he almost didn't open the fifth box.

But when he did, he saw her jewelry box sitting on top of her favorite books.

Carefully, he lifted out the smooth, varnished wood box. He remembered the Christmas when their parents had given it to her. She'd been so excited about having a big-girl jewelry box. When she'd opened the lid, they'd all laughed at her surprised expression. She hadn't known it would play music.

As he lifted the lid, her favorite song, "Amazing Grace," began to play. He felt a lump form in his throat and had to close the lid quickly. Carefully turning the box over, he flipped the switch that shut off the music.

Opening it again, he went through the contents, wondering why he was wasting his time. There wasn't much in it, just some cheap costume jewelry. Ginny had been buried in the Black Hills gold earrings and necklace that she'd loved and the Montana sapphire ring she'd gotten from all of them on her sixteenth birthday.

As he started to close the box again, he saw that a corner of the velvet interior had come loose. His heart began to pound, his fingers trembling as he pulled at it, hoping he was wrong. That Destry was wrong.

The corner of the velvet came up easily, making his stomach drop at the sight of a tarnished silver heart-shaped locket and chain coiled on a piece of paper. As he gingerly pulled out the locket, he saw the words hand-printed on the notepaper under it and felt his heart drop.

CHAPTER NINE

A CANOPY OF BLACK VELVET, bejeweled by more stars than most people had ever seen, filled Montana's big sky as Destry drove toward the W Bar G.

She felt wrung out. Her worry for her brother and seeing Rylan with Kimberly had taken everything out of her. She'd heard rumors since Rylan had returned home. Word on the grapevine had been that he was ranching with his father and brothers during the day and spending at least part of his nights at the Range Rider Bar.

She'd also heard that he'd been seen with several women in the area. Nettie Benton at the store had made a point of telling her. Apparently it wasn't enough that Rylan had tried for years to get his fool self killed riding anything that held still long enough in the rodeo—he'd come home still looking for adventure?

Fortunately, since he'd been home, the worst he'd done to himself was drink too much, get into fights and hook up with Kimberly, apparently.

What bothered Destry was that his behavior was so different from the cowboy she'd known all her life. He'd changed after his sister's death. They all had. But now it wasn't just her brother she wasn't sure she knew anymore.

A cool breeze blew down from the mountains, the air scented with wood smoke from one of the ranch houses she passed. It was a good night for a fire to ward off the cold. Destry yearned for a warmth that the heater in the truck couldn't provide.

She shoved away thoughts of Rylan, only to find herself worrying about her brother again. Carson was in trouble. That man who'd been threatening him when she'd come out of the bar had looked like a thug. Worse, her brother's attitude scared her.

"Give up," he'd said. "*I* have."

The defeat she'd heard in his voice had rocked her to her core. Just that morning he'd seemed hopeful when she'd mentioned him clearing his name.

Now she feared he was in more trouble than even she could have imagined, if the only way he could pay his gambling debts was to sell the W Bar G.

She thought about what Rylan had said about her not being able to save her brother from himself. That he would take her down with him.

Destry feared he might be right, since, as determined as she was, she hadn't been able to stop Rylan and the rest of this community from finding Carson guilty of Ginny's murder without even a fair trial.

Like a shot straight to her heart, she again was reminded of the image of Rylan with Kimberly tonight on the dance floor. She'd heard about the women on the pro circuit who followed the riders, as rabid as any rock groupies. But actually seeing Rylan with another woman...

She forced the image away again as she reached the fork in the road. To the right, the road led to her father's house up on the mountain. To the left, it wound down to the homestead house where she lived.

It was late. There would be no point in trying to

talk to Carson tonight with him half loaded. But she had to be sure he'd gotten back to the ranch safely. She wouldn't be able to sleep until she was.

Swinging the pickup to the right, she headed up the mountain road. A wedge of moon hung high over the ranch, the bright stars glittering around it. In the shadow of the Crazy Mountains, the pines stood like dark sentinels against the skyline.

Normally she loved nights like this, all the different fall smells, the landscape captured in cold silence. But tonight she felt unsettled and scared. The things her brother had said...

The pickup Carson had driven into town was parked beside the house. She would have turned around and left then, but she saw lights on in WT's den. Was Carson having it out with their father? The thought scared her. Her brother had sounded so desperate tonight. She feared what would happen if the two of them locked horns.

The big house was quiet as she slipped in the front door. Only a few lamps shone in all that spaciousness as she headed across the stone entry. The smell of charbroiled beef steaks lingered. She moved through the large living room with its stone fireplace and Native American rugs and artifacts.

She was partway down the hall when she heard the voices. Her father's was raised in anger. She debated whether to turn and leave or go in and try to keep the two of them from killing each other.

Then she heard her brother say from the partially open door to her father's den, "Destry has a right to know the truth."

"What truth is that?" Destry asked as she stepped into the den.

THE LAST THING CLETE Reynolds wanted was trouble in his bar, but when the band took a break, he could feel a change moving through the place. He didn't need to hear the talk at the end of the bar to know it was about Carson Grant.

Trouble was brewing. It was one reason he kept a sawed-off shotgun and a baseball bat behind the bar at the Range Rider—as well as a can of high-dollar pepper spray. The spray was for the women.

He'd started carrying the spray after an episode with a couple who'd been sitting at the bar drinking and bickering. Pretty soon the wife said something to the husband and he smacked her, which, as the old joke went, was considered foreplay in some parts of Montana.

Before Clete could put an end to it, one well-meaning male patron from down the bar stepped in, no doubt thinking he was going to be a gallant protector. The moment he butted in, the wife began pummeling the poor fool with her high-heeled shoe. So much for date night.

Ever since then, Clete kept pepper spray under the bar for the angry girlfriends and wives.

He'd come to have a sixth sense when it came to trouble. Sometimes it was a single raised voice. Other times it was the sudden quiet that came before a storm. Or, like this evening, it was more like an electric current moving through the place, making the hair on his neck lift and his skin prickle.

Several rowdy patrons had been working themselves up after seeing Carson Grant. Now tensions were running high. All this bar needed was a spark, and it would blow like a roman candle on the Fourth of July.

As if he'd conjured up that spark, Clete turned at the

sound of the front door opening and saw the Thompson brothers come in. They were always spoiling for a fight.

He glanced at the clock on the wall. Even set at bar time—twenty minutes fast—it was going to be a long night the way things were going. Before now there'd only been grousing about Carson Grant's return.

No one in the county was a fan of WT Grant, but they put up with him for Destry's sake. Most everyone liked her, just as they had liked her mother, Lila. Prior to Ginny West's murder, they'd at least tolerated WT's son, Carson.

But Ginny's murder had changed that. Several of the more raucous residents had been talking about paying the W Bar G a visit.

Now that the Thompson brothers had walked into the already charged air, Clete feared a vigilante posse would soon be heading for the ranch.

Clete had enough problems of his own, he thought. He didn't have any idea where his wife, Bethany, was at this moment, but he had a sneaking suspicion that she was with another man.

Right now, though, he had to keep the Thompson brothers from tearing up his bar.

As Clete reached for his sawed-off shotgun, the front door swung open and a breath of cold fall air rushed in along with Sheriff Frank Curry.

"WHAT TRUTH?" DESTRY asked again as both her brother and father turned to look at her.

"This it between you and WT," Carson said, heading for the door. He slowed enough to squeeze her shoulder as he passed. His lip looked swollen from his earlier altercation.

"There's something you need to tell me?" she said to her father, remembering what Carson had said earlier.

WT looked paler than he had a few moments before. He wheeled away, turning his back to her, as he went to the bar. "You want a drink?"

"Am I going to need one?"

His movements slowed for a moment, his shoulders slumping a little. "You shouldn't eavesdrop."

"I wasn't. I was worried about you and Carson in the same room together. I didn't expect you to be talking about me."

He turned from the bar with a drink in his hand. Hadn't he been drinking more lately? Or had she just not noticed before?

"What truth is it I need to know?" she asked, holding her ground.

"It's late. I really don't want to get into this now."

She put her hands on her hips, digging in her heels. "I think you'd better tell me. I suspect this is something that you've needed to tell me for some time. Be honest with me. You got Carson back to run the ranch."

He gave her an impatient look. "He's my son."

His son. She stood, breathing hard. *Give up, I have,* her brother had said. But that wasn't her. She would fight for the ranch if that's what it took. WT had always made it clear that he expected his *son* to come back to the ranch. But she'd never dreamed WT meant to give it to him, lock, stock and barrel.

She shook her head. "You're leaving him in charge of the ranch."

Her father said nothing, making it clear that Carson had been right.

"What about me? You just hope to marry me off to anyone who'll have me?" she asked.

"Hitch McCray has had his eye on you for years and he stands to inherit the McCray place," he said. "That's some fine land and part of it is adjacent to that piece I just purchased."

"I see. So if I want a ranch, you expect me to marry it."

"That's what women do."

Destry balled her fists at her side, overcome with years of anger at her father. He'd fought her at every turn when it came to the running of the ranch, but she'd helped make it one of the most productive ones around in spite of him.

"You think Carson will do a better job of running the ranch?" she asked.

WT looked away. "I'm not saying that. I'll admit he's made some mistakes in the past."

"Mistakes?" She stared at him in shock. "You don't mean Ginny's murder." She felt her eyes widen in alarm. "You think he killed her."

"What I think doesn't matter."

"And yet you plan to give the ranch to him believing he's a *murderer?*"

"He's my *son.*"

"And I'm your *daughter,* not to mention I am actually capable of running the ranch and I don't have a murder charge hanging over my head." She stopped herself from saying Carson only wanted the ranch to sell it so he could pay his gambling debts.

Hot angry tears burned her eyes. She willed herself not to cry, damned if she would let him see how much he'd hurt her.

"I don't expect you to understand." With a curse, he said, "You've always been just like your mother."

Destry had heard that her whole life. She apparently looked like her mother and acted like her. But until that moment, she'd always thought her father meant it as a compliment.

"This isn't just about the ranch, is it?" she demanded.

WT shifted his gaze away.

Given his attitude toward her, she'd suspected it for sometime. "It has something to do with me. Why you treat me the way you do. It isn't just because I look so much like my mother, is it?" She'd always thought he couldn't bear to be around her because she reminded him so much of the wife he'd loved and lost in a horseback riding accident. Now, though, she suspected that had never been the case. "Since you're being honest with me…"

He trembled with rage as he met her gaze. "If you're so damned determined to know the truth, then fine. You aren't my daughter. You're some bastard's your mother slept with. She didn't even bother to try to pass you off as mine."

His words were delivered like a blow. They knocked the air out of her. She rocked like a young sapling under a gale wind. For years she'd known something was wrong, even suspected it had something to do with her mother. But not this.

"I don't believe you." Even as she said the words, she did believe him. It all made sense, why he never wanted to hear her mother's name, why he'd destroyed all the photographs of his wife, why he treated Destry the way he had since as far back as she could remember. Why he was giving the ranch to Carson.

"You wanted to know. Now you do." He took a gulp of his drink and coughed as it went down the wrong way.

"Did she tell you I'm not your daughter?" she asked.

He laughed at that. "She didn't have to."

"Did my brother know, too?" Was this what her brother had wanted to tell her the night he came down to the homestead house and helped her stack wood? If so, how could he keep something like this from her?

WT narrowed his gaze. "Your brother was young but I suspect he knew more than he's ever told me." He sounded bitter and angry about that. If Carson had seen something and hadn't told, WT would never forgive him for not coming to him. It wouldn't matter that Carson had been just a boy.

She stared at WT. She'd made excuses for him, telling herself not to take the way he treated her personally. He was a bitter man who treated most everyone poorly. But the pain of WT's rejection had never been as sharp as it was now that she knew his feelings toward her *had* been personal.

She'd never had her father's love, but she'd never missed it, either. As far back as she could remember, she'd had people who loved and took care of her. W Bar G's ranch foreman, Russell, had taught her to ride a horse. Ranch hands had taught her to rope and brand and cut cattle. Her brother had taught her to swim. Margaret had taught her to cook enough that she would never starve.

She'd had Rylan for her best friend. She'd never felt unloved. If anything, she'd felt badly for her father because it had been clear to her early on that he was in a lot of pain. She'd felt for him and blamed herself for looking so much like her mother.

"You're the spitting image of Lila," Margaret had told her when she'd asked why her father could barely look at her sometimes. "It's just hard for him because of that. Don't pay the old fool any mind."

And it wasn't as if WT was nice to other people. He was abrasive to everyone and didn't apologize for it. Except maybe to Margaret. Margaret was also the only person Destry had ever seen stand up to him.

"Who is my father?"

"Don't you think if I knew who he was that he'd be dead?"

She didn't believe him. He knew. Or at least he suspected. But for some reason he hadn't confronted the man. Her heart was pounding as if she'd tried to outrun a storm on a fast horse. If she wasn't WT's daughter, then who was she?

The thought shook the once solid ground on which she'd built her life. She had no right to the ranch. No wonder WT had never considered leaving it to her. With a horrible sinking feeling, she realized she was about to lose everything she loved.

She'd already lost so much. Her mother. Rylan. And now not just her father, but also her whole identity. But to lose the ranch, too?

"You can't just turn the W Bar G over to Carson."

"It's late and I'm tired," WT said and coughed again.

"I love my brother, but there is something you have to know."

WT's drink glass slipped from his hand and hit the floor, shattering with what sounded like a gunshot. Ice cubes clattered across the floor.

With alarm, Destry saw his face. All the color had washed from it. His hand had gone to his chest, and he seemed to be desperately trying to catch his breath.

RYLAN CAREFULLY PICKED up the piece of notepaper from where it had been hidden under the velvet of Ginny's jewelry box. The words were handwritten in ink, the letters slightly slanted. Neat, but appearing to have been scrawled in a hurry—or in anger. He didn't recognize the handwriting.

The small piece of paper was faded to sepia. It was also wrinkled, as if at some point his sister had wadded it up to throw it away. Why hadn't she? Why would she keep something like this, let alone hide it? A frisson of fear rushed along his nerve endings as he read the words printed on the notepaper once again.

For the lips of an adulteress drip honey, and her speech is smoother than oil; but in the end she is bitter as gall, sharp as a double-edged sword. Her feet go down to death; her steps lead straight to the grave

What the hell? *Her feet go down to death?* He shuddered.

Why would Ginny have kept this? Especially why would she keep it hidden in the same place as a tarnished heart-shaped locket?

Both of these had to mean something to his sister. Something she hadn't wanted anyone to know about.

Rylan slumped back onto one of the boxes as he considered what he'd found and, more to the point, what it meant.

It meant Ginny had secrets. Just as Destry had said. Secrets that could have gotten her killed?

He shook his head at the thought as he picked up the locket and pried it open in the hopes that a clue would be inside. The locket was empty. Even under the overhead bulb of the basement he could see that the piece of jewelry was cheap. He tried to remember if he'd ever seen his sister wearing it. He couldn't recall seeing it around her neck. If it meant something special to her, then why hadn't she worn it?

Rylan groaned at the implication. He thought of Carson Grant's suspicion that Ginny had been seeing someone. Possibly a married man. What if it was true and the locket was from the mystery man? The note certainly would support that theory if someone had found out about them.

Was it possible Carson had given Ginny this note? He couldn't see Carson Grant quoting the Bible, not that hotheaded young man he'd been at twenty. But he could see Carson losing his temper if Ginny really was seeing a married man. Didn't this give Carson even more motive?

He stared at the note and the locket, wondering what to do with them. How about putting them back where he'd found them and keeping his mouth shut? The last thing his parents needed was this. How could he open this can of worms now? But Destry's words to him echoed in his head.

"Are you so set on vengeance, that the truth be damned?"

As he sat staring at what he'd found, he realized he had no choice. His father had told him that the sheriff was reinvestigating the case. He couldn't keep this to himself, no matter where it led.

He thought of Destry. Her brother might have been right about there being another man in Ginny's life. But that only gave Carson Grant even more motive to kill Ginny in a jealous rage.

IT WAS LATE. LATE ENOUGH that Bethany thought it would be all right to call him. Still, she was shaking when she dialed his number and was relieved when he answered and not his wife.

"I got another one of those notes," she said before he could chew her out for calling the house.

"What are you talking about?" he asked, keeping his voice down. She heard a door close on his end of the line. She could tell he was distracted. He hated when she called him at home. But this last note had scared her.

"I told you about the note someone left under my windshield wiper. I saw it when I came out of the Branding Iron after my shift." She felt a stab of anger at the realization that he hadn't remembered the other note she'd told him about. He also hadn't tried to contact her since they'd gotten together earlier. "You remember the Branding Iron, don't you?"

The café was where they used to visit when she was working and the café was empty. He'd stop by and they'd just talk. After a while, she'd realized that he was flirting with her. Before then, she'd thought of him as being too old and too married. But he'd become even more forward when the cook, Lou, was out having a smoke behind the café.

She'd been flattered by the attention. He was sweet and shy at first. He made her feel as if she was the only woman in the world. The flirting had led to a secret rendezvous away from the café and finally to his cousin's apartment in Big Timber.

"Of course, I remember the Branding Iron." The way he said it made her heart kick up a beat or two. It had been romantic, the way he'd seduced her over time. She could still remember the night he'd put the locket on her and shivered at the memory.

"So tell me about these notes?" he asked as if this was the first time he'd heard about them.

"The first one was just weird. But this one kind of scares me."

"Bethany."

"Just listen to the note, okay?" She cleared her throat and read:

> *He who sleeps with another's man wife; no one who touches her will go unpunished. Those who confess their sins and turn from them will receive mercy.*

It had been under her windshield wiper, just like the last one, when she'd come off her late shift at the Branding Iron tonight. She'd put off calling him, afraid she would only make him mad.

"So, what do you think?" she asked into the dead silence coming from the other end of the phone.

"I think we definitely shouldn't see each other for a while."

"What?"

"I don't think these notes have anything to do with us, but if they do..."

She hadn't imagined it when she'd thought he was

pulling away from her earlier. "There's someone else, isn't there?" she cried.

"Don't start this again. We're both married. Of course there is someone else! We should never have gotten involved to begin with and you know it. We're better people than this."

"There *is* someone else. I can tell."

"I have to go. Please, let's do the right thing. Don't contact me again." He hung up.

She stared at the phone, fighting tears. He was breaking up with her.

As many times as she'd said she wasn't going to see him again, she felt as if someone had pulled the rug out from under her. She'd always thought she would be the one to end it. She never dreamed he would.

She touched the locket at her throat. There *was* someone else. And not his wife. But who?

CHAPTER TEN

DESTRY PACED.

"Wearing a hole in the floor isn't going to help," her brother said from where he was slumped in an alcove chair.

"I can't sit. This is all my fault. If I hadn't confronted him—"

"It's not your fault." Carson sounded weary. They'd had this conversation a half dozen times already as they waited for the doctor outside WT's bedroom door. "I'm sure he's fine. I wouldn't be surprised if he pulled this so you'd be afraid to argue with him for fear you'd kill him."

"How can you say that? He looked as if he was having a heart attack."

Carson shrugged. "I know him. He isn't past pulling something like this because he feels guilty about what he's doing to you. So he told you everything?"

"I don't want to talk about it right now. I can't, okay?"

"Fine with me." He closed his eyes. His lack of concern bothered her. Did he really care nothing for his own father? Or was this his way of coping?

A door opened down the hall. Carson sat up as the doctor came out, closing WT's bedroom door behind him.

"How is he?" Destry asked.

"Your father is resting comfortably," Dr. Flaggler said.

Her father. The words made her ache. "Did he have a heart attack?"

"No. Just shortness of breath. Probably along the lines of a panic attack. I understand you and he were having a discussion?"

"WT doesn't have discussions. He has arguments," Carson said.

The doctor shot him an impatient look. "Whatever you want to call it, your father needs to take it easy."

Her brother shoved to his feet. "In other words, he told you to tell us not to argue with him, right?"

The doctor frowned. "Has your father talked to you about his health?"

"No," Destry said. "Is there something we should know?"

He cleared his throat and glanced back at the closed bedroom door. "Your father is a very stubborn man. The last time I saw him he promised me that he would talk to you about his condition."

Her eyes widened in alarm. "The last time you saw him? I didn't even know he'd been to see you. Is his condition serious?"

"Your father's airplane accident and years in a wheel-chair have taken a toll on his body," the doctor said. "I encourage you to have an honest talk with him about his health."

"Without upsetting him, right?" Carson said snidely, but quickly sobered. "Wait a minute. Are you telling us he's dying?"

Destry felt her chest hitch. No matter their blood, WT was the only father she'd ever known.

"Just try to keep him as comfortable as you can and

as…calm." The doctor put his hand on her shoulder and squeezed it before walking away.

RYLAN KNEW IT WAS TOO EARLY in the morning. He'd tried to talk himself out of what he was about to do. But he was already in his truck on his way to the W Bar G as the sun was coming up.

Last night, he'd had hell getting to sleep after what he'd discovered in Ginny's jewelry box. He hated to think what the note or the hidden locket meant. A part of him still wished he'd just put both back in the jewelry box where he'd found them.

He knew he was probably going to wake up Destry, but he couldn't put this off any longer. The thought of her sleepy-eyed, hair a jumble falling around her shoulders, set off a sharp, painful ache inside him.

Rylan shoved the image away as he passed the road up to WT's Folly and continued down the mountain to the ranch road and the homestead house. It was a two-story log structure surrounded on three sides by aspens, pines and cottonwoods.

The front yard was shaded, the sun gilding the tops of the trees. A figure slinked across the front of the house, stopping to peer into one of the windows.

Rylan blinked, confused for a moment by what he was seeing. The pickup rumbled over the cattle guard and down the ranch road. The man must have heard him coming because he took off running toward the trees that flanked the side of the house.

Speeding up, Rylan raced into the yard and jumped out to rush into the trees after the man. He had only an impression of the intruder: big, definitely male.

It was still dark in the thick stand of trees. About half

the leaves clung to the limbs of the aspens. They rustled over his head, sunlight flickering through them as he ran. The man had too much of a head start.

As Rylan burst from the trees at the edge of the creek, he stopped short. There was no movement in the trees on the other side. A gust of wind whirled leaves around him, sending them skimming across the water's surface. Over the sound of the wind and the rushing water, Rylan heard a vehicle engine start up in the distance.

The man was gone. But he'd left a fresh boot print in the soft dirt. It wasn't the only print, Rylan noticed with a curse. He'd been here before.

DESTRY WOKE WITH A START. She lay in bed listening to the familiar creaks and groans of the old house. So what had awakened her?

Through the sheer curtains of the second story window, she could see the sun was still low on the eastern horizon. She glanced at the clock, surprised it was so early. She hadn't gotten home from the big house until late after her father's spell, which meant she hadn't been to sleep long.

The events of last night came back in a rush of shock and grief. WT was ill, so ill he might be dying. She'd upset him enough that she could have killed him. She closed her eyes, not wanting to deal with any of it yet this morning.

The sudden banging on her front door startled her up into a sitting position. Going to the window, she looked down to see a pickup parked in the yard. That must have been the sound that had awakened her.

The banging became insistent. She grabbed her robe

and tied it as she headed down the stairs. Throwing open the door, she was shocked to see Rylan standing there.

"Were you asleep?" he asked, sounding either winded or upset. She couldn't tell which as he stepped past her into the house.

"What's wrong?"

"That's what I was going to ask you. As I drove up I saw a man peering in one of your lower windows."

"A man?" She felt half asleep, exhausted after last night and off balance with Rylan standing in her living room staring at her. "Are you sure it wasn't my brother?"

"Would your brother have taken off through the trees when he heard me drive up?"

"Maybe, if he saw you racing up this time of the morning," she said. There was no way her brother was up at this hour unless there was trouble at the big house, but then he or Margaret would have called. And Carson wouldn't have taken off into the trees even if he had seen Rylan.

Destry knew that the man she'd seen the other night had come back. It sent a chill through her. Lack of sleep and the recent emotional roller-coaster ride she'd been on, added to Rylan's surprise visit, had her feeling vulnerable. It wasn't a feeling she was comfortable with.

Wrapping her robe more tightly around her, she went into the kitchen and busied herself by putting on a pot of coffee. Someone had been out there again. Had he been peeking in the windows the last time, too?

"This isn't the first time he'd been on your property," Rylan said, following her. "I found older boot tracks by the creek. They matched the ones of the man I saw looking in your window. You don't seem surprised."

She was more surprised that Rylan was here.

With a shudder, though, she tried not to imagine what could have happened if he hadn't shown up when he did. She set the can of coffee back on the shelf above the coffeemaker and closed the cupboard before she turned to face him.

"I thought I saw someone watching the house before I went to Denver. He's been back once since then."

"Did you call the sheriff?" He didn't wait for an answer. "Of course not. You think whoever it is, you'll just handle it yourself."

"The sheriff can't do anything," she said. "If I called him when I saw someone out there, by the time he got here, it would be too late."

Rylan swore and dragged off his Stetson to rake his hand through his thick blond hair. Watching him, she was reminded of those same fingers caught up in her hair in a moment of passion. She quickly pulled her hair up, knotting it at her neck.

THE WOMAN WAS IMPOSSIBLE. Rylan swore under his breath as he watched her tie up her mane of hair. Just as he'd pictured, she had that sleepy-eyed look that made him want to drag her to him and kiss her senseless.

"You've got yourself a Peeping Tom or something worse and you don't seem all that concerned."

Her look said she had bigger things to worry about right now. He noticed the shadows under her eyes. Apparently she hadn't been sleeping any better than he had.

"I'm having Grayson Brooks put new locks on the doors later this week when he comes to build some stalls up at the barn. He's busy up at the store taking care of a window where a bear tried to break in."

"This peeping tom's been in your house?"

She hoped not. "No, but since I don't even know where to find a key for the front door, I thought it might be a good idea to get new locks."

"You have any idea who was out there?" he asked.

"No," she said with a shake of her head.

"Could this have something to do with your brother?"

Her hands went to her hips. She had an athletic body, full in all the right places, and great hips. "Isn't it possible that not everything comes back to Carson?" she snapped. "It just so happens that I thought someone was watching my house *before* my brother came back."

He didn't want to argue with her about her brother. "Still, you'd be smart to stay up at your father's house until Grayson changes the locks."

"I have my shotgun. Loaded. A pistol by my bed. And I'm planning to sleep with one eye open. But thanks for your concern."

He ground his teeth at the woman's mule-headed stubbornness.

"Is there some reason you're here at this hour of the morning?" she asked impatiently.

He slapped his hat back on his head, having second thoughts about coming out here. But he wasn't going to let her rile him so he would leave. What he'd come out here for was too important.

"I got to thinking about what you said the other day." It was damned hard to admit that he might be wrong. Especially about her brother. "What you said about Ginny having a secret…"

Destry nodded and moved out of the kitchen to take

a chair at the table. He finally had her undivided attention apparently.

He cleared his throat. "I need you to look at something." Reaching into his pocket, he stepped to her and laid the yellowed piece of once-crumpled notepaper on the table, dropping the silver heart-shaped locket and chain next to it. He watched her closely as she looked from the note and locket to his face.

"Have you seen that before?" he asked as she lifted the locket by its thin silver chain.

THE SILVER WAS TARNISHED. The only thing unusual about the locket was that the heart wasn't perfectly shaped. "Is it Ginny's?" Destry asked.

"I found it in her jewelry box—hidden under the lining."

She felt herself start. Hope burned through her. So it was possible that Ginny had a secret lover just as her brother had said.

Rylan clearly still didn't want to believe his sister had any secrets, she thought, seeing the hard set of his jaw. And yet he was here, showing her what he'd discovered. Clearly the discovery had upset him.

He pointed to the piece of notepaper he'd put on the table. "I found that with it. Do you recognize the handwriting?"

She glanced at the note, then up at him. "Carson didn't write it, if that's what you're asking. He's left-handed like you. This is definitely not his handwriting."

Rylan said nothing as she picked up the note. She had only glanced at the writing before. Now she read the words.

*For the lips of an adulteress drip honey, and her
speech is smoother than oil; but in the end she is
bitter as gall, sharp as a double-edged sword.
Her feet go down to death; her steps lead straight
to the grave*

Startled, she looked up at Rylan. "This sounds…
threatening."

"Why would she hide something like this?" he asked,
as if hoping she would come up with a reason other than
the one staring him in the face. He'd come to the wrong
house if he hoped for that.

"You *know* why. Carson was right about Ginny seeing someone else. Apparently, if the note is any indication, a married man."

Rylan shook his head as he pulled out a chair and
sat down. "I called some of Ginny's old friends. None
of them knew about her dating anyone but Carson."

"She wouldn't have 'dated' this man if he was married."

"Ginny was too smart to get involved with a married man," he said adamantly. "There has to be another
answer."

Destry didn't argue the point. She knew that intelligence had little to do with love.

"Maybe he wasn't married, but he wasn't free. Whoever wrote this knew about the two of them," she said,
holding up the paper. "But if he wasn't married, then
why else call her an adulteress?"

"If the note was even to Ginny."

Destry gave him an impatient look. "Why else would
she have kept it?" A thought struck her. "What if she

showed it to her lover? He'd know that someone had discovered their secret. He might panic."

Rylan didn't say anything for a long moment. He leaned forward, placed his elbows on the table and dropped his head in his hands. Destry fought the urge to place a hand on his broad shoulders. She loved this man. She wanted to comfort him. But there was eleven years between them and a whole lot more.

"There's something I haven't told you," he said, his words muffled.

She held her breath as he raised his head, his eyes shiny and filled with a bright pain that broke her heart.

"Ginny was pregnant."

Her breath came out in a rush. "Was it Carson's?"

Rylan nodded.

Destry felt her heart break for her brother. Had he known Ginny was pregnant? That she was carrying his baby?

As the coffee finished brewing, she rose from her chair, needing a cup for the warmth and a few moments to lasso in her anger. "If he'd known about the baby, he would have wanted it. He says Ginny was the only woman he will ever love."

Rylan said nothing, clearly not believing a word of it.

She took down two mugs, filling one. As she held it up, Rylan shook his head. She put the second mug away. Wrapping her fingers around her cup, she hoped the radiating heat chased away the chill she felt after reading that note. What had Ginny gotten herself into?

Rylan got up from his chair, and for a moment, she thought he was leaving. Instead, he walked over to the windows facing the creek.

"You have no idea who this other man might have been?" she asked as she took her seat at the table again.

He shook his head but didn't turn around. She studied his broad back, the long muscled legs clad in faded denim, and felt an overwhelming rush of desire. She took a sip of the hot coffee, wanting to scald away her need for this man.

"If this man was married, then he has a motive to want to keep your sister quiet about the affair," she said, even though Rylan wouldn't have come out here so early in the morning if he hadn't already figured that out himself. "Especially if she thought it was his baby."

As she looked at the note and locket, her heart swelled at the realization that there really was another suspect other than her brother. If the real killer was found... "You have to take this to the sheriff."

"I've been wondering what made your brother think Ginny was seeing a married man."

She shook her head as he turned to look at her.

"Ginny told me that she'd thought someone had been following her, spying on her."

"If Carson had been following her, then he would know who she was seeing. He would have had no reason not to tell the sheriff eleven years ago."

Rylan sighed. "I'll take this to the sheriff, but this doesn't clear your brother. If anything, the pregnancy makes him look more guilty. Given what the locket and note suggests, if he'd found out about the baby and thought it wasn't his, I can only imagine what he might have done."

"Even with this evidence right in front of your face, you're still determined my brother is guilty?" She shoved back her chair and got to her feet. She studied him for a moment and then, with a shake of her head, said, "I used to think I knew you."

"Ginny's death changed us all," Rylan said with a curse.

"Yes, it changed us. But not the way it changed you and my brother." She started to step away, but he grabbed her arm, pulling her around to face him.

"I'm still the same man you fell in love with."

She looked into his eyes. "I don't think so."

"Like hell." He dragged her to him with one arm around her waist. His mouth dropped to hers in a demanding kiss that stole her breath. She could feel the thunder of his heart against hers. Wrapped in his strong arms, she lost herself in the kiss. She felt the passion, the chemistry that had always made her pulse pound. The kiss fired that old aching need for this man she couldn't have.

It swept her up, made her forget for a moment the gulf that lay between them. He drew her closer, pressing his body to hers, deepening the kiss, and with desire burning through her, all she wanted was for him to sweep her up in his arms and carry her upstairs to her bed.

The realization made her draw back. She was shaking with both passion and fear at what would happen if she gave in to her need for this cowboy. "You should leave now."

He shook his head, clearly as overwhelmed as she was by the desire the kiss had ignited. "Destry—"

"You are never going to believe my brother didn't hurt Ginny, no matter how much evidence you find otherwise." She picked up the note and the necklace. The locket felt light. She wondered—

"I already looked inside."

Destry handed the locket to him and crossed her arms, waiting for him to leave, needing him to leave before they did something they would both regret. "I'll ask my brother if he gave her the locket or knows anything about the note."

He took out a West Ranch business card and pen, scribbling something on the back. "There's my cell number. Call me." He seemed to hesitate, as if there was something more he wanted, needed, to say.

Destry held her breath. When he finally walked to the door, he stopped and turned. "Please don't stay here alone tonight." His voice was soft, caring. She remembered the way he was with the horses on the ranch. A gentle man with a soft, slow hand. "I don't think you're safe."

"Thanks for your concern, " she said, unable to look at him. She feared she might call him back. "But I can take care of myself."

"That's what my sister thought."

CHAPTER ELEVEN

DESTRY DROVE INTO CHURCH as she always did on Sunday mornings. The small, white wood-framed community church sat at the far edge of Beartooth. It had a steeple with a bell that Pastor Tom rang each Sunday morning and looked like something out of an old Western movie.

As she entered the building, she didn't take her usual wooden pew up front, but sat at the back. There was no use pretending that nothing had changed from other Sundays. She felt the stares, saw the curious looks and whispers. She didn't want to sit through the entire service, feeling as if everyone was staring at the back of her head.

Kate LaFond, the new owner of the Branding Iron Café, sat at the organ playing a hymn Destry recognized. Kate had taken over since Grayson Brooks's wife Anna's health had gotten too bad for her to play or even attend church.

Destry looked around until she spotted Grayson, the local contractor, also sitting alone at the back of the church. He was a large, nice-looking man with an easygoing manner. He smiled at her and looked as if he might come over to sit by her. She picked up a hymnal on the pew beside her.

She didn't want to have to visit with anyone this morning. Rylan's unexpected visit had left her off-kilter, like a washing machine out of balance. It wasn't every day that she was awakened by Rylan West. Unfortunately, she thought, with no small amount of disappointment.

Her hope was to simply enjoy the service. She wasn't going to worry right now about her brother or think about Rylan or WT. Maybe she didn't know Carson. Maybe she never had.

She barely knew *herself* this morning. She thumbed through the hymnal for a moment, unable to hold off the reminder that WT apparently wasn't her biological father. Looking around the congregation gathered, she wondered if one of the older men might be her father. The thought sent a shiver through her. She feared she'd never look at an older man in the community without wondering.

She pushed the thought away as she took in the parishioners gathered today. There was Nettie and Bob Benton from the Beartooth General Store. Both were in their late fifties. Natives of the area, they lived in a house on the mountain behind the store. Nettie was chattering away. Bob didn't seem to be listening.

Destry spotted Rylan's father, Taylor, but not his mother, Ellie. The two younger West boys were also not in attendance, either, it seemed. That was unusual. Nor was Sheriff Frank Curry here, also unusual.

Pastor Tom Armstrong spotted her, nodded and smiled, but she was glad he didn't come over. In his early fifties, Tom had come to the cloth late in life after growing up in California. He claimed he enjoyed preaching because it kept him on the straight and narrow.

He still had that blond, blue-eyed West Coast look

and was quite handsome, which didn't hurt when it came to getting more of the twenty- and thirtysomething young women to attend Sunday service.

Destry noticed his wife, Linda, in the front row pew. Linda was a tall, statuesque woman, quite a bit older than her husband. They'd come to town about fifteen years ago and moved into the parsonage on the hill behind the small community church.

She was glad to see that neither Kimberly nor the rest of the Lane family were in church today. She tried not to think of Kimberly in Rylan's arms at the bar as Tom took his place behind the lectern and the church quieted. He opened his Bible, welcomed everyone and announced the hymns. They all stood and sang, one of Destry's favorite parts of Sunday service. She loved the hymns and the feeling they gave her as she heard the congregation's voices raised in song.

It seemed like more than a coincidence when Tom announced that the sermon was about forgiveness. She wondered if next week's service would be on being her brother's keeper and if she would heed its message.

Destry started for the door at the conclusion of the service. She was almost there when Pastor Tom caught her arm.

"Destry, so good to see you."

She looked past the pastor to see that Linda had cornered Grayson Brooks. Destry knew that Linda had become good friends with Grayson's wife, Anna, when they'd moved here. Linda looked upset, and Destry wondered if Anna's health had worsened. Linda and Grayson certainly seemed to be having a very intense conversation. Linda had a grip on Grayson's arm that looked almost painful. Nearly as painful as the look on his face.

"How are you?" Pastor Tom asked now as he drew Destry aside.

"Fine." The word came out automatically.

He smiled as if he knew better. "I'm always available to talk if you feel the need."

"Thank you." He'd made the same offer after Ginny's murder and Carson's exodus from Montana. But Destry hadn't wanted to talk about it. Maybe especially to a pastor. She hadn't wanted to admit that she'd been making love with Rylan the night his sister was killed and that had made it all the worse.

"How is your brother?"

She didn't know how to answer that. "Carson's trying to adjust to being home." Past him she saw that Linda had released her hold on Grayson Brooks and was now watching her.

"Then he's staying?" Pastor Tom sounded pleased.

"I'm not sure." If WT had his way, yes.

"Well, the offer stands if you need anything or your brother needs someone to talk to. Sometimes it helps to talk to someone who doesn't have a dog in the fight, so to speak."

"Actually, I wondered if you are familiar with this." She'd looked up the Bible quote after Rylan had left this morning and written it down. She handed him the piece of paper to read.

He looked at it, then handed it back. "I'm familiar with a lot of quotes from the Bible. Is there a particular reason you wanted me to look at that one?"

"I believe someone left it as a threat."

He paled. "That is very upsetting. Was this recent?" He was definitely upset, she noticed.

But before Destry could ask him anything further, Linda joined them. She slipped an arm possessively through her husband's and asked, "Did you enjoy the sermon?" Linda always wore flats, no doubt so she didn't tower over her husband.

"I did, thank you," she said.

Linda gave her a smile, then turned to her husband. "Tom, Mrs. Murphy needs a word with you. If you'll excuse us, Destry?"

"Destry," Tom said quickly, "I was hoping you'd stop by sometime soon, since you're chairwoman of the clothing drive, so we can get the bins emptied out."

She said she would and watched Linda drag her husband over to the elderly Mrs. Murphy. Tom looked back at her once, worry etched on his handsome face.

"She can't stand to see her husband talking to a pretty young woman," Nettie Benton said beside Destry, startling her. "It's that green-eyed jealousy. I feel sorry for Pastor Tom, don't you? I really doubt he gives her any reason to worry, but you never know about men, do you?"

Destry didn't have a chance to respond as Bob dragged his wife out, saying they had to get the store open. Nettie prided herself on the Beartooth General Store being open seven days a week, even though the hours often varied.

"Me and God have an understanding," Nettie was fond of saying. "I pay my respects to him and then I make sure people have what they need, even on Sunday."

As Destry followed them out of the church, she saw

Grayson drive away and wondered what Linda had been so intently talking to him about. Only three vehicles were still in the lot by the time she made her way to her truck.

But as she grew near, she caught a glimpse of a straw Western hat through the window of her truck cab. Someone was leaning against the other side of her pickup waiting for her.

Her first thought was Rylan, not that he'd been in church this morning. But he would have known where to find her. She seldom missed church services.

As she came around the front of the truck, she was disappointed and immediately uneasy to see that it was Hitch McCray.

She slowed, remembering what he'd said at the bar.

"You're a hard woman to get alone," Hitch said congenially enough as he took a step toward her. "Why don't we go somewhere so we can finish our talk."

Destry shook her head. "I don't think so."

He grabbed her arm to stop her from moving away. "You know your father wants to see the two of us get together. So what is the problem?" he demanded, raising his voice.

Her father? She almost laughed at that. She jerked free of his hold. "Have you been coming out to my place sneaking around watching me?"

He let out a snort. "Why would I do that?"

"That's what I was wondering. You told me at the Range Rider that you'd been watching me."

His eyes widened. "And you thought that meant I'd been out to your house, sneaking around and looking in your windows?"

"Have you?"

A nasty grin curled at his thick lips. "What if I have? Sounds to me like you're hoping I have been."

"Is there a problem here?"

They both turned to see Rylan's father, Taylor West. He was a big man, much like WT, with a quiet, patient way about him that Destry had always admired. He'd apparently been heading for his pickup when he'd heard Hitch's raised voice.

"No problem," Hitch said, taking a step back. Under his breath, he added, "We aren't finished."

Destry smiled her thanks to Taylor West and walked back around to the driver's side of her pickup, but he called to her before she could climb behind the wheel. Reluctantly, she turned, fearing a confrontation she wasn't up to.

Hitch had unnerved her. The more she'd thought about it, the more she feared it had been Hitch prowling around her place. She shuddered at the thought. Well, she'd be ready for him next time. She had her old shotgun loaded with buckshot. It would be the last time he came sneaking around.

An engine roared and Hitch took off, tires throwing gravel and kicking up dust. Destry turned to face Taylor West as he looked after Hitch's retreating pickup for a moment, then shifted his attention to her. He had taken off his hat and now turned the brim nervously in his fingers.

The church parking lot felt eerily quiet. The rest of the parishioners had left. Out of the corner of her eye, she saw Pastor Tom following his wife up the mountainside to the parsonage behind the church. He looked as if he had the weight of the world on his shoulders.

A magpie let out a squawk from a nearby pine tree,

then flew away in a flurry of black-and-white wings. Destry looked at Taylor West, waiting.

"Mr. West," she said, bracing herself. Rylan had taken after his father. Taylor West was tall, lean and broad-shouldered strong. Like Rylan, he was also handsome from his blond hair to his brown eyes, with a strong jawline and high cheekbones.

She'd heard Taylor West had been offered a modeling job years ago but turned it down. She imagined that the whole idea had embarrassed him. If WT had been asked, he'd have jumped at it.

"Please. You're old enough to call me Taylor." There was a warmth to his gaze that she'd seen too many times in his eldest son's brown eyes, a kindness and sincerity. He cleared this throat. "I have a favor to ask. I hope you don't mind."

A favor?

"I heard your brother was back. I'm worried something terrible is going to happen after what transpired at the funeral."

"I'm worried, too."

"I was hoping you might talk to Rylan," he said, taking her by surprise. She'd thought he was going to ask her to talk to Carson, talk him into leaving again. "He might listen to you. I know he cares about you."

She smiled at that, wishing it were true.

AT HIS FATHER'S INSISTENCE, Rylan was expected at his parents' house for Sunday lunch. He loved his mother's cooking and would gladly have accepted under most circumstances. It was what he heard in his father's voice that had him feeling anxious this particular Sunday.

"We've been talking about Ginny," Taylor said

after the dishes had been washed. His father cleared his voice. "Given what you found hidden in Ginny's jewelry box…"

Rylan looked at his two younger brothers. Jarrett was twenty, his younger brother a recent high school graduate. Their births were staggered more years than either his father or mother had hoped. Ellie'd had trouble getting pregnant after each of her children.

"Are you sure you want to do this in front of the boys?" Rylan asked.

"They're part of this," Taylor said and looked to his wife, who nodded her agreement. "We've been trying to remember those days before Ginny's death in case there is something that will help find her killer," his father continued.

"I think we need to accept that your sister was seeing someone besides Carson Grant," his mother said. Ellie was a small, gentle woman with honey-brown eyes and an easy smile.

Rylan hated that she had to go through this. "That's all I've been thinking about." That and Destry Grant. He wanted to argue that, even if they were right and Ginny had been seeing someone else, it didn't mean Carson hadn't been the murderer, but he figured they all knew how he felt since he'd voiced it enough times.

"I knew your sister didn't want to go back to college," his mother said. "She'd dreamed for years about her wedding. All she wanted was to get married and have babies. But Carson was too young. He wasn't ready and Ginny had realized that."

"So it makes sense that she might have been attracted to an older man," Taylor said.

"We've been trying to remember if we'd seen her with anyone," his mother said.

"I have to admit, I wasn't around all that much," Rylan said. He'd had too much going on himself with Destry.

"I saw her talking to people at church," his brother Cody said.

They all turned to look at him.

"Like who?" his father asked.

Cody shrugged. "The pastor."

"Yes, son," Taylor said as if to move on, but Rylan had noticed that his mother had paled.

"Did you remember something?" Rylan asked her.

She shook her head, but he could tell something had upset her.

"Hitch McCray," Jarrett said. "He was always going up to her and trying to get her to go out with him."

"He wasn't married, though," Rylan pointed out.

"But he was unavailable because of his mother," Taylor said.

"I saw her talking to Grayson Brooks," Cody said.

"The contractor?"

"This is crazy," Rylan said. "Ginny talked to a lot of people."

"Not Bob Benton. Ginny thought he was creepy," Jarrett said.

"She told you that?" his mother asked.

"No, but I saw her reaction to him. He was like Hitch, always watching her when no one was looking, and once I saw him go up to her in church. She took off like a shot when Bob's wife, Nettie, walked up."

Rylan looked at his brothers, realizing they were just kids when Ginny died. Jarrett had been thirteen,

Cody only seven. But sometimes kids noticed more than adults. "Bob, I guess, isn't bad-looking, but he's dull as dirt."

"Maybe dull was exactly what your sister was looking for after Carson," Taylor said.

"Clete Reynolds liked her," Jarrett said. "He used to flirt with her during the sermons."

Ellie got to her feet. "None of this proves anything and I hate talking about our neighbors this way."

After a moment, Rylan followed her into the kitchen. She was standing at the sink, gripping the edge of the counter, her head down.

"Are you all right?" he asked.

"It's just so hard even talking about this." She turned to look at him.

"You remembered something earlier. Mom, you have to tell me."

She swallowed, still looking pale and upset. "I'm sure it's nothing."

"It was something to do with Pastor Tom, wasn't it?"

Her eyes filled with tears. He could see how hard this was for her. "It was a week or so before your sister died. I saw him trying to talk to Ginny. She appeared to be arguing with him and finally pulled away from him. I wasn't the only one who noticed. Pastor Tom's wife, Linda, was watching them. I saw her expression. She'd looked upset and…"

"Jealous?"

His mother nodded. "Pastor Tom has always been so kind and caring, he wouldn't—"

"He's a man, and maybe his wife has reason to be jealous," Rylan said, turning to head for the door.

"Wait, what are you going to do?"

"Talk to him."

"I don't think you want to talk to him about this with his wife around. She goes to a women's support group in Big Timber on Mondays. Linda is usually gone most of the day."

"I know you and Anna Brooks started that group years ago, but I didn't think you still went."

"I don't usually. Anna isn't well enough to attend anymore, but Linda, as the pastor's wife, gives these young women spiritual comfort. She struggled with infertility for years and finally gave up hoping she and Tom would have children. Me, I stop in on occasion, bring cookies, try to do what I can. I was blessed with four children, but I haven't forgotten the ones I miscarried. A mother doesn't."

CHAPTER TWELVE

AFTER CHURCH, DESTRY drove up to the big house to find Margaret and Cherry in the kitchen. "How's WT?" she asked after saying hello to Cherry.

"His usual contrary self," Margaret replied. If she'd noticed that Destry hadn't called him Dad, she didn't acknowledge it. "He's in his den, going over some paperwork."

"Shouldn't he be taking it easy today?" she asked, unable not to be concerned about him. "Maybe I should stick my head in—"

Margaret gave her a warning head shake. "He told me he didn't want to be disturbed."

Destry helped herself to one of Margaret's buttermilk biscuits, slathering fresh creamery butter on it, then a thick layer of peach jam before adding the bacon and the top half of the biscuit. As she took a bite, she reveled in the salty and sweet mixture, the buttery flaky biscuit melting in her mouth.

Last night she couldn't have swallowed a bite, but today, like WT, she was determined to get on with her life. She might not share WT's blood, but when it came to stubbornness, they were two of kind.

She'd had a lot of time to think this morning on the ride to and from church. She'd never taken anything lying down, and she wasn't going to this time.

"You always have to grab the bull by its horns, don't you?" WT would say when she'd dig her heels in over changes she wanted to make on the ranch.

Cherry looked up from the magazine she was reading. "Is your ranch using the radio frequency identification tag system yet?"

Destry blinked, then noticed the magazine Cherry had been reading. She almost laughed. "No. You've taken an interest in cattle?"

"Well, according to this article, all a cattle thief needs is a horse, a dog and a trailer and he can walk away with ten thousand dollars worth of beef in a night. A brand can be changed, but if a vet injects an RFID into the animal, it can be scanned and the cow tracked. It sounds like a very sensible system. I'm surprised you haven't implemented it."

"I've talked to WT at length about it, but he's stubborn," Destry said. "He thinks it's a waste of money. He has it in his head that no one is going to rustle his cattle."

Cherry sighed. "That explains why he didn't want to discuss it with me, then." She smiled. "Not that he wants to discuss anything with me." She got up. "Thank you for breakfast," she said to Margaret. "I think I'll go work out."

After they were sure Cherry couldn't hear them, Destry and Margaret shared a laugh.

"Can you imagine how WT reacted to Cherry asking him about RFID tagging?" Margaret said with a shake of her head.

Destry could well imagine. No one could convince WT of anything. Except maybe Margaret. Just the thought made her voice something she'd often wondered. "So what does WT have on you?" Destry asked, studying her. She was a few years younger than WT, a pretty woman, talented, smart, strong and reliable. She could do so much better than working here.

"I beg your pardon?" Margaret asked with a laugh.

"There has to be a reason you put up with him. I'm thinking it must be blackmail, but then why wouldn't you have poisoned him by now?"

Margaret shook her head, smiling. "WT and I go way back."

"No, that's not it," Destry said and, with a start, wondered why she hadn't seen it before. The spark in Margaret's eyes when WT was around wasn't irritation or even anger. "You're in love with him."

It seemed so improbable, and yet that was it, Destry realized.

Margaret didn't bother to deny it. "Your biscuit is getting cold," she said and turned back to the chocolate cake she was preparing for dinner. Chocolate cake was WT's favorite.

Destry finished her biscuit without another word on the subject. "Where's Carson?" she asked as she took her plate over to the sink. She needed to ask Carson about the silver locket, then she planned to call Rylan. She wanted to tell him about Pastor Tom's odd reaction at church when she'd told him about the Bible verse.

"He's gone for a hike."

Destry didn't bother to hide her surprise. "We're talking about Carson, right?"

The housekeeper laughed.

"Any idea where he went on this hike?"

"I saw him head up the creek trail about ten minutes ago."

Destry glanced out the window, but she couldn't see him. "I think I'll see if I can catch him."

THE TRAIL BORDERED THE creek, going from the grassy foothills into the thick pines before breaking out to reveal a waterfall that tumbled over a sheer rock face. It was a short easy hike—until you reached the falls.

She hadn't gone far when she saw her brother making the last of the climb to the top of the waterfall. A moment later, he appeared at the railing. Years ago, someone had built a wooden fence at the top edge of the falls. It had rotted over time and needed replacing, but since WT owned this piece of land, he'd seen no reason to make the repairs.

"You and everyone else have no business going up there anyway," he'd said when Destry had suggested it. "You could fall, railing or no railing, and kill yourself." Sometimes WT's logic amazed her.

Now, seeing her brother standing so close to the edge frightened her. It wasn't like him to go for a hike. Especially up here.

She hurried up the rest of the trail, climbing to the top of the falls without any trouble. She was used to the high altitude.

If Carson saw her coming, he gave no indication. Even when she walked up behind him, he didn't acknowledge her presence.

"Carson," she said a few feet behind him, afraid she might scare him.

"Hey, sis," he said without turning.

She moved to his side and looked out over the valley. It took her breath away. The land dropped to the Yellowstone River in a series of streams edged with

yellows, golds and reds. The only green was the clear,
snow-fed waters of the creeks and finally the river on
its way to the Gulf of Mexico.

But when she looked over at her brother, she realized he wasn't seeing any of it. He had a faraway look
in his eyes. His swollen lip a reminder of the trouble
he'd brought home with him. She'd come up here to
ask him about the locket, but there was something she
needed to know first.

CARSON HAD GROANED inwardly when he'd seen his sister coming up the trail. He knew it was no coincidence
that she'd hiked up here today, which meant she'd been
looking for him.

"Something on your mind?" he asked, just wanting
to get whatever it was over with.

"How long have you known I'm not WT's daughter?"

He couldn't miss the accusation in her voice and
sighed. "Didn't know exactly. Suspected. Come on, the
way he's always treated you. How could *you* not suspect?"

"He's a bastard to everyone." She let out a humorless
laugh. "Why should I be special?" Her voice broke as
if she remembered what the doctor had said.

"I'm sorry, sis."

"You could have told me."

"Maybe I hoped, especially after his accident and
you coming home to help him out here…." He swore
under his breath. "I'd hoped he would change."

"How can WT be so sure I'm not his daughter?" she
asked, her voice breaking as she stared out at the land
as if unable to look at him.

"You'd have to ask him that."

"I did. He says he just knows. If he's not my father, then who is?"

"I honestly don't know."

"There must have been rumors over the years," she asked, stealing a glance at him. "How could our mother and her lover, if there was one, have kept it a secret in a community as small as this one? I would have heard rumors growing up, wouldn't I?"

"Destry, I don't know. You're asking the wrong person."

They fell silent, the only sound the rush of the water over the rocks and the dull roar that rose with the mist from the bottom of the falls far below them.

"What was she like?" Destry asked after a while. "I don't even have a photograph of our mother."

He hated the pain he heard in her voice. "I wasn't that old when she died, but I remember her as being kind of quiet. I think I remember her smile, maybe even her laugh."

"Do you think she ever loved him?"

"I suppose so, at first."

"He must have loved her to be so bitter. And yet love shouldn't turn a person into what he's become."

"Do we really have to do this?"

"I'm trying to make sense of my *life*," she snapped. "I thought I was his daughter. Now I find out he's cutting me out of his life. And we both know what you'll do once you get your hands on the ranch."

Carson rubbed his forehead and sighed again. "I don't have a choice, sis. I need the money."

"Have you asked Dad—WT—for it?"

"Even if he'd give me more money right now, it

wouldn't be enough to cover even the interest on what I owe."

She shook her head. "You lost so much that your only way out is to sell the whole ranch?"

He looked away, feeling like the dumb son of a bitch he was. Did she have any idea what it was like living in WT's shadow? He'd wanted to show the old man that he could be just as successful. Once he got a large enough stake, he'd planned to start a business of his own or buy a company. At least that's what he'd told himself.

"I got in too deep," he said, unable to look at her. "I thought I could get myself out." He shook his head. "I'm in serious trouble, Destry."

Her expression darkened, as if she thought he might be in even more serious trouble than just with gambling debts. "There's something I need to ask you."

He braced himself.

"Did you give Ginny a silver heart-shaped locket and chain?"

He felt the question pierce his chest like a poison arrow. "Why would you ask me that?"

"Just answer the question." She was staring at him, looking for any hint of a lie.

But this was something he could never lie about. "No." He thought of the diamond engagement ring he'd bought. The stone had been small, all he could afford at the time. He'd carried it around with him for weeks. "I didn't give her a silver locket."

DESTRY STUDIED HER BROTHER. It was the pain in his expression when he'd answered that made her believe him. "I need to get back." She was anxious to call Rylan, anxious to hear his voice. She stepped away, but her brother's words made her stop and turn to look back at him.

"That man gave her the locket, didn't he?" Carson said. "The married man I suspected she was seeing."

"We don't know. Rylan found it hidden under the lining of Ginny's jewelry box. He found a note, too. It was a Bible verse about adultery. It sounded threatening. Do you have any idea who might have written the note to her?"

"Probably just some do-gooder around here, someone you brushed elbows with this morning in church."

"Whoever wrote the note must have known about the affair and who Ginny was seeing. Rylan is taking what he found to the sheriff." She waited for his reaction.

"I don't blame you for not trusting me, but please don't stop believing that I'm innocent of her murder," he said as he turned his back to her to look out again into the distance. She noticed that he'd moved closer to the rotten railing. "You're the only one I have left."

Destry felt her breath catch. "Don't get so close to the edge." She took a step toward him, suddenly afraid of what he might do.

Mist rose into the chilly air from the cascading water, allowing only glimpses of the frothy white pool at the bottom of the cliff. He stood on the precipice as if considering the distance to the ground far below him. If he leaned out any farther… She shuddered, desperately wanting to pull him back but afraid to touch him for fear it would have the opposite effect.

"Carson, step back. You're making me nervous."

He didn't seem to hear her.

"Carson!"

He grabbed the railing, one of the small log limbs

coming off in his hand. She reached for him but before she could grasp his arm, he stumbled back.

"Someone should fix that railing," he said as he tossed the limb aside.

Destry couldn't reply, her heart was pounding so hard, her breath still trapped by the lump in her throat.

"I'm sorry, sis. I didn't mean to scare you."

She was shaking her head as she finally found her voice. "I can get you enough money to hold off your creditors for a while."

"I'm not taking your money." But she saw relief, gratitude and, ultimately, guilt wash over his expression. "I can't ask you—"

"You aren't asking. WT pays me what he does the ranch hands. He says if I'm going to act like one, I should get paid like one. Since I have few expenses…"

"It would just be a loan. Once I have the money from—" He broke off. "I'll pay you back with interest. If you want, I could sign something."

"I might not be more than a half sister, but I'm your *sister*."

"Sorry. I feel like enough of a jackass as it is. Your offer is so generous, given what I'm putting you through, that I don't know what I'm saying, okay?"

She smiled, although it hurt. She didn't want to fight with her brother. He was her only blood relative. She loved him. But she was angry with him and concerned about the man he'd become.

"You haven't been asking around about a poker game again, have you?"

He looked chagrined. "A weak moment. Not to worry. The old man hasn't given me a cent. I couldn't gamble even if I wanted to."

His words didn't relieve her mind. "How do I know you'll give my money to the man you owe and not gamble it away?" she asked.

He looked hurt. "You have my word."

His word? She didn't think his word and a dime could get her a cup of coffee. She feared that if he could, Carson would lose not only the money, but also the ranch in a poker game. As it was, she didn't doubt that once he sold the place, he would gamble it away. She looked out over the ranch and fought the burn of tears. The worst part was that there would be nothing she could do to stop him.

"I need your help with something," she said. Her brother looked wary. "I need a DNA sample from WT. Will you get it for me?"

"Are you sure you want to do this?"

"I have to know for sure."

Her brother nodded, studying her for a long moment before he sighed and said, "Just tell me what you need. I'll do it."

CARSON EASED OPEN HIS father's bedroom door and quietly slipped inside. The room was dim, the drapes drawn. The smell of age—or more likely impending death—seemed to cloak the room, making him nauseated.

He moved quickly to the bathroom, listening for any sound of his father's wheelchair outside the room. When he'd come into the house, he'd heard WT in his den on the phone and decided now might be the perfect time.

His plan had been to see what brand of toothbrush his father used, then bring a replacement. That plan changed the moment he'd stepped into the bathroom. He had no intention of coming back in here.

WT's toothbrush was in its holder next to the sink. Using a tissue from the box between the two sinks, he carefully wrapped the used toothbrush, then hesitated. What would WT think when his toothbrush was missing?

Carson wasn't sure he cared, but still he looked under the cabinet and was relieved to see that Margaret had stocked several packages of new toothbrushes.

It only took a moment to replace one in the holder beside the sink. He figured, even if his father noticed, he'd think Margaret had done it.

As he started to leave, he spotted his father's hairbrush. There was always a chance the lab tech wouldn't be able to get DNA from the toothbrush. He pulled some hair from the brush, put it in a tissue as well, and slipped both tissues into his pocket.

No way was he going to get caught in his father's bedroom. But as he was about to leave, he saw his image in a full-length mirror on the far wall and froze.

It often surprised him when he saw himself. It was as if he expected to be that young man who'd left here eleven years ago. Or maybe he just wished it so. Wished those years away, wished Ginny back from the dead, wished—

"What the hell are you doing?" he asked his image as he stepped closer until he could look directly into his own eyes. Even that surprised him, that cold look he got back. "Helping my sister," he answered back.

Yeah, you're real helpful. You're helping yourself to the ranch, the ranch your sister loves. "You really are an SOB, Carson Grant."

The image in the mirror didn't bother to argue.

He had reason to feel guilty. He knew Destry was wasting her time with the paternity test. It would only make everything official. There was little to no chance Destry was WT's daughter. Carson knew that because he remembered a lot more about their mother than he'd told Destry—or the old man.

CHAPTER THIRTEEN

EARLY MONDAY MORNING, Sheriff Frank Curry stood in front of his old farmhouse and stared out at the land in surprise. Sometimes fall came on so fast he didn't notice that the grasses had dried and yellowed or the lush green leaves of the cottonwoods had turned to rusts and golds that scattered on a breath of breeze, leaving the limbs bare.

This year was like that. Or maybe he was just getting old. His short marriage short years after Lynette dumped him seemed like a lifetime ago. Just the thought made him feel old when only recently he'd felt like a teenager again.

He smiled, thinking of Lynette. She had been a beauty in her younger days, with her long red hair like a flame. She'd changed over the years, but he still felt that spark that would never go out. When he looked at her even now, he saw that beautiful, young, lively woman she'd been. He wondered if a lot of men thought of their first loves in that way, forever frozen in that moment past.

Frank sighed, took off his hat and raked a hand through his still-thick blond but graying hair before settling his Stetson back on his head.

He looked toward the Crazies—and the W Bar G—

bracing himself for the day ahead. Whenever he had to butt heads with WT it made for a tough day.

That spring afternoon at the creek so many years ago tugged at him like a noose around his neck. That moment in time had set his life on a course he'd been fighting for years and branded him with its memory, like a scar that had never healed.

He could almost smell spring on the air when he recalled it. The water had been running high and cold that year. He and a group of boys had gone to their favorite spot where the creek ran between the granite boulders and the pines to form deep dark holes.

He'd never been that fond of water. But he'd been smart enough to know that he would never hear the end of it if he didn't go in. All of the other boys, even younger ones than him, had already jumped in.

He'd watched them disappear into the rushing dark water only to bob up moments later downstream in a burst of air before swimming quickly to the shore. Their bodies had been covered with goose bumps, their teeth chattering from the cold, as they'd pulled their clothes back on, all of them looking cocky and self-assured, laughing as if invigorated by the snow-fed stream.

Frank had seen that his turn was coming up fast. His fingers had trembled as he'd slipped out of his boots, unsnapped his Western shirt and discarded it, then shimmied out of his jeans. He'd put his clothing on a large rock, just as everyone else had. He'd stood in his white shorts, trying to talk himself into jumping in.

"Come on, Curry, we haven't got all day," one of the boys had yelled.

He'd stepped to the edge of the water as the boy in front of him had jumped in and waited for a few mo-

ments until the boy's head had bobbed to the surface.
Then he'd stepped out onto the boulder next to one of
the deepest holes and froze as he'd stared in the cold,
dark water.

"Frankie's not going to do it." WT Grant's voice had
filled the air. "He's chicken." WT had started clucking
and the others had begun to laugh and join in. A couple
of them had threatened to throw his clothes in with him.

Frank had held his breath, closed his eyes and
jumped.

The icy water had stolen his breath, shocking his
eyes open. All he'd seen was darkness. It had taken a
few moments before he'd realized that he'd sunk like
a rock to the deep bottom and hadn't bobbed up for
some reason.

The water around him had been almost black with
darkness. Instinctively, he'd begun to swim hard for
the surface. But it had been as if he'd dropped into a
bottomless well. He could feel the water rushing him
downstream, see light above him, *far* above him. But
as hard as he'd swum for it, the surface had eluded him.

Panic had seized him. He couldn't hold his breath
any longer. He'd felt as if he was going to burst. Suddenly water had rushed into his mouth and nose and
everything had begun to fade to black.

Even now, he could remember that feeling, knowing
he was drowning. That's when he'd felt the arm close
around his neck and drag him up and into blessed air.

He'd gulped, then choked and coughed, the icy creek
water heaving out of him and, all the time, hearing
the scared silence around him. That day Waylon "WT"
Grant had jumped in fully clothed to save his life.

That's why everyone in the county thought he

couldn't be trusted when it came to WT. Frank laughed under his breath at that. What he and WT had between them was much more complicated than that.

Frank was startled out of his thoughts as one of his crows called to him from the branch of an old cotton-wood next to the barn. He recognized the bird by its call. It was the one he'd named Billy the Kid after his deputy, Billy "The Kid" Westfall, a cocky, loud young man with an itchy trigger finger.

Frank had inherited Billy when he took the sheriff's job. The grandson of one of the town's elite, Billy had a job as long as his grandfather was alive, and there was little Frank could do about it if he hoped to remain sheriff.

The bird Billy the Kid cawed at him and flapped his wings, upset over something. Probably the weather, Frank thought as he looked past the mountains and saw dark clouds obscuring the peaks of the Crazies.

But it was the other storm brewing that worried him as he slid behind the wheel of his patrol pickup and headed for the W Bar G.

WT WAS ALREADY IN A foul mood long before he looked up and saw the sheriff's patrol pickup drive up. The reason he hadn't told Destry or anyone else about his declining health was he didn't want them walking around feeling sorry for him.

Margaret and Carson hadn't mentioned the doctor's visit last night or asked how he was feeling. Margaret was smart enough not to. Carson didn't give a damn.

The sheriff's visit wasn't a surprise. WT had been expecting it ever since he'd heard that some new evidence had turned up in Ginny's murder case, and Frank had called to say Carson needed to come home. It would be better for everyone involved if they didn't have to go after him.

WT had agreed. He'd just figured he would handle it, one way or another. He wanted Carson home for his own selfish reasons.

"What the hell do you want?" he asked, answering the door.

"Mind if I come in for a moment?" Frank asked.

"If this is about Carson…" When the sheriff said nothing, WT swore and wheeled into the living room, the lawman behind him.

"I need to speak to Carson," Frank said behind him.

It was too early for a drink, but WT made himself one anyway. The doctor had told him to quit drinking. He laughed to himself at that. He figured alcohol was the only thing keeping him alive. He didn't even bother to offer Frank one. The man was a known teetotaler.

"If you think you're going to railroad my boy—"

"Carson isn't a boy anymore. Nor am I railroading anyone. I came out here to talk to your son. I would think you'd want this resolved. Last night I had to put some fires out at the Range Rider. A lot of people think your son got away with murder. Some of them are talking vigilante justice just like in the old days. The best thing I can do for your son is find out who killed Ginny West. Unless, of course, you know something I don't?"

"Have you forgotten that you owe me?"

The sheriff's gaze narrowed. "I'm never going to forget that you saved my life. But that has nothing to do with this."

"Well, Carson isn't here right now. But let me give you some good advice. If you want to remain sheriff, then I suggest you get rid of any evidence that might incriminate my son or—"

"I'm going to pretend I didn't hear that. Have Carson give me a call."

WT let out a string of curses.

"Oh, and make sure he doesn't run again. It will only make him look more guilty, and this time I'll see that he gets brought back in handcuffs."

As the sheriff left, WT sat staring down into the cut-crystal glass in his hand for a moment before throwing it at the closing door. The glass shattered, the rich amber whiskey droplets suspended in the air for an instant before splattering against the door and running down the wall.

NETTIE WAS ABOUT TO turn on the store lights to begin another day at work when she spotted the sheriff sitting in his pickup just down the road. She watched him for a few moments, wondering what he was doing, until her curiosity won out.

Opening the front door, she walked down the street. The fall breeze sent the golden dried leaves of a large old cottonwood next to the creek fluttering across the truck's hood. Frank appeared to be simply sitting there, staring into space.

She heard the soft seductive rustle of leaves, felt the warm sun on her back as the breeze stirred her bottled-red hair. It could have been a fall day years ago when Frank had stopped by the house on his motorcycle to pick her up to do one fool thing or another.

"You don't have anything better to do than daydream?" she asked, as she stuck her head into the open passenger-side window.

Frank laughed. "I'm watching those young crows over there."

She looked past him to see two birds hopping around on the ground in the fallen leaves. "Fascinating. Why can't you just admit you're daydreaming?"

He laughed. "It *is* fascinating. Come join me." He reached across to open the passenger-side door. "I'll show you."

Nettie lifted a brow. But this was Frank Curry, a man who, even at sixty-one, didn't need a line to get a woman into his pickup. She glanced back at the store and then slid in, moving closer at his encouragement so she could have a better view of the birds.

"Did you know crows are smarter than cats and most children?" he asked. From the children she'd experienced in her store, she couldn't argue that. "Crows are more like us than any other species, even primates. I've been studying them for years." He grinned. "Gives me something to do on a stakeout—besides daydream."

"So you're on a stakeout now?" she asked.

"Actually, I was hanging around in case you had any more trouble from bears."

She couldn't help being touched by his concern. "The grizzly hasn't come back, thankfully."

"I saw that the FWP trap is still empty. Haven't heard of any bear sightings in the area. Maybe the bear wandered back up into the mountains already."

She watched the birds hopping around in the leaves. "So what's so fascinating about these two crows?"

He seemed pleased by her question. "Well, they're young, so they're playing like kids do. See the way they chase each other around, pulling at each other's tails?

Watch that one. He'll pick up that leaf, then the other one will chase him. Whoever has the leaf is it."

He was right about the birds, she thought, watching them, and he smelled nice as if he'd just come from a shower.

"Crows have been known to make their own tools, like taking a plant stem and using it to probe in holes for insects," he said. "In one study I read about, crows in captivity will bend a piece of wire to make a hook, then use it to pull a bucket of food closer to them. Making tools is a sign of just how intelligent they are."

She'd known men with *less* intelligence. Sometimes she wondered if Bob would sit in his chair and just starve to death if she didn't cook for him.

"So you like crows." This side of Frank surprised her, but then he had always been a man of many interests in the old days.

"I like watching crows because they're so human. If you feed them, they'll bring you small presents, pieces of shiny glass or trinkets they've found. But if you're mean to them, they'll poop on your car."

She laughed, wondering how serious he was about these birds, how serious he'd been about her. He'd once told her that she had broken his heart when she married Bob.

"The thing about crows, they're territorial when it comes to their families and loved ones," Frank said and glanced in his rearview mirror. "Crows pair for life, but the males fool around some. If they get caught, though, there is hell to pay. Just like humans, crows have been known to kill one of their own if they suspect he's been trespassing in another's territory."

Nettie pulled her attention from the two young crows to look at Frank. "Are you trying to tell me something?"

He chuckled and pointed to the pickup's rearview mirror. "I just saw your husband go into the store. I think he's looking for you."

She didn't want to leave the warmth of the pickup or the spell Frank had cast. But she slid across the seat to the passenger side and reached for the door handle anyway. "Thank you for the lesson on crows."

"Any time."

As she shoved open her door, the two young crows took off in a flurry of black wings, and she heard Frank sigh and start his pickup engine.

RYLAN HAD MENTALLY kicked himself after his visit to Destry's house Sunday morning. She'd taken his concern for her as him butting into her life, her business. She had a point, though. He had no right to tell her what to do—even if it was for her own good.

He'd gone home and worked hard the rest of the day, thinking he could work off his frustration—and his growing worry about her. It hadn't worked. It was so like her to shrug off his concern, as well as the fact that someone had been watching her house watching her. She was stubbornly convinced she could take care of herself. She'd been like this since they were kids.

"I wouldn't climb that tree if I were you," he'd said one day. And sure as the devil she'd climbed clear to the top and almost gotten herself killed.

That was Destry Grant. Impossibly mule-headed and just as impossible to forget.

Someone had been hanging around Destry's house spying on her. He recalled that one of Ginny's friends had told him that his sister had had the same problem—months before she was murdered.

That thought shook him to his core. Just a coincidence?

It scared him to think what could have happened if he hadn't gone out to see Destry just after daylight yesterday morning. What if he hadn't scared the man away? And what if he didn't happen by the next time?

As he parked in front of the sheriff's department, he shoved away thoughts of Destry. All thinking about her did was rile him up.

He glanced over at the small plastic bag he'd put the note and the locket in, hoping either could really help find his sister's killer. But what were the chances of that happening? Even if he trusted Sheriff Frank Curry, even if the trail hadn't gone cold, even if Carson Grant wasn't the killer, he feared it was too late for him and Destry.

He fished out his cell phone as it rang. Destry. He braced himself for the sound of her voice and what it did to him. "I was hoping I'd hear from you."

"I talked to my brother. Carson swears he didn't give Ginny the locket." He wondered what was the point of having her ask Carson. Did he really trust her brother not to lie?

"I believe him, Rylan. He was upset. He thinks the other man gave it to her, that's why it was hidden, just as I do."

"Well, thanks for asking him. I'm on my way into the sheriff's office right now. I'll let you know how it goes. Everything all right with you?" Was he trying to make conversation just to keep her on the line because he was worried about her? Or because he liked the sound of her voice?

"Everything is fine."

Why didn't he believe that? He'd seen the dark shadows under her eyes. Something was keeping her awake at night, and he doubted it was the Peeping Tom.

"There is something else," she said. "I showed the quote to Pastor Tom after church. I didn't tell him anything about it except that it had been left as a possible threat. He got upset. I could tell he wanted to talk to me, but Linda came up and dragged him off to talk to someone else."

"You think he might know about the notes?"

"Ginny was in church almost every Sunday. I was wondering if she might have confided in the pastor about the notes, maybe even about her pregnancy and the man she was involved with."

"I think we should talk to Tom."

"I was thinking the same thing."

"You don't mind going with me?"

"Of course not."

"Okay. I'll give you a call after I talk to the sheriff." He snapped the phone shut, telling himself he was a damned fool in more ways than he wanted to admit. Spending time with her was pure hell, and yet every time he saw her or talked to her, he couldn't wait until the next time.

Sometimes he thought he could feel the gulf between them narrowing. But he knew the moment something else came up about his sister and her brother, that gap would only widen further.

As he pushed open the door to the sheriff's department, he was glad he'd shown his father the note and silver locket.

Taylor West had immediately told him he must take them to the sheriff.

Now Rylan just hoped his father was right and that Frank Curry could be trusted.

"Can I help you?" the sheriff's department dispatcher asked from behind the thick sheet of glass.

When had Montana become so dangerous that people were forced to work behind bulletproof glass? "I need to see the sheriff."

"He's out but—" She looked past him and smiled. "Here he is now."

Rylan turned to come face-to-face with Sheriff Frank Curry. Now that he was here, he worried that he was wasting his time, since Frank Curry was as thick as thieves with WT Grant.

"You wanted to see me?" the sheriff asked.

"It's about my sister's murder."

With a nod, the lawman said, "Why don't we step into my office."

Rylan followed him, telling himself all that mattered was catching Ginny's killer and putting him behind bars.

"Sit down," the sheriff said as he settled into his chair behind his desk. The chair groaned under his weight.

Rylan took one of the straight-back wooden chairs across from him. The small room had a musty smell, the building old and dark. Maybe the dispatcher was behind a wall of bulletproof glass, but he didn't get the feeling that anything else about investigating had changed from the days of the old West.

Frank Curry looked like an old-timey sheriff. He wore jeans, boots, a uniform shirt and gold star, his gray Stetson resting on a hook by the door. He could easily have been on the hunt for Butch Cassidy and the Sundance Kid instead of Ginny West's killer. He even had a thick drooping blond mustache flecked with gray and a weathered Montana look about him.

"I'm sorry about your sister," the sheriff said. Maybe it was the kindness in his eyes or something in his voice, but Rylan relaxed a little.

"That night, the night my sister was killed…" Rylan began.

"You were with Destry Grant up at the old abandoned ski lodge."

He stared at the sheriff. "How did you—"

"Destry told me a few days after."

Destry had come forward? Why hadn't she told him? Because he'd cut off all contact with her, and not long after that, he'd left to rodeo.

"So you know that Carson Grant's only alibi is Jack French?"

The sheriff nodded.

"And you know Jack would say whatever Carson told him."

Frank Curry merely smiled.

"But that's not why I'm here," Rylan said and reached into his pocket. He'd put the note and the locket in a small plastic bag. "I found this hidden in my sister's jewelry box."

The sheriff took the bag.

"Carson said there was another man in my sister's life. He swears he didn't give Ginny the locket. Destry believes him. Maybe—" He stumbled over the words, hating that Carson might have been right as much as even the thought that his sister might have been seeing a married man. "—Ginny was seeing another man, possibly a married man."

The sheriff opened the bag, inspected the locket, then read the note. "May I keep this?"

Rylan nodded. "It doesn't prove there was anyone else…" He saw something in the sheriff's expression. "Wait a minute, did you find evidence of another man?"

Frank seemed to measure his words. "It's an ongoing investigation."

Even if that was the new evidence, another man's DNA at the murder scene didn't prove that the man had killed Ginny, though. Just as it didn't clear Carson of the murder. Rylan pointed this out to the sheriff.

"True. You have any idea who might have given your sister this locket?"

He shook his head. "No." But the hidden locket, the note all pointed to a secret lover. A man they all knew? The thought terrified him since Beartooth was such a small, close-knit community.

Rylan got to his feet, remembering what the sheriff had said about Destry. She'd come forward eleven years ago to refute her brother's claim that she was his second alibi. She'd told the sheriff everything.

He'd just assumed she'd kept quiet, covering for her brother. It had felt like a betrayal, but as it turned out, he was the one who'd betrayed her by not trusting her, by taking off the way he had.

The sheriff rose and extended his hand. "I'm glad you're home."

Was he as glad Carson Grant was home? he wondered as he left the sheriff's department.

Rylan felt more confident in the sheriff. Not that he was going to stop digging for answers on his own.

Had he known Destry told the sheriff the truth that
night, would it have made a difference eleven years ago?
Would he have left?

He didn't know. He felt as if he'd abandoned her after
promising to always love her. And yet, it wouldn't have
changed anything. Her brother would still be a suspect
in his sister's murder. Destry would still side with her
brother.

It would be just like it was now. A stalemate. As
long as her brother was under suspicion, there was no
chance for them.

DESTRY ACHED TO SADDLE UP and ride up into the Crazies—where she always went when she was upset. But
she couldn't leave. Rylan hadn't called yet. She felt at
loose ends.

In the kitchen she made herself a sandwich but only
had a few bites before she put the rest in the refrigera-
tor. She was too anxious to eat. She poured herself a
glass of milk. Somehow milk had always soothed her.
The milk was cold and sweet. WT loved to drink milk
late at night.

"Father like daughter," Margaret used to say when
she caught the two of them in the kitchen in the middle of the night.

WT would always grunt and tell Margaret to mind
her own business. Destry had never thought anything
of it. Until now.

She ached from the sense of loss. She looked around
the house. Her mother had lived here, decorated this
place, and yet there was so little of her still here. She
knew nothing about the woman who had given her birth.

Worse, she knew nothing about herself. *Who was she if not WT's daughter?*

The thought came as a jolt each time, shaking the foundation under her as well as making her question her entire life.

Who was her father?

If only she had known her mother, maybe she wouldn't feel so adrift now. As she stepped to the sink to rinse out her empty milk glass, it slipped from her hand and fell, breaking on impact. Shards of glass ricocheted across the floor.

She'd never been this clumsy, she thought with a curse as she grabbed the roll of paper towels and began to clean up the glass. On her hands and knees, she was reaching for a piece of the broken glass that had fallen in a small indentation in the floor, when she saw something she'd never noticed before.

The indentation was crescent-shaped, as if someone had purposely carved it in the wood. She moved closer to inspect it and saw the slightly wider space between the boards. Was it possible?

Slipping her fingers into the indentation, she pulled. A section of floor lifted a fraction. The years had filled in the edges. No wonder she hadn't noticed it in all this time. The trap door had apparently not been opened in a long time.

Destry shoved the table out of the way and pried at the edges with a butter knife from the drawer. She tried to raise it again. A section of the floor about three foot square lifted just enough that she knew she'd found a door that opened to whatever was under the house.

She tried again and thought she'd have to ask her brother for assistance when it finally gave.

The door creaked slowly open on rusted hinges. An earthy, musty smell rose into the kitchen like a ghost. Leaning the door back so it stayed open, Destry took a flashlight from the drawer and shone it down into the darkness.

Cobwebs had nearly closed off the opening. She reached for a broom and brushed the cavernous gap free before shining the light into the hole again. This time she saw something. Several large old trunks.

The top stair creaked under her weight, and for a moment, Destry thought better about going down into the space below the house. It could be a long time before anyone thought to check on her.

She tested the next stair with her weight, then the next. The trunks called to her like mythical sirens. As she eased down the stairs, she shone her flashlight around the space. The walls were earthen, smelling of damp soil. She heard the scamper of mice. A cobweb brushed across her face and hair, making her jump.

Wiping it away, she took a calming breath. She'd never liked cramped places, especially damp, musty ones. But she was too close to quit now. Just a few more steps.

As she put her weight on the last step, she felt it give and grabbed for the railing, grasping only air. The step snapped, pitching her forward and into the darkness.

CHAPTER FOURTEEN

DESTRY LAY IN THE COLD, damp dirt for a moment. She'd dropped the flashlight. It now lay a few feet away, the beam cocked at an angle shooting slightly upward, away from her.

She didn't move for a moment, allowing herself time to catch the breath that had been knocked out of her. Something small with a lot of legs ran across her hand. She sat up, brushing furiously at her fingers, then her sleeve and the front of her shirt.

Shoving to her feet, she brushed at her jeans, fighting panic. Alone down here, what would have happened if she'd hurt herself badly?

Well, she wasn't hurt. She was fine, although strangely she still felt more alone than she had, more afraid of not just the creepy crawly things in this cellar, but larger, more all-encompassing fears as if the worst was yet to come.

Limping a little, she stepped to the flashlight and picked it up. The cold dampness seeped into her bones. Flicking the light over the larger of the trunks, she moved to it and pried at the lid with one hand as she kept the flashlight steady, half afraid of what she would find, half afraid all this had been for nothing.

The lid rose with a groan, an aged stale scent from another time rising with it. Destry shone the light over

the contents. Clothes. The dresses appeared to have
been her mother's, or possibly her grandmother's, from
some of the styles. She dug through them, held one
dress up to her and sniffed the fabric. But there was no
hint of the women who had come before her.

She closed the lid and pried open the other trunk and
was disappointed that it was much the same. Digging
through the clothing, she found a few items that could
have been her mother's. None, though, held any clues
as to the woman Lila Gray Grant had been.

Discouraged, she started to close the trunk lid when
her gaze lit on the corner of what appeared to be a shoebox under all the clothes. She dug it out to find someone
had trimmed the box with a piece of lace. With trembling fingers, she lifted the box out, slipped off the lid
and shone the light inside.

She knew at once the photograph was of her mother.
Lila Gray Grant was wearing a leather Western jacket,
the same one Destry had found in the back of the closet
when she'd had the bedrooms remodeled upstairs.

Her mother stared up at her, smiling happily from an
old snapshot. The photo was crinkled, the color faded,
but to Destry it was the most wonderful thing she'd
ever seen. She stared down into her mother's face—a
face so like her own.

As she touched her mother's face with her fingertips, she felt her eyes fill. While she couldn't miss the
resemblance to her mother, Lila had been a striking
beauty. In the photo, her mother was smiling, her eyes
bright, her face aglow.

The shot looked as if it had been taken at one of
the yearly fall harvest festivals held at the fairgrounds.

Destry glanced then at the two men in the photograph. She'd expected one of them to be WT.

But it was Russell, their ranch foreman, who stood next to her mother. The other man, Sheriff Frank Curry, stood to the other side. All three appeared to be in their early twenties.

While her mother was smiling at the camera, both Russell and the sheriff were looking at her mother with nothing short of adoration in their eyes.

BOB BENTON HAD BEEN having the nightmares for several days now—ever since he'd heard Carson Grant had returned. He'd wake in the wee hours before dawn sweating and shivering, more afraid than he'd ever been in his life.

"Night terrors, that's what they're called," Doc Carrey had told him just this morning as the two had had coffee at the Branding Iron. Doc was retired from pediatrics and had bought a ranch outside of Beartooth, so he now handed out free medical advice from the counter at the café most mornings.

"Do you remember anything about your dreams?" Doc had asked.

He'd lied. "Crazy stuff. Just bits and pieces that make no sense. Like strange noises. And smells."

"Smells?" Doc had turned from his coffee to study him. "What kind of smells?"

Bob had had to shake his head. Blood. "I can't even describe them." He'd shifted his gaze, glancing across the street to the store where Nettie would be opening the front door any minute. He didn't want her knowing about the nightmares. She'd want to know what was causing them and would pester him relentlessly until he came up with some answer. His fear was that she already knew, had known for years.

"Nasty smells," he'd said finally. An image came to him from one of the nightmares. Dark wings against a midnight blue sky. "Vultures, I think."

"Vultures? Could be crows. They're considered a sign of death. You should ask the sheriff. He knows all about crows." Doc had taken a bite of his flapjack and chewed for a moment. "But I doubt your dreams have anything to do with vultures *or* crows. You get to a certain age and you start thinking about death. Completely natural. I wouldn't take the dreams too seriously. You're only in your late fifties, right? You should have another thirty years ahead of you at least, if you take care of yourself."

Bob had made a noncommittal sound, wondering how he would be spending those thirty years.

"Like I said, I wouldn't worry about it," Doc had said, going back to his breakfast. "I'm sure it's just a passing phase."

Before he'd retired, Doc had probably told every mother that it was just a passing phase over the years. "Well, thanks for your help," Bob had said and headed across the street to the store. It made Nettie mad when he wasn't there to help right after opening time, even though they seldom had a customer until later in the morning. Nor did he do much to help.

Partway across the street, he spotted the sheriff's pickup parked at the curb down the street from the store. There were two people in the cab, the sheriff and a woman sitting next to him. He blinked as he recognized Nettie's fiery red head. When she'd started turning gray, she'd begun dying it to match her original color. That was Nettie.

He turned away, telling himself that whatever the reason she and the sheriff had their heads together it didn't concern him. But as he hurried into the store, he had trouble catching his breath—just like in the nightmares—and for a moment, he was crippled with fear.

Clutching the doorjamb, he fought the wave of dizziness that overtook him. His heart still pounding, he made his way behind the counter and sat down on the stool Nettie kept there, afraid he was going to black out.

First night terrors? Now panic attacks?

The image of Nettie sitting so close to the sheriff flashed before him. What was she telling her former lover? What her husband cried out during the night? Was she repeating what she heard to Frank at this very moment?

His stomach cramped, and the next moment he found himself throwing up in the wastebasket behind the counter.

"BOB?" NETTIE CLOSED the store's front door behind her and stood for a moment as her eyes adjusted to the dim interior lighting. It had been so bright and sunny outside. She thought of the young crows, their feathers iridescent in the sunlight, their dark eyes shiny with what Frank Curry believed to be intelligence. "Bob!"

She heard the toilet flush at the back of the store, and a moment later her husband came out drying his hands on a paper towel. Nettie couldn't help the instant irritation she felt. He'd washed his face as well as his hands, apparently, because that lock of gray hair that always fell over his forehead was still dripping.

When he'd started going gray, she'd tried to get him to color his hair. He'd refused, saying something about acting his age.

She'd known it was a dig about her dying hers red. "Don't kid yourself, you've always been old," she'd said. "It would take more than hair dye to make you young, let alone fun."

Now as she looked at him, she noticed something odd. He'd aged. It took her by surprise, because, apparently, she hadn't really looked at him in a long while. This morning he appeared pale and smaller, as if he'd shrunk. She knew she was unfairly comparing him to Frank and maybe always would.

"What's wrong with you?" she asked, although she could have filled volumes without any help from him.

"Nothing." He looked annoyed, frowning at her, before tossing the paper towel into the small wastebasket that should have been behind the counter by the door.

"What are you doing with that?" she demanded. He'd put a new plastic bag in it. Wasteful, she thought, since he'd taken out the trash last night before closing and had put in a new bag. She'd checked since he often forgot.

"Putting it back where it goes," he said as he walked over to place it under the counter. "I'm not feeling well. I'm going home."

She stared at him, thinking for the first time in a long time that she didn't want to work today, either. She'd like to go on a picnic up in the Crazies. Go bird-watching with Frank. Eat that picnic lunch beside the creek and then go skinny-dipping in Saddlestring Lake as she and Frank had done when they were young and in love.

"You can manage without me," Bob said.

Yes, she thought. She could. She just wished she'd

realized that thirty years ago when she'd chosen security over passion.

"I'll come back later if I'm feeling better."

"Don't bother." She hadn't meant for her words to come out so sharply. "Stay home and get to feeling better. I'll be fine."

He studied her for a long moment, then nodded and headed for the door.

"Bob?"

He stopped but didn't turn. "Yes, Nettie?"

She started to question him about the nightmares he'd been having and the odd things he'd been saying. She settled for, "Call me if you need anything."

He didn't answer as he opened the door and left.

AT THE SHERIFF'S DEPARTMENT, Frank Curry pulled open his desk drawer and took out the worn Bible. It had been his father's. The leather felt warm to the touch as he opened it. His father used to keep it beside his chair where he would open it to a random page and begin reading.

Often he would read aloud, his deep voice rich and full in the tiny house where Frank had grown up. Wallingford Curry hadn't been one of those fanatical Bible thumpers. Quite the contrary. He was simply a man of God who believed in grace and goodness as well as evil and hell.

It only took Frank a few minutes to find Proverbs 23-27. His father's Bible was the King James version, so the quote was a little different.

For a harlot is a deep pit, and a seductress is a narrow well. She also lives in wait as for a victim, and increases the unfaithful among men

Frank dragged the box marked Ginny Sue West over to his desk and lifted the top. He took a breath and let it out slowly as he picked up the top sealed plastic bag.

The victim's clothing had been sent to the crime lab in Missoula eleven years ago. He'd sent the new evidence marked as Urgent. His hope was that the new evidence would provide the proof he needed to not only make an arrest but also get a conviction.

The autopsy was attached to his report. He didn't bother with any of that right now but dug out the small sealed plastic bags with the purse's contents. The purse had been found in Ginny's pickup.

Pulling out the one with the partial scrap of notepaper, he flattened the plastic and the torn piece of paper inside. The scrap of paper had been found in Ginny's purse-sized Bible, the New Living Translation.

Ginny had been a regular churchgoer, so he hadn't thought much about the piece of torn paper—or the words printed on it. At the time he'd thought she'd simply used it to mark her place.

Now, though, he turned to his computer and typed "bible verse," and the three words that were readable on the scrap of paper, "like a robber."

Proverbs 23-28 came up at the top of the page.

A promiscuous woman is as dangerous as falling into a narrow well.
She hides and waits like a robber,
Eager to make more men unfaithful.

The scrap of paper had now taken on a whole new importance in light of what Rylan West had found hidden in his sister's jewelry box. Apparently Ginny had received at least two such notes.

Frank pulled out the note Rylan had found and compared it to the partial one found in Ginny's purse. The handwriting was identical. The notes were from the same person.

His phone rang. He saw that it was the crime lab and braced himself as he took the call.

"DESTRY?" CARSON KNOCKED again. No answer. He'd tried the door, not surprised to find it unlocked. "Destry?" he called as he opened the door and stepped in. No one out here locked their doors even at night.

He heard her voice, though faint. "Where are you?"

"Down here."

He stepped into the kitchen, surprised to see a gaping hole in the wood floor. As he moved closer, he glanced down and saw the old wooden stairs. His sister was standing on the dirt floor of what couldn't be called a basement.

"What the devil are you doing down there?" he asked as she started up the steps. He could see that the bottom stair was broken, and his sister's clothes were covered in dirt. "Did you fall down there?"

"Just from the bottom step," she said as she climbed up. She had a shoe box tucked under one arm.

"What's that?" he asked, hoping it was full of cash. Surely this wasn't where his sister kept her money.

"Some old photographs of our mother."

He had a sick feeling. "Oh, really?" She was eyeing him as if she knew he hadn't told her the truth regarding their mother and the man she'd been involved with.

"I brought what you asked me to get," he said, hoping to change the subject as she dropped the hatch door, put the shoebox on the table and shoved the table back into place.

He took out the tissue-wrapped samples and handed them to her. She hugged him as if surprised he'd done it—let alone done it so quickly. "Thank you."

"You sure you want to do this, though?"

"I told you. I have to know. I have a friend who works in a lab in Livingston. I've already contacted her and she's agreed to run the tests for me. I'll take them to her right away."

"How long before you know something?"

"She said a paternity test like mine shouldn't take more than twenty-four hours."

He nodded thoughtfully. "That quick?"

"It's just a preliminary one, but it will tell me what I need to know."

"Then what?"

She shook her head. "No matter how they turn out, WT wouldn't believe the test results. So basically, it changes nothing."

Carson chuckled, and touched his healing lip. "You do know him, don't you?"

"I'm not doing this for WT. I'm doing it for myself." She sighed, realizing what the results might say about her mother. "I just wish I'd known our mother."

"She would have been so proud of you." He looked away. Earlier he'd gotten a call from the collector the casino had sent after him. The threats were getting more specific. He felt desperate and feared what the man might do.

"I hate to think how disappointed our mother would be in me," he said.

"Don't say that. I can't help feeling that if she'd lived, none of this would have happened."

Carson laughed and gave her a hug. "You really are such an irritating optimist. Don't you get tired of always seeing the glass half full?"

"I'm not always optimistic," she said, thinking about the ranch she loved. She wasn't fool enough to believe even a paternity test could change WT's mind about the ranch. Carson's gambling debts aside, she could see that he was angry and just wanted to be rid of the ranch.

"I'll get you a certified check after I take the samples to my friend at the lab."

He looked down at his worn boots, wishing there was another way, and yet more grateful than she would ever know. "Thank you."

"Was there a reason you stopped by?" she asked.

"Just wanted to see you." He'd come for the money, hoping she hadn't changed her mind. At least now he'd know when he could make a payment on his debt.

He took a step toward the door, glad she hadn't mentioned the photographs in the box. "You should get those samples to the lab."

She nodded as if she knew he was more interested in her getting him a check.

He didn't know what else to say. She would give him her own money even knowing he was planning to sell the ranch out from under her. "You're something, you know that?"

DESTRY WAS SOMETHING, all right. Naive. Foolishly trusting. Possibly just pain stupid. But Carson was her brother and he needed her help.

She realized she hadn't mentioned the photo of her

mother, Russell and the sheriff. A part of her suspected it wouldn't come as a surprise to her brother anyway.

The phone rang and she hurriedly picked it up. She was anxious to get the DNA samples to her friend at the lab in Livingston, but brightened when she heard Rylan's voice on the phone. They agreed to meet in Beartooth. Pastor Tom was anxious to talk to them about the note, Rylan reported.

Destry quickly showered and changed and drove into town. Rylan was waiting for her just down the street from the church.

They found Pastor Tom in his study there. He motioned them in, offering them chairs, clearly nervous.

"So what is this about some note that was left for someone?" he asked as he took his chair behind his desk. He didn't seem to know what to do with his hands, first moving things around his desk, then finally folding them in his lap.

"Destry showed you the Bible quote?" Rylan asked.

Tom nodded. "She didn't say where it came from, though."

"It was found in some of my sister's things."

The pastor's eyes widened. "Your sister, Ginny."

"You know about the notes, don't you?" Destry said. "Ginny showed them to you?"

Tom quickly shook his head. "No. This is the first I've heard that Ginny received one of them."

"Have other people gotten them?" she asked in surprise.

"Several of the parishioners have complained about receiving them. They assumed I was behind them." He glanced from her to Rylan and back again. "I would never do something like that."

"So you have no idea who wrote the notes?" Rylan said, sounding disappointed.

"No. I believe in counseling my congregation, not badgering them." He sounded angry and upset.

"You counseled Ginny when she came to you?" Destry asked.

The pastor's expression gave him away.

"We know she was pregnant," Destry said quickly. "What we need to know is if she told you the name of the man she believed fathered her baby."

"What she told me was in confidence."

"I realize that," Rylan said, jumping in. "But if there is even a chance that man killed her—"

"We have found evidence that indicates she was having an affair with a married man, possibly someone older. If you can just confirm that much," Destry said, watching him closely.

Pastor Tom sighed. "She didn't tell me who the man was. All I can tell you is that she was concerned about the people this would hurt when it came out and how her family and friends were going to take the news. I'm sure the man was, as well. But she was especially concerned how Carson was going to take it."

CHAPTER FIFTEEN

RYLAN WALKED DESTRY out to her truck. The pastor's last words seemed to ring like a death knell. Ginny was worried about how Carson was going to take the news.

"Just say it," Destry snapped as she opened the driver's side door.

"I don't want to argue with you." He wanted to kiss her. He'd seen her face when she'd heard what the pastor said. He'd instantly wanted to comfort her. She wasn't her brother's keeper.

"Isn't it possible Ginny didn't want to hurt Carson? Isn't it possible she cared about him?"

Rylan nodded, stepping to her to touch her cheek as he pushed an errant lock of hair back from her face. His fingers tingled. He quickly drew them back as her expression darkened.

"What do you want me to say?" he asked.

"Say what you're really thinking."

He shrugged and looked away for a moment. "Carson hurt Ginny once during an argument not long before she was killed. Ginny swore it was an accident, that she pulled away and tripped. But even so, why wouldn't she be afraid of him? She broke up with him and yet he continued to stalk her."

"Because he was worried about her," Destry said. "I know that isn't an excuse. But he suspected the man she was seeing was married. Did you happen to notice that the pastor seemed more than a little nervous when we brought up the notes and almost guilty when we asked about Ginny?" Destry demanded.

He had, but like his mother, he didn't want to believe it was Pastor Tom. "If he looked guilty, it was because he didn't help her and she got killed."

"Or he looked guilty because he was. If he was the man Ginny was seeing, the man who fathered her baby, then who would have more to lose by a scandal than Pastor Tom Armstrong?"

Rylan stared at her, her words hitting him hard because they had a ring of truth to them.

"We both knew Ginny. She wasn't the type to have an affair with a married man unless that man was someone trustworthy, someone she felt close to, someone with possible marital problems. If you'd been to church lately, you'd know that Tom's wife is a very jealous woman. I don't know if she has always been that way, but she certainly is now. I'm wondering if she has reason to be."

His own thoughts. But he couldn't help playing the devil's advocate. "Tom would have come forward when Ginny was murdered," Rylan said with more conviction than he felt. "He couldn't have lived with such a lie all these years. According to my mother, Linda and Tom tried for years to have a child. If he thought Ginny was carrying his baby—"

"But she wasn't carrying his baby," Destry interrupted. "It was Carson's."

"No," Rylan said, shaking his head. "Tom would have come forward."

"Why? Once Ginny was dead, there would be nothing gained by his admitting the truth and everything to lose. His worries were over. Convenient, wouldn't you say? And who would suspect the local pastor?"

"Destry, if you have a minute," Pastor Tom called from the church side door. They both turned, no doubt looking guilty. "I was hoping you could take the items we've collected for the clothes drive to the community center. The women on the committee are down there now sorting through things."

"I can help," Rylan said. "You don't think he overheard us, do you?" he whispered as they walked back to the church.

"I hope not." She shot Rylan a look, though, as they followed the pastor back into the church. Tom didn't look well. He was pale, perspiration beading on his forehead, and his hands were shaking as he opened one of the wooden bins at the back of the church where area residents could put clothing for the yearly drive.

"Are you all right?" Destry asked him.

"I'm sorry, but talking about Ginny just makes me realize that I should have done more to help her. I blame myself."

"You shouldn't," Rylan said quickly. "You tried to help her."

He shook his head. "I didn't do enough. If I had, she might still be alive today. Here, I have some bags we can put the clothing in."

"We all feel that way," Rylan said as he opened a second bin and began to pull clothing from it.

Destry held open a bag as Tom began to pull clothing out of the first bin. Both bins were stuffed full to overflowing, surprising her since on Sunday neither had been this full.

Suddenly Rylan let out a gasp. She and Tom turned as Rylan pulled out what appeared to be a blue-and-white letterman jacket. All the color washed from his face as he held it up, and she saw not only the dark stain down one side, but also the name monogrammed on the front: Ginny.

AFTER SHE RETURNED HOME, Destry was too worked up to hang around the house. Finding Ginny's letterman jacket in the church clothing drive bin had left them all shaken. Rylan had called the sheriff at once.

When Frank Curry arrived, he'd asked them to keep what they'd found to themselves. "I'll talk to your parents," the sheriff had told Rylan.

By now the jacket was on its way to the crime lab in Missoula. Destry couldn't get the large dark stain out of her mind.

It was late afternoon by the time she dropped the paternity samples with her friend in Livingston. Fearing that the jacket would incriminate her brother even more, she felt all the more desperate to find out who Ginny West had been seeing.

She stopped in a couple of jewelry shops in Livingston but saw no silver lockets that resembled Ginny's. Who knew how old the locket was before Ginny had gotten it. Whoever might have given it to her could have had the piece of jewelry for years. Or could have bought it anywhere.

Still, she checked the few shops that sold jewelry in Big Timber as well, but with no luck. Then she stopped by the bank and picked up the cashier's check for her brother and headed home.

By the time she neared the Crazy Mountains, the

sky was liquid silver in the twilight. She felt exhausted, wrung completely out by all the events of the past few days. With a chill, she realized that she'd taken the wrong turn back on the highway.

Startled, she saw that she was on the road where Ginny's body had been found. She slowed as she topped the hill a few miles from Beartooth. Even in the dim light of the fading day, she saw the wooden cross in the weeds beside the road.

She brought the pickup to a stop at the edge of the road. As she got out, she shivered less from the cold than this desolate spot. A chill wind blew down from the mountains, though, a reminder that winter would soon be breathing down her neck.

The thought filled her with dread. She had no idea where she would be come winter. Or where Carson would be. The ramifications of everything that was happening had begun to set in. She felt numb, chilled to the bone.

Being here where Ginny had died, only made her feel more depressed. The Crazies cast a long shadow, making the pines lining both sides of the narrow road appear as dark as the inside of a boot.

The small, once-white homemade cross had been erected at the edge of the trees near the spot where Ginny West had died. Destry felt even colder standing near the shadowed dense pines. What was she doing here? It wasn't as if she thought she could find any evidence after eleven years.

She breathed in the sharp scent of pine as she stood at the edge of the road, staring at the dried yellow grasses in the shallow barrow pit and trying to imagine how anyone could have dumped Ginny out here.

Ginny had still been alive when her body had been left here. She'd tried to crawl out of the ditch. Destry shuddered at the thought.

Carson couldn't do such a thing, she told herself and hugged herself against the cold and the growing darkness.

A hawk screeched from high over the tops of the pines, making her jump. An instant later, she heard the crunch of gravel and spun around, as a man stepped from the darkness of the pines.

Startled, she let out a cry and stumbled back, sliding in the loose dirt and dropping partway into the barrow pit.

"Sorry, didn't mean to scare you," Nettie's husband, Bob, said as he seemed to appear out of nowhere. "I was just out for my nightly walk."

Destry stumbled up out of the barrow pit, trying to still her pounding heart.

Bob looked past her to the cross. She followed his gaze. The cross, although weathered with age, seemed to glow as if it had absorbed the last of the day's light.

"I always get a little spooked when I walk past here," Bob said. "It's just such a…lonely spot."

She nodded, wondering why he walked this way if it bothered him. "I've never come out here before." She hadn't wanted to see it, hadn't wanted to think about the person who'd killed Ginny West.

"I heard the pastor's wife won't even drive down this road."

Destry felt a chill run the length of her spine. She'd forgotten the pastor's wife and Bessie Crist had found Ginny's body. Linda and Bessie Crist had been on their way to visit a sick friend when they'd seen what they'd thought was a dog that had been hit beside the road.

"Well." Bob pulled his coat around him as if suddenly chilled. "I best get back. Don't want to worry Nettie. You going to be all right?"

She nodded, realizing that was the most she'd ever heard Bob Benton say. At the store and church, Nettie did all the talking.

It had gotten dark, the temperature dropping as night fell over the valley. She told him goodbye and headed for her pickup. Even with the heater going in the truck, she couldn't shake the cold that snaked up her spine as she headed back to the ranch.

CLETE KNEW HE WAS DRIVING too fast. At one point, he thought about calling Bethany and making sure she was home. But he wanted to surprise her. Or was it catch her?

The night was black, the stars and moon obscured by the low clouds. The wind had kicked up as it often did, coming down out of the Crazies in a roar. The Native Americans had been afraid of these mountains and the wind that howled out of them. Some believed they were the ones who had originally named the mountain range, believing any man who went into them was crazy.

As he neared the house, he saw that the lights were on. Bethany's SUV was parked out front. No other vehicle was in sight, but that didn't mean her lover wasn't parked around back or behind the barn or even down the back road out of sight.

Just the thought of her in their bed with another man...

Clete fought to control his temper.

"You scare me sometimes," Bethany had said after a fight early on in their marriage.

He scared himself since he knew what he was capable of and never let himself forget. He'd backed off, pulled away and had known it was part of the reason he'd become distant. If he cared too much... He knew that was crazy, but he'd seen his parents go through it. Their love had turned toxic with his father's jealousy turning to physical abuse. Clete had promised himself he would never let that happen with Bethany.

That is why he drove up in the yard and sat in his truck for a few minutes trying to calm down. After he felt a little less tense, he climbed out. With a start, he saw Bethany in the dark shadows of the porch. She must have heard him drive up and come out. He wondered how long she'd been standing there, watching him, waiting.

As he closed his truck door and walked toward her, he couldn't help remembering the first time he'd kissed her. She'd been nothing more than a kid when she'd come up to him at the Fall Harvest Festival and tried to get him to buy her a beer.

Bethany had always been gutsy. He liked that about her. *Loved* that about her. She'd told him that night on the dance floor that he was going to marry her some day.

He'd laughed because she was so young and yet so serious.

"Is everything all right?" she asked now from the darkness. She sounded worried. "You're home so early."

"Is that a problem?"

She seemed to shrink at the sharp edge in his tone.

He watched her reach for the doorknob behind her as if she just wanted to get away from him.

"I wanted to surprise you," he said, softening his tone.

"Well, you did. I'm glad you got off early. Dinner's not ready yet, though."

He realized there was only one thing he was hungry for as he followed the sweet scent of her perfume into their house.

It wasn't until later, lying next to her in the damp crumpled sheets, that he realized she must have just gotten out of the shower before he drove up. Nothing suspicious about that, right?

As DESTRY PULLED INTO the yard, she saw in her headlights that someone had left her a note.

The night was dark, only glimpses of the moon peeking through the clouds. It was another cold evening, the air scented with the smell of snow. As she looked toward the Crazies, she knew the peaks would be dusted with fresh snow come morning.

Getting out of the truck, she looped her purse over her shoulder, her hand slipping inside where she felt the cold metal of the gun, and its weight reassured her. Nothing moved in the trees. The wind whispered in the tops of the pines and sent fall leaves skittering across the yard, but nothing ominous came out of the darkness.

At the door, Destry pulled off the note. It felt heavy. She realized why as she saw two large house keys taped inside. She used one to open the door, turning on a light so she could read the note.

Rylan's handwriting. She recognized it even though it had been a long time since she'd last seen it. He was left-handed, so his writing was distinctive and yet completely different from her left-handed brother's.

She read: *"I hope you don't mind. I changed your locks. You might want to start locking your doors. Just a thought. Rylan."*

Destry stared at the note and smiled. He'd changed her locks? She couldn't help being touched. As she closed and locked the door behind her, she realized she'd left the door unlocked earlier—just as it had been when her brother stopped by.

This was rural Montana, no one locked their doors. Few people, herself included, could even find the keys to their doors. She would lock her doors at night, but she'd be damned if she would during the day.

She felt the cold keys in her hand and smiled again at the thought of Rylan changing her locks. She was more than touched by his concern, she thought, her smile widening.

Maybe he hadn't changed as much as she'd thought. At least their feelings for each other hadn't. She thought again of the kiss and felt warmth rush through her veins. As irritating and stubborn as the man was, she still loved him.

If she closed her eyes, she could recall the feel of his bare skin under her fingertips just as she could the beat of his heart as they lay entwined the night they'd made love. She'd clung to that memory for eleven years, but the desire they'd shared was just as strong now as it had been then.

Dropping the keys into a dish by the door, she reminded herself not to get her hopes up. As long as Ginny's killer ran free, none of them could move on.

She started up the stairs when she saw him. A large

dark figure moved past the windows beside the back door. For a just an instant, she froze, her heart lodging in her throat. But she quickly willed herself to move as she raced across the room to snatch up the shotgun.

The sky had darkened to blue velvet, but there were enough stars and the moon to see for some distance as she threw open the door and stepped out, shotgun in hand. A stiff wind whirled her stray hair around her face, reminding her of earlier today when Rylan had brushed it from her eyes.

She swatted that thought away as she lifted the shotgun and took aim. The man must have heard her coming because he was hightailing it toward the creek. She raised the shotgun toward the sky and pulled both triggers. The man stumbled as if hearing the boom and fearing he'd been shot.

"Next time I won't miss," she yelled after him, then shut the door and locked it as the man disappeared into the far woods.

NETTIE BENTON SHOT UP in bed with a start. Instantly, she froze, listening. The window facing the store was cracked open where she could hear if there was any trouble down the mountain.

But as she listened, she heard only the wind in the tall pine trees outside. One of the branches scraped against the side of the house. Was that what had awakened her?

Carefully, she slipped out of bed. Clouds scudded across the midnight-blue sky, giving her only glimpses of stars and a sliver of silver moon.

When she looked through the pines toward the store

on the hillside below, she could see the faint light she'd left on inside the back door but nothing else.

Nettie considered going back to bed but knew she wouldn't be able to get a wink of sleep until she checked the store. If someone was down there trying to break in again, maybe it hadn't been a bear the first time and maybe the robber was back. She would love nothing better than to catch the thief and show that Frank Curry. Her money was on one of those wild Thompson kids.

She glanced toward the bed. Bob must have gone into the guest room to sleep again, no doubt complaining that she snored. Or more likely so she wouldn't hear him cry out from one of his nightmares. Last night she'd awakened and would have sworn he was calling out the name Ginny.

Carson coming back had everyone talking about Ginny again, she told herself. Nor was there any reason to wake Bob. She could handle this herself, she thought as she hurried to the back door, pulled on one of the down coats from the hooks, slipped on a pair of mud boots and rushed out of the house.

The wind howled around her, rocking the tops of the pines and sending dust scurrying across the narrow path in front of her. She hadn't realized it would be so dark in the trees. Too late to go back for a flashlight now, though.

Watching for any movement in the thick pines next to the store, she made her way quietly down the steep hillside toward the back of the store. She hadn't gone far when she realized she should have brought a weapon.

She was almost to the back of the store when a sound stopped her. Something grunted on the hillside off to her right. The wind picked up the hem of her nightgown, making it flutter at her ankles.

Her whole body tensed, her stomach dropping, as a huge grizzly ambled down the hillside through the pines. It stopped to overturn a dead log as it scrounged for ants.

Nettie gauged the distance back uphill to the house. She was closer to the store and it was downhill. But with growing panic, she realized that she hadn't grabbed the keys to the store when she'd left the house. Fortunately she kept a key hidden in a hollow space in one of the logs by the back door of the store.

Another grunt.

Nettie knew better than to run but covered the distance to the back door as fast as she could. The grizzly had seen her, though. She didn't doubt that for a moment. It had probably picked up her scent the moment she'd left the house. Fortunately, it must not have thought her a threat because it hadn't even looked in her direction, let alone charged her.

She frantically reached back into the log opening and felt around for the key. A limb cracked behind her, and she caught the distinct putrid smell of the grizzly bear. She could hear it moving slowly toward her, crunching the dried pine needles under its huge paws.

Her fingers trembled as she dug out the key. But before she could get it into the lock, the key slipped from her hand, dropping to the ground at her feet.

Panicked, she fell to her knees, felt around wildly, scooped it up and pulled herself to her feet. She couldn't hear the grizzly now, but she didn't dare turn to look. The scent in the air was so strong, she swore she could feel the bear's nasty breath on her neck.

Nettie fumbled the key into the lock, turned it and the doorknob at the same time, and practically threw herself into the back of the store.

As she turned to close the door, she saw the grizzly's steering-wheel-sized head peering in at her, its nostrils flared, eyes bright in the faint starlight. She slammed the door, locked it and leaned against it as she fought to catch her breath and still her thundering heart.

She was shaking so hard her teeth were chattering. Behind the store, she could hear the bear foraging around in some empty boxes her husband hadn't taken care of yet.

Anger overcame the fear. She'd wake Bob up and get him down here, that's what she'd do. But as she picked up the receiver she heard a loud crash outside as a massive limb blew off one of the old cottonwoods along the creek.

With a curse, Nettie listened for a dial tone. The line had gone dead. She slammed down the receiver. Not only was she trapped here in the middle of the night, her husband didn't even know she was gone—let alone that she was in trouble.

The bear was still digging around in the boxes, hoping to find something to eat. What would he do when he finished? Grayson had nailed a piece of plywood over the back window. She just hoped it held in case the grizzly decided to break in. There were other windows, most too high for the bear to try to get through, though.

Sighing, Nettie padded into the main part of the store in the dark since the electricity had gone out with the phone. A little starlight lit her way down the grocery aisle to the front window.

The street was empty. The Branding Iron was dark.

So were the upstairs windows of the apartment where Kate LaFond lived.

Nettie started to turn away when she saw a light bobbing along behind the café. She recognized the figure armed with a flashlight and, of all things, a shovel. Kate LaFond was heading for the ancient stone garage set off to one side behind the café.

What in the world was the woman up to at this hour? And what was she doing with a *shovel?*

Just then the store backup generator came on, along with the store's lights. Nettie was caught in the glare. How had it slipped her mind that the backup generator that kept the freezers and coolers running would come on—along with the security lights?

She ducked and turned out the lights, but soon enough that she hadn't been seen? As her eyes adjusted to the darkness again, she glanced across the street but saw nothing. Either Kate was working in the pitch dark of the old garage. Or she'd decided not to dig tonight because she knew she'd been seen.

CHAPTER SIXTEEN

EARLY THE NEXT MORNING, Destry called Rylan to thank him for changing the locks at her house. She suspected after finding Ginny's letterman jacket, he'd needed something to occupy him.

"Not sure why I bothered. Your house was unlocked when I came by to replace them."

"Which made it lot easier for you, huh," she joked. "Anyway, I don't think I'm going to be having any more problems."

"I'm afraid to ask."

"I threw some buckshot in his general direction and told him next time I would take aim."

"I hope whoever the dumb bastard is realizes you're serious."

"How are you doing?" she asked.

"Okay. It was just such a shock seeing her jacket with…"

Destry knew he was thinking about the blood. There'd been so much of it. "Anyone could have put that jacket in one of the clothing drive bins."

"But why now? Why after all these years?"

She'd been wondering the same thing. "A guilty conscience?"

"You still suspect Pastor Tom."

"The more I've thought about it, the less sure I am,"

she had to admit. "Did you see his face when you pulled out Ginny's jacket? I thought he was going to pass out. And last night I ran into Bob Benton and he reminded me that it was Tom's wife and Bessie Crist who found Ginny."

"Yeah, I remember that."

"Well, I'm thinking I might go talk to Linda and Bessie. Since they were the first people on the scene, maybe they might remember something now that didn't seem important back then—or that they didn't notice at the time."

"I want to go with you," he said.

"Are you sure?" She would imagine it would upset him to hear how his sister had been found again. "I can—"

"I'm sure."

Her phone beeped in her ear. "I'm getting another call. Can I call you back?"

He said she could and she took the other call. "Hello?"

It was her friend who worked at the lab.

Blood thundered in her ears. "You got the paternity results."

"Do you want me to mail them?"

"Can you tell me…" Destry held her breath. Although, after finding the photograph of her mother, didn't she already know what her friend was going to say?

"There's no match between your DNA and the sample you brought me."

Destry nodded. Confirmation. WT had been right. She wasn't his daughter. "Thank you," she managed to say. "I appreciate you doing this for me." Her hand shook as she replaced the phone.

So, who am I?

When the phone rang again, she thought it would be Rylan. Instead, a recorded message came on. "This is a collect call from Montana State Prison. If you will accept a call from...Jack French...press one. If you—"

Jack? She hadn't heard from him since he'd gone to prison. She pressed one.

"Sorry I had to call collect," he said.

"It's not a problem. I'm just surprised." She had a sudden mental image of Jack. The cowboy was too handsome for words and always grinning. Talk about happy-go-lucky, that was Jack French. He took nothing seriously. How else had he gotten arrested for some late-night cattle rustling that had landed him in prison?

"I heard Carson was back," Jack said now. He sounded older, possibly even more mature. She wondered if this experience had changed him. He'd been working the prison cattle ranch, and, according to people who'd heard from him during his sentence up there, it wasn't much different than working for WT Grant, except the guards treated him better.

"How did you hear that?" she asked, amazed how information traveled so quickly across a state as large as Montana—even to prison.

"We talked before he left Vegas. How is he?"

She didn't know how to answer. Fortunately, Jack didn't give her a chance.

"Listen, I've been doing a lot of thinking. Time on my hands, you know," he said with a laugh.

"About the night Ginny died."

Silence. "Yeah."

Her heart leaped to her throat. "Carson wasn't at the ranch all night, was he?" She already knew the answer, realized she'd suspected it the moment her brother had involved her in his alibi.

This time the silence was longer, so long Destry feared they'd been disconnected or, worse, that Jack had changed his mind and hung up. After all, Carson had always been his best friend.

"Jack, you have to tell me the truth, no matter how bad it is. I have to know so I can help him."

"That's why I called you. It's been hell keeping his secret. That night I tried to talk him out of following Ginny. He suspected she was meeting some married dude."

"So he did go into town." The words were as heavy as her heart.

"Yeah." Jack cleared his throat. "When he came back, oh, man, he was a total basket case. I've never seen him like that. He kept saying she was gone. There was blood on his shirt sleeve."

Destry covered her mouth with her hand for a moment, tears burning her eyes. "Did he tell you what happened?"

"All I could get out of him was that he'd seen her and that he'd blown it and she was gone."

"Jack, you don't think he…" She couldn't bring herself to finish.

"Naw, Destry. Did you know he came up here to visit me a few times and he wrote me, too? He couldn't kill her, you have to know that. He *loved* her."

She wished she could be as convinced as Jack. Carson had lied about going to town. What else had he lied about?

She thought of Rylan. He'd always suspected that Carson had lied. That he was still lying about what happened that night. Once Rylan knew that Carson had not only gone into Beartooth, but also that he'd seen Ginny that night, had gotten blood on him, he wouldn't believe anything her brother said. Destry wasn't sure she did anymore. She felt sick.

Could Carson have put Ginny's letterman jacket in that clothing bin at church? The church was open all the time. Anyone could have gone in and left it without the pastor or Linda seeing them.

After she hung up with Jack, she called Rylan, thankful to get his voice mail. She was too upset to talk to him right now. She left a message, saying she had something she needed to do but to let her know if he could go to Linda's and Bessie's later this morning.

At the big house, she saw the sheriff's car parked out front. Fear gripped her. Frank couldn't have gotten the report on the jacket this quickly.

She tried not to panic as she hurried inside the house. "What's going on?" she asked when she saw the three somber faces in the living room.

"I was just asking your brother to come down to my office for a talk," Sheriff Frank Curry said. He sounded irritated, and Destry guessed this wasn't the first time he'd tried to get Carson to his office. "We're waiting for his attorney."

Destry glanced at her brother. He appeared shaken. WT looked as if he might bust an artery, he was so furious.

"Could I talk to my brother alone for a moment?" she asked. "Don't worry, we'll be right back."

The room fell deathly silent. Destry looked to her

brother. Her anxiety increased when he wouldn't hold
her gaze.

"Just make sure he doesn't go out the back door,"
the sheriff said.

"He won't," she said and motioned for her brother to
come with her. He rose slowly, clearly not wanting to
talk to her any more than he did the sheriff.

As she led him down to WT's den, she told herself
he couldn't have killed Ginny. Yes, he'd lied about leaving the ranch, lied about seeing Ginny that night. That's
why he looked so guilty.

Carson went straight to the bar and poured himself
what she guessed wasn't his first drink.

"Do you think that's a good idea?" she asked.

"At this point, it can't hurt."

"The sheriff wouldn't be here unless he'd found evidence implicating you," she said to his back. "But you
swore you didn't leave the ranch that night. Jack swore
it as well, and you threw me into the mix for good measure. I need to know the truth."

Carson sighed before turning around, drink in hand,
to face her. He looked shamefaced. "Are you sure, Destry?"

"I know you left the ranch that night and the sheriff
must, too." Her voice broke. "Tell me you didn't hurt
Ginny."

He raised his gaze slowly until their eyes met, his
exactly like his father's.

"Stop lying. Tell me the truth, Carson."

CARSON TOOK A GULP OF his drink and then seemed to
brace himself. "I *loved* Ginny." His voice broke. "It was
killing me to know there was someone else."

"You never even suspected who it was?" Destry asked.

He shook his head. "But I knew he was married because there was some reason they couldn't be together except secretly."

Destry nodded and waited.

"Ginny wanted to get married, have kids. I was twenty, too young, so I put her off, telling her we'd get married after college. Then, out of the blue, she broke up with me. When I pressed her for answers, she finally told me that there was this man that she'd…" He swallowed and looked away. "That she'd slept with him."

"What did you do?" Destry asked, afraid she already knew.

"We fought. I tried to hold her. She shoved me away and fell and hurt her wrist."

Destry remembered that Rylan had been upset with her brother in the weeks before Ginny was murdered. He'd also mentioned that Carson had hurt Ginny one other time. "Oh, Carson."

"I wanted to know who he was, so I started following her. That night I followed her. She was driving one of the ranch trucks. She parked it behind the bar, then sneaked down to the old Royale theater."

"What were you planning to do?"

"Maybe I planned to confront him. I don't know." Carson put down his empty glass and scrubbed his hand over his face. "It was pitch-black inside the theater, but I knew my way around from when I was a kid."

Every kid in the county must have played on that stage, she thought, fear making her sick inside. The rumor was that a hair clip belonging to Ginny had been found in that room under the stage.

"I didn't go in right away. I guess I was afraid of what I might do if I found her with him. When I finally went in, it took me a while to find her."

"Who was she with?"

He shook his head, his Adam's apple working as he swallowed. "She was alone, a single candle burning in that room under the stage. He'd been there but he'd left. When I found her, she was crying and upset. He'd broken it off. I told her not to worry, I would take care of her. I took her in my arms and one thing led to another. But afterward…" He looked away, and she feared what was coming.

"She told you she was pregnant."

He nodded, apparently not surprised that she knew about the pregnancy.

"And you changed your mind about wanting her," she said, filling in the blanks.

"No, I just wanted her to tell me who the father was. I wanted to… I don't know what I wanted to do. Punch him in the face."

"But she wouldn't tell you?"

"No, so I stormed off. I left her lying there and headed back to the ranch. But halfway home, I realized it didn't matter who the other man was. I loved Ginny. I would love her baby, no matter whose it was. I turned around and went back."

Destry held her breath.

"She was gone, but I could see that there'd been a struggle. I lit the candle. There was blood…" He stopped and shook his head, his eyes bright with tears. "I knew something horrible had happened to her."

"Why didn't you call the sheriff? Why didn't you—"

"I couldn't. I'd just been with her. I had her blood

on me. Who would believe that I hadn't been the one who'd hurt her?" His gaze implored her to understand. "I was young and stupid. I thought I saw someone at the window. I ran." His voice cracked, and she could see him fighting tears.

"Her killer must have just left with her. Maybe was even still in the building. Or maybe he was the person you saw at the window. If you'd called the sheriff..."

"Don't you think I've told myself that a million times for the past eleven years?" he snapped. "I was a punk kid, running scared. Your boyfriend had already told me that if I ever laid a hand on her again... Once he told the sheriff..." Tears welled in his eyes. "I loved Ginny. If I had called the sheriff. If I had gone looking for her. If I had just tried, I might have found her before she died. I might have saved her."

"Was her letterman jacket there?"

He looked surprised. "No, why?"

"It turned up in one of the clothing bins at the church."

Carson looked sick. She got up and went to him, putting her arms around him. She understood now the demons that had haunted him the past eleven years and the change she'd seen in him. "It isn't your fault she's dead."

"If I hadn't left her there—"

"You might both be dead."

The den door opened behind him. "Your attorney's here," Margaret said.

Destry straightened, her brother rising and turning away to wipe his tears. "We'll be right there."

Would the sheriff believe him? She'd believed him eleven years ago when he'd told her he'd been at the ranch all night, just him and Jack. Then he'd dragged her into it, making things even worse between her and Rylan. But she'd believed him because she hadn't wanted to believe he was capable of murder.

"I'm sorry I involved you," Carson said, as if reading her mind. "I wasn't sure anyone would believe Jack."

They hadn't. Nor had it helped dragging her into it. Everyone had always believed he'd killed Ginny. Carson had a temper. He'd admitted to hurting Ginny once, even though it had been an accident. He'd made love to her that night, but afterward when she refused to give him the man's name, he must have been furious.

"Jack has had some second thoughts about that night," she said. "He called me this morning."

Carson nodded. How long before Jack recanted his story to the sheriff, since clearly it had been eating away at him all these years? "I told him when we talked recently that I don't want him lying for me anymore."

"The sheriff must know that you were with her that night," Destry said.

His eyes welled with tears again. "She told me the baby was her lover's, but I knew she just wanted it to be his. I think she had this crazy idea that he was going to marry her."

LATER THAT DAY, LINDA Armstrong opened the door and seemed surprised to see Destry and Rylan standing there. The parsonage was small, wood-framed and painted white like the church with a small stoop out front. Destry had never been inside. Few people had. Linda preferred to hold any gatherings down at the church, saying the parsonage was just too tiny.

"If you're looking for the pastor, he's down at the church," Linda said.

"Actually, we wanted to see you." Destry noted that Linda was dressed up as if she was going somewhere. "I'm sorry if we caught you at a bad time. We can come back."

Linda seemed to hesitate. "I have a few minutes." She stepped back to let them enter. "What is this about?"

The house was simply furnished and sparsely decorated. In the living area there was a large cross on one wall and several plates with Bible quotes on them, nothing else on the walls.

"We need to ask you about the night you found my sister," Rylan said. "I know it's been a long time, but I was wondering if there was anything else you might have remembered."

Linda looked surprised by the question. "I have done my best to forget everything about that night. I don't understand why you would want me to relive it."

"We're trying to find Ginny's killer," Rylan said.

Linda lifted a brow, her gaze shifting to Destry. "Isn't that the sheriff's job? And anyway, I thought everyone already knew..." But she didn't finish the thought.

"If you could just tell us about that night, maybe something will come to you," Destry said, realizing the pastor must not have told his wife about what they'd found yesterday in the clothing bin.

"I told the sheriff this eleven years ago," Linda complained. "It was...awful. I saw what I thought was a dog that had been hit at the edge of the road. Bessie Crist was with me. She can tell you probably better than I can. I was so upset, I can't swear to anything. I just remember slowing down and there in my headlights..." She shuddered. "I thought she must have been hit by a car. I still wonder if that wasn't the case."

"The coroner confirmed that her injuries indicated foul play, not a hit-and-run," Destry said.

Linda sniffed. "I'm running late for an appointment."

"You didn't notice another vehicle leaving or hear anything when you got out of your car?" Destry pressed.

"I've never heard such quiet. It was completely still. There wasn't even a breath of breeze." She sighed. "I'm sorry, but I really can't add anything more and I have to go."

BESSIE CRIST WAS A tiny gray-haired woman with bright blue eyes and a ready smile. She served Destry and Rylan coffee and bite-size sugar cookies that she'd baked only the day before.

"It's almost as if I knew I was going to have company," she said as she settled into the chair across from them.

They sipped the coffee, complimented the cookies and finally got around to their reason for being there.

Destry put down her cup and said, "We hate to ask, but—"

"Linda called to tell me you'd been to her house asking about that night. She said not to let you upset me." Bessie shook her head. "Linda worries too much about other people." She reached over and placed her hand on Rylan's. "You poor child. It must be so terrible for you to lose your sister like that. What can I do to help?"

"We'd appreciate anything you can remember about that night," Destry said. "We still don't have a clear picture of what happened."

"Well," Bessie said. "It was one of those dark nights where the headlights are just a swatch of gold pointing into the darkness. I spotted her. Linda was too intent on her driving I suppose. I saw what I thought was a dog that had been hit beside the road. Linda didn't want to stop. She was afraid the dog might be rabid and bite one of us."

"So she thought the dog was still alive?" Destry asked.

Bessie blinked. "I suppose so. I told her we couldn't just leave the poor thing."

"So you saw movement?" Rylan asked, sitting forward.

Bessie frowned. "No, I don't think so, but Linda would know better than me. When she stopped, Linda told me to stay back while she went and checked. I saw her stooping down. She had her back to me so I couldn't see what it was. It wasn't until later when I saw that her arm was bleeding that she told me she'd fallen down and cut it, she'd been so upset at seeing Ginny like that."

"How was it that the two of you were on that road that night?"

"Linda had called me and said poor Mrs. Burke wasn't doing well and she needed to drive out to see her and did I want to go along. I'd always enjoyed Mrs. Burke's company, plus she makes a wonderful cup of coffee. So I readily agreed to the drive. I don't drive much myself anymore. Can't see all that well."

"So what happened then?" Destry asked.

"I got out to see if I could help, but Linda said to get her phone and call the sheriff. I dug her cell phone out of her purse but couldn't get it to work. So she came back to the car after a few minutes and punched in 911. That's when I knew, when she told the dispatcher it was

Ginny. I took a blanket out of the backseat and carried it over to your sister to cover her up until the sheriff and the ambulance arrived."

The room fell silent for a few moments. "It wasn't until the next day that I heard it hadn't been an accident. *Murder.*" Bessie shivered and hugged herself. "Imagine, murder here in Beartooth. I told Linda whoever killed that girl had to be a stranger," Bessie said emphatically. "A stranger passing through."

That, unfortunately was harder to imagine since Ginny's ranch pickup had been found behind the Range Rider and Ginny wouldn't have gotten into a car with someone she didn't know and trust.

Rylan was quiet on the ride back to town. They hadn't learned anything new. Instead, he'd been forced to hear the details of how his sister's body had been discovered dumped beside the road.

She felt badly for him and wished there was something she could say. But like him, she felt sick after hearing the details and could understand why Linda had been so adamant about not wanting to relive them— maybe especially if she suspected her husband had been involved with Ginny?

Destry knew she wasn't basing that suspicion on anything but the pastor's suspicious behavior when they'd asked about the Bible quotes. Certainly not any evidence. Given how upset Pastor Tom had been when Rylan had found the letterman jacket, she was less sure of him as a suspect.

Rylan dropped her at her pickup. "Thanks. I'm not sure I could have done that alone."

"Anytime," she said and climbed out. "Thanks again for changing my locks."

He nodded distractedly. She watched as he headed for the Range Rider as if he needed a drink. Or was he meeting Kimberly there?

RYLAN STEPPED INTO the Range Rider. He didn't need a beer so much as he needed a distraction from his thoughts. Hearing about his sister from the two women who'd found her had left him shaken—and furious. He hadn't wanted Destry to see him like this.

"What'll you have?" Clete asked as he came down the bar to where Rylan had taken a stool.

"Just a beer. Whatever you have on tap." The bar was quiet this time of day. A couple of regulars were at the other end watching some daytime game show on the small television.

"So, how are things going?" Clete asked as he set a frosty glass of beer down on a bar napkin in front of him.

"They're going." Rylan took a sip of the beer. It was cold and tasted wonderful on this fall day. The morning had been cold, but as the day wore on it had warmed up.

He and Clete both turned as the front door of the bar opened. Clete's wife, Bethany, came in on a gust of fall breeze that smelled as if someone was burning dried leaves. It instantly transported him to another fall when he and Destry had been in high school. Destry with flushed cheeks and bright eyes as they raced through the fallen leaves.

Rylan sipped his beer as Clete and Bethany exchanged a few words. He heard Clete ask her why she wasn't working her shift at the café and Bethany told him Kate asked her not to come in because it wasn't busy.

As Bethany started to leave, though, he caught a glimmer of light flash at her throat. Before Rylan could stop himself, he stood and grabbed her arm, turning her to him.

"Where did you get that necklace?" His tone was sharper than he'd meant it to be. He'd just been so surprised to see a locket like the one he'd found hidden in his sister's jewelry box.

Bethany froze. *"What?"* Her hand went to the heart-shaped locket at her neck. All the color seemed to wash from her face as she closed her fingers over it, balling the heart in her fist as her gaze shot to her husband behind the bar.

Clete was watching the exchange, no doubt having heard the shock and surprise in Rylan's voice.

"Sorry," Rylan said quickly, letting go of her. "It's just that I think I've seen one like it and I was wondering where you got it."

Clete leaned across the bar toward her. "Let's see it."

"It's just an old locket I had lying around," Bethany said nervously.

Rylan watched the exchange, confused. He hadn't meant to cause a problem between them, but clearly he had.

Clete motioned for his wife to remove her hand so he could see the locket. She did it with obvious reluctance. From his expression, he'd never seen the locket before and was just as curious as Rylan as to where she'd gotten it—and no doubt why she was reacting the way she was.

"Like I said, it's just some old thing I've had."

Clete nodded, but he didn't seem to believe her any

more than Rylan did. The silver wasn't tarnished like Ginny's had been. The locket looked new.

He could think of only one reason Bethany would lie about it and quickly changed the subject, figuring he would catch Bethany alone and talk to her when Clete wasn't around.

As she left, he saw that Clete was upset. What the devil was going on between the two of them? He could only guess, if he was right about the locket and her lying.

Bethany, he realized with a start, reminded him of his sister. Hell, she'd even looked like Ginny when the two of them were in school together. He remembered a time when Ginny had complained that Bethany was dressing like her, had even had her hair styled like hers.

There was a resemblance even now, he realized. The reddish-blond hair, the fair coloring, the sprinkling of freckles. Both women had that girl-next-door look about them.... Like Destry....

CHAPTER SEVENTEEN

ON HIS RETURN FROM the sheriff's office, Carson had gone straight to the bar in his father's den. He was still shaking, only too aware of how close he was to being arrested for Ginny's murder. Once the DNA results came back on Ginny's letterman jacket—

He turned at the sound of the door opening behind him. The last person he wanted to talk to right now was WT.

"Cherry." He should never have brought her here, knowing the kind of trouble he was in.

"Your father said you had to go down to the sheriff's office. Is everything all right?"

"I think there's a good chance I'm going to be arrested."

"For your high school girlfriend's murder. But you didn't do it."

"No, but I lied about seeing her that night. I lied about a lot of things at the time."

"You were young."

He laughed at that. He'd been lying to himself for years.

"This isn't working out, is it?" she said. "I knew you were hung up on what happened before you left Montana, but since you've been back here, I've seen the change in you."

"The thought of being arrested for murder changes a person."

"That's not it. This place means more to you than you pretend it does."

"Sorry, but when did you get your degree in psychology?" He hadn't meant the words to come out so sharp.

She merely smiled. "I know you, Carson. There's more keeping you here than your father's money."

He wanted to argue that she was wrong as he watched her take off the diamond engagement ring he'd bought at a Vegas pawn shop. That life felt a million miles away and suddenly not as glittery as it had seemed when he and Cherry had been a part of it.

"What are you doing? If you can just wait—"

She held the ring out to him.

He shook his head. "Keep it. I don't want it."

Cherry studied him for a long moment. "I do love you and I hope you get all this figured out. I understand why you feel the way you do about your father, but your sister cares for you. Don't hurt her." She turned to leave. "I'm going to pack and then you can take me to the nearest airport. It had better not be three hours away," she joked.

"An hour and a half." He was glad that they could still share a laugh together.

Carson watched her go, hating that she was right. He hadn't resolved the past. He wasn't sure he ever could.

His cell phone rang. He opened it without looking to see who was calling and instantly regretted it. The threats were getting more detailed. Time was running out, his desperation growing along with the interest on his gambling debts.

Destry would get him some money. It would hold

them off temporarily. But then what if he still didn't have his hands on the ranch?

A thought whizzed past. Maybe there was another way. If he could get a stake, maybe he could win back enough at the local poker game to keep the wolf away from the door and stall for even more time.

With a jolt, he realized this turn of events might work in his favor. Wouldn't WT pay to have Cherry gone? If he played his cards right, he could make this work for him. He could redeem himself.

At the sound of the old man's wheelchair coming down the hallway, Carson prepared himself for battle.

Cherry didn't understand the problem was between him and his father. Even though he'd been young when his mother had died, he remembered only too well how things had been between WT and her. He'd seen the way WT had treated her. That's why he'd kept his mother's secret and would take it to his grave.

It was also why he'd promised himself he would pay his father back for being so horrible to his mother. That day was almost here, he thought as WT wheeled into the room. Maybe Destry wouldn't have to get hurt, too.

WT SAW CHERRY FLOUNCE out of the den and overheard her say she was going to pack. He watched her head in the direction of her room and couldn't wait to see the woman gone.

He suspected his son felt the same way. Carson had never planned to marry her. The bluff had been wasted on him. Or if he had, being in Montana on the ranch had changed both of their minds.

"You were right about Cherry," Carson said as WT wheeled himself over to the bar.

"So, she *is* a stripper?" WT said, purposely misinterpreting what his son was saying. He saw Carson grit his teeth and fight back the anger that always simmered just under the surface. Cherry had turned out to be a lot smarter than he'd first thought. She might not have been so bad for Carson after all. But her life was in Vegas. Carson's was here.

"I can't marry her."

WT said nothing. Was he supposed to act surprised by this?

"I need to let her down easy though, especially after bringing her all the way up here and promising her a big wedding," Carson said.

WT wished Carson wasn't so transparent. And yet it made things easier often, didn't it? "I can run her off for you, or if you're feeling generous, you can drive her into Big Timber. I'll pay for the bus trip back to wherever you picked her up."

"I told you. I *love* her. I can't do that to her. If you won't help me, then maybe I should go back to Vegas and marry her, let the chips fall where they may."

Carson was bluffing again, but WT didn't call him on it. Getting rid of Cherry would be worth every penny because the woman wasn't cut out for ranch life. She would lure Carson away eventually.

"How much?" he asked, as his son started out of the room.

Carson stopped but didn't turn. "Five thousand dollars."

WT swore and put up an appropriate fight, but he would have paid twice that much to get the woman out of his son's life. "Fine," he said after a few minutes of negotiation. "I'll write you a check."

After Carson left, WT rolled over to the window. There was fresh snow on the tops of the peaks and fewer leaves on the cottonwoods and aspens every day. Winter was coming. He knew firsthand how inhospitable this country could be. He'd survived the blizzards, the howling winds that screamed down out of the Crazies, the scorching summers that baked the earth and starved the land and animals.

He'd seen the way the younger generations were leaving the land for what they considered a better life and higher wages. The mass exodus reminded him of the stories his father had told about the 1920s when thousands of farmers and ranchers had been starved out. They'd left everything, fleeing. But his family had stayed and fought, barely surviving.

He'd changed that. He'd thrived here at the base of the Crazy Mountains, and damned if he'd let anything happen to his ranch. While other ranches were being sold and divided up into twenty-acre tracts, his wasn't going to be one of them, if he had to fight until his last dying breath.

As he surveyed what he'd accomplished, he waited for that surge of pride he used to feel and frowned when it didn't come. All of this didn't feel like enough, never had. He'd hoped when his son came home, he would feel differently. He'd been waiting years for Carson to return and take over the ranch.

His fear had always been that Carson was too much like his mother. Just the thought of Lila made his stomach roil, even though she'd been gone almost thirty years now. Gone, he thought, but not forgotten since he was reminded of her every time he looked at her daughter.

Now, though, he feared Carson had taken after him—in all the worst possible ways. WT shoved away those thoughts, reminding himself how far he'd come from that old house where he'd been raised. Look where he lived now. He smiled to himself, remembering how his new house had been the talk of the county.

Just as his son had been the talk of the county, his thoughts darkening quickly again. It had been eleven years since the "trouble," as he liked to think of it. Plenty of time for the heat to die down, just as he'd assured Carson.

But the sheriff's latest visit had made him worried that his son might be headed for prison. Worse, there wasn't a damned thing he could do about it.

"You what?"

"I forgot I was wearing the locket," Bethany said into the phone. "When I stopped by the bar to see Clete… Well, it was really weird. Rylan West saw the locket and he had such a strange reaction to it."

The sigh on the other end of the line was heavy with anger. "What are you trying to do?"

"I wasn't—"

"You just happened to forget to take it off?" He sounded furious. She wished she hadn't called. Why had she told him, anyway? He probably would have never found out.

"It's not that big of a deal. I came up with a story."

"A *story?*" He didn't sound as if he had any faith in her.

"I said it was mine, that I hadn't worn it for a long time and had forgotten about it." She could hear him moving around the room. She wondered where his wife was. She must be in another part of the house because he hadn't gotten mad about her calling him at home.

"What did you do with the locket?" he asked, emphasizing each word as if she was a child.

"I hid it."

"I want you to get rid of it."

She shook her head, even though he couldn't see her. "But *you* gave it to me."

"Yes, unfortunately, and I now see that it was a huge mistake on my part."

"I won't *wear* it again."

"Bethany, clearly I can't trust you to get rid of it, so I want you to bring it to me." She heard a noise in the background like that of a door opening and closing. "I'll let you know when. Wait for my call." He hung up.

She put down the phone and looked at the small heart-shaped locket, the delicate silver chain curled around it. She'd been so touched when he'd given it to her that she'd cried.

"I never thought anyone like you would ever care about me like this."

"Why would you say that?"

"Because you're smart and successful and people look up to you. Me, I'm just…nobody."

"Bethany," he'd said lifting her chin so their eyes met. "You're special. I've never met anyone quite like you."

"I just wish we didn't have to keep this a secret." The moment the words were out of her mouth she'd seen her mistake. He'd become angry, explaining to her, as he had so many times before, that the only way they could see each other was if they kept their feelings secret.

"You have to trust me. The timing is all wrong.

Maybe someday, but for now… You do trust me, don't you, Bethany?"

She'd nodded and he'd kissed away her tears, then he'd made love to her. She'd felt cherished and…well, special.

Now she picked up the locket and chain, cradling it in the palm of her hand. It felt cool to the touch, just as it had the day he'd put it on her. She didn't want to give it back. She couldn't. After he called and she went to meet him, she'd say she'd forgotten it.

What if he really did break off the relationship like he had said? He was already upset about the notes and had said they should stop seeing each other. She'd thought he was overreacting, but now she was worried that he might really mean it. The thought sent an arrow to her heart. He was all she had to look forward to each day. Clete didn't care. He pretended to. She thought about last night. Last night she'd loved him just as she had at the beginning.

But last night he'd been jealous, worried that a man had given her the locket. Now that he thought that wasn't true…

She sighed and got up to tuck the locket in the back of her lingerie drawer. Clete would never look in there.

She closed the drawer, a mixture of dread and apprehension as she waited for her lover's call.

CHAPTER EIGHTEEN

CLETE REYNOLDS NODDED and smiled when necessary but was only half listening to the conversation at the bar.

He regretted not confronting his wife last night about the silver locket she'd been wearing yesterday. He'd suspected Bethany was up to something for some time now. He tried to pinpoint exactly when he'd become suspicious. After working in a bar, he knew the signs. It was the little telltale things.

The first time was the night he'd caught a whiff of unfamiliar aftershave when he'd walked into his house. Bethany had just been getting home. She was hanging up her coat when he'd smelled it. He hadn't been able to place it.

Bethany had seen him sniff in her direction and frowned. "What?"

"Nothin'." He'd let it go. Bethany hadn't seemed the type. She wasn't tall and leggy. Or slim, for that matter. Let's just say the woman filled out her shirts and jeans. She was more a homegrown girl, not the kind men whistled at on the street or did double takes because she was a raving beauty. Bethany was simply... cute, sweet looking.

The second time he noticed something was when he realized she'd changed clothes since she'd stopped by the bar only an hour earlier. Her hair had been different, too.

Earlier it had been styled. Now it was pulled up in a ponytail and looked damp, as if she'd just stepped out of a shower. Which was impossible since he knew for a fact she hadn't been home.

He'd taken her out behind the bar and, lighting a cigarette, casually asked her about it. She'd said she and her friend Cassie had taken a dip in the creek because it was so hot out.

Last night, he'd been determined not to do whatever it took to get the truth out of her. He didn't need a repeat performance of what he'd done at a bar in Missoula after he'd realized his girlfriend was cheating on him and he would never play football again. He didn't need another stint behind bars—even overnight—because of another unfaithful woman.

So he'd waited until he'd cooled down. Let her think she was pulling the wool over his eyes. If he bided his time, he would catch her.

But now as Clete stood listening to the same bar talk he heard every night, he wasn't sure he wanted to catch her. Maybe whatever was going on would just play itself out. Maybe it already had. He suddenly couldn't bear the thought of losing her. If he confronted her, would she choose her lover or her husband?

DESTRY NEEDED TO CLEAR her head, and the best way she knew how was on the back of a horse. Her talk with her brother had upset her more than she wanted to admit. She feared he was facing prison, or worse, the death penalty. She shuddered at the thought.

She found their ranch foreman Russell Murdock in

the tack room. The familiar scents of the barn filled her. She breathed them in, stopping to visit her horse for a moment before stepping to the doorway of the tack room. Russell was putting away a halter.

"Hey, there," he said when he saw her. He gave her a big smile, just as he had since she was a girl. Russell was a big man like WT, handsome and easy-going.

When she was a girl, she'd wished he was her father rather than WT. Russell had definitely acted more like one, that was for sure. As she studied him, she knew, until she learned the truth, she would look at every older man in the county, speculating as to whether or not he could be her father from now on.

"Going for a ride?" he asked.

She nodded.

Russell smiled and leaned back against the tack room wall as he took her in. "I know that look. Bad day?" He'd always made time for her, always had lots of patience, as well. "If you're wondering about those new stalls your father wants built, Grayson Brooks is on his way out to start working on them. He said he'd planned to put new locks on your doors today, but that you'd called him and canceled?"

"Rylan already changed my locks."

Russell lifted a brow. "That was nice of him."

She had to laugh. Russell had always known how she felt about the cowboy.

"I saw the sheriff's patrol rig in front of the house. I don't mean to pry." He shoved back the brim of his hat, his face open. Since the time she was small he'd told her if she had a problem she was always welcome to come to him. He'd been good to his word.

She felt her face heat as she recalled asking him if

what she'd heard about sex was true. She'd grown up around animals all her life, so she knew about them. It was just hard to imagine people doing the same thing. She must have been all of eight. Russell had been great about answering her question. She was forever grateful to have him in her life.

"Carson might be in more trouble than we thought," Destry said now. "I suppose you know WT isn't well."

He nodded. "Margaret told me, but I figured something was up when he got Carson home."

"He wants Carson to take over the ranch."

Russell said nothing for a moment. "What does he want for you?"

"Marriage. To Hitch McCray."

Russell sighed, his gaze locking with hers. "Between you and me, Sweet Pea, you aren't seriously considering that, are you?"

He hadn't called her that in years. "Not a chance," she said with a curse.

Russell cocked a brow at her. He'd threatened to wash her mouth out with soap when she was seven if she didn't quit swearing like the ranch hands. She felt even more love for this man who'd filled in for the father she should have had. She couldn't imagine what her life would have been like if Russell hadn't always been around since the beginning.

"How well did you know my mother?"

Russell let out a surprised sound. "Why are you—"

"But you liked her."

"Your mother was a very special woman. Of course, I liked her, but the only man Lila ever loved was WT."

She studied him. "No secrets between us, isn't that what you always said? Nothing I can't ask you."

He smiled. "Nothing's changed."

"Is there any chance you might be my father?"

"You're WT's daughter," he said.

She shook her head. "You've been more of a father to me than WT, so I just thought…"

Russell glanced past her. "Looks like your brother's fiancée is leaving."

She turned to see Carson loading Cherry's suitcases into the back of the sports car.

AFTER BOB BENTON HAD found his wife sleeping on the office floor rug down at the store this morning, he'd stared at her, surprised that she could still astound him after all these years of marriage.

"What were you thinking, coming down here alone? What if it had been some criminal breaking into the store?" he'd demanded after waking her up and insisting to know what was going on.

"I'd take care of it the way I take care of everything else around here," Nettie had snapped as she'd stomped out the back door and headed up the mountainside to the house.

Bob had watched her until she'd reached the house, then he'd gone into the office to call the Montana Fish, Wildlife and Parks to tell them about the grizzly. Not that they could do anything. They'd already put out a trap, but clearly it wasn't working.

With that done, Bob had taken care of the boxes he'd failed to break down the day before and got ready to open the store.

The temperature had dropped again last night, and even with the sun out now, it was going to take a long time to warm up. As he unlocked the front door and put up the Open sign, he felt another panic attack coming on as he saw the sheriff's car parked across the street at the Branding Iron.

He couldn't stay here. He'd thought about going south for the winter, but he knew Nettie would never leave the store. Until that moment, he hadn't thought about going alone.

Why couldn't he just pack up and leave like the rest of the snowbirds who spent only a few weeks in this godforsaken country each year? That could be the answer to all his problems, he realized.

He brightened, even though it meant a change of plan. He was going to Arizona. Who knew what awaited him down there in the sunshine? Maybe a sparkling pool and young women lying around it in tiny swimsuits.

Nettie had already told everyone that she was going to work in this store until she fell over dead. Someone would find her dead one morning when she failed to put out the Open sign. He'd always thought that *someone* would be him.

What if the sheriff got suspicious? Bob stopped in the middle of the chip/cracker/cookie aisle waiting for the panic attack to come again. Would people really question why he'd left without Nettie? No one who knew her, he told himself. Not even the sheriff.

Relief washed over him. He'd spent his last winter in this damned place. His last summer, as well, because once he left he wouldn't be coming back—even if Nettie would let him. He was putting this place and the nightmares behind him. Arizona would be a new beginning.

"WHAT ARE YOU SO HAPPY about?" Nettie demanded when she returned to the store to find her husband whistling. As far as she could remember, she'd never heard the man whistle once in his life.

"FWP is coming out to check the bear trap," Bob said and smiled as if that was the source of this unexpected glee.

She studied him. Bob Benton was never cheerful. He hadn't been when she married him, and that certainly hadn't changed during their many years of marriage. She recalled his moody, odd behavior, all the nights he'd gone for long, late-night walks, coming back more worked up than when he'd left.

"You'll never guess what I saw last night," she said, unable to keep it to herself any longer. "Kate LaFond was digging up something in her garage in the wee hours of the morning." Or burying something, she couldn't be sure which from this distance.

Bob didn't answer, but that was nothing new.

"I told you she's hiding something."

"Kate's just messing with you, Nettie, don't you see that? She probably saw you over here watching her." He wagged his head sympathetically. "Or you just dreamed it. It's none of our business anyway. I cleaned up those boxes in back," he said as he headed for the back door. "Got the cash register ready to go for you, and now I'm going to go pack."

She'd been too angry with him for trying to brush off what she'd seen that she hadn't been listening—that was until she heard the word *pack*.

"Pack?"

He turned then to look at her. It struck her that he even appeared different somehow. Taller, as if a weight had been lifted off his shoulders.

She frowned as she considered him. What had gotten

into *him?* If she didn't know him better, she would suspect he'd fallen in love as part of some delayed midlife crisis.

"I'm going south, Nettie."

"*South?*" she repeated, wondering what the devil he was talking about.

"Arizona. I'm thinking I might buy a place down there with the money my father left me."

Nettie scowled, remembering how Bob's father had left everything to Bob—making sure she was cut from his will. And that, after all the years she'd taken care of his worthless son. Her blood still boiled at the reminder.

"Did you hear me, Nettie? I'm leaving right away, before the first snowfall."

Was he serious? Apparently he thought so.

"The truth is…I'm not sure I'll be back."

She didn't know what to say. The one thing he hadn't mentioned was her going with him. Because he knew she wouldn't? Or because he didn't want her to?

"Just like that?" she finally managed to ask.

"It's been a long time coming. I think you know that." His smile was a little sad. "I never was your first choice anyway."

She couldn't argue that. She was just surprised that Bob had known.

"I hope I haven't ruined your life, Nettie." His words came out hoarse with emotion.

"What are you talking about?" she asked, feeling a tremor of worry move through her. Bob had been acting more than a little strangely lately, not to mention the nightmares. "What have you done, Bob?"

He shook his head, turned and left, closing the door behind him.

Nettie thought about going after him. Instead, she stood alone in the middle of the store waiting for the reality of his leaving to hit her. After a few moments, her eyes filled with tears, and she began to laugh and cry. Unable to settle on one or the other, she sat down in the middle of the store aisle and continued until all she felt was a huge sense of relief.

RYLAN CALLED DESTRY, but there was no answer. He left a message and waited around for a while for her to call back. When she didn't, he considered trying to find Bethany and talking to her alone about the locket. But he realized she might be more apt to tell Destry the truth than him.

So he did the only other thing he could. He saddled up and went for a ride. The West Ranch ran adjacent to the W Bar G, both connecting to forest service land and the Crazies.

He rode up through the pines but hadn't gone far when he saw her. "Great minds think alike," he said as he caught up to Destry.

She laughed, though she didn't seem all that surprised to see him. They rode along together as they climbed up through the pines to an open ridge.

Destry swung down from her horse to walk to the cliff edge.

"This always was one of your favorite spots," he said, joining her. The view was incredible. Destry had always said she felt as if she could see to the end of the planet from here. It seemed that way on a clear, cloudless day like today. The afternoon breeze stirred the stray tendrils of hair beneath her Western straw hat.

He'd been anxious to tell her about Bethany and the

locket he'd seen, but now he didn't want to spoil the moment with talk of the murder or what had kept them apart all these years.

To his surprise, when he looked over at her, there were tears in her eyes. "Destry, what is it?"

She shook her head.

"I've noticed that there is something going on with you. Please, you know you can talk to me."

She glanced over at him. Her blue eyes glistened. She made an angry dash at the tears with her sleeve.

When she didn't answer, he stepped to her, took her shoulders in his hands and turned her to face him. "What is it?"

She tried to avoid his gaze, but he pulled her closer, until there was nothing she could do but meet his eyes.

"It's the ranch. I'm going to lose it."

"Lose it?" he asked in surprise. He knew that the W Bar G was doing great with Destry running it.

"WT's not my father."

"What?"

She shook her head. "Apparently my mother had a lover before I was born. WT has known about it all these years. It explains his lack of interest in me."

"How long have you known this?"

She shrugged. "I guess I've always suspected something was wrong. I just never thought... When I realized he'd gotten Carson back to take over the ranch, I confronted him and he told me."

Rylan took a moment to digest this. The ranch had become Destry's life. To lose it... "He's giving your brother the ranch? So it isn't really lost. Your brother wouldn't kick you off." The bastard better not, if he knew what was good for him, he thought.

"Carson is in trouble and plans to sell the place to pay a large debt he has."

Rylan had to bite his tongue to keep from swearing. If he could have gotten his hands on Carson at that moment—

"I don't know who my biological father is," Destry said, her voice breaking. "I don't know who *I* am."

"I do," he whispered as he drew her to him and, cupping her beautiful face in his hands, kissed her softly. "You're Destry Grant and I admire the hell out of the woman you've become. Never doubt what a strong, capable, amazing person you are. I never have."

DESTRY FELT AS IF SHE could finally breathe as they rode through the pines and the growing twilight. It had helped to tell Rylan. She smiled to herself remembering his words.

He'd held her for a long while before he'd told her his news.

"You aren't going to believe this, but that locket I found in Ginny's things? I saw one exactly like it."

Her heart kicked up a beat. "Where?"

He explained that when he'd gone to the bar, Bethany had come in to see her husband. "She was wearing one that I swear is identical. When I said something about it, she… Well, I think she lied to me about where she'd gotten it. I think she lied to her husband, as well."

A brisk breeze leaned the grass over and ruffled the horse's mane. Destry felt goose bumps skitter across her skin. "We have to find out where she got it."

"Yeah, that's what I was thinking. I don't suppose you want to—"

"Yes."

He'd grinned over at her. "Let's see if Clete is working at the bar tonight when we get back. I definitely think we need to talk to her when he's not around."

Rylan left her partway down the mountain, saying he would ride on down to her house and wait for her there.

Destry headed toward the barn and corrals. Earlier as she'd been about to ride out, Grayson had stopped her to ask about the new stalls. Now, as she led her horse into the barn, she saw that he had finished one of them and left her a note to let him know what she thought.

He'd done a beautiful job, she thought, as she unsaddled her horse. She'd have to remember to call him and tell him.

Knowing Rylan would be at the house waiting for her, Destry finished unsaddling her horse, put away her tack and headed for her pickup. She hadn't seen her brother since he'd loaded Cherry's suitcases into his sports car. She wondered if she would see him again. It would be just like Carson to disappear again.

Right now, though, she was just anxious to get down to the house and Rylan. His news about Bethany having a locket like Ginny's felt like the first real break they'd gotten.

RYLAN RODE DOWN THE mountain, his mind reeling with everything Destry had told him. As he came out of the pines and down into the valley, he breathed in the day, trying to imagine how he would feel if he didn't have his family and the ranch.

As he rode through the sun-paled grasses, he saw tracks where a vehicle had recently crossed this pasture. The tracks led to the east along the fence line. He hadn't

gone far when he saw the barbed wire gate lying on
the ground. There were fresh tracks into the property.

His heart began to pound. Riding through the
downed gate, he galloped toward the homestead house.
He couldn't see it from here because of the thick band
of trees between him and the house. Reaching the edge
of the trees, he looked for a vehicle but didn't see one.

Maybe the gate had been down for some time. Destry said she'd chased her stalker away, but he feared that
firing her shotgun hadn't been a strong enough message. Maybe the man didn't know Destry, didn't realize that next time she wasn't kidding about not missing.

Getting off his horse, he led it into the dense trees,
looking for any sign that the man had returned. He
hadn't gone far when he found both fresh footprints
and older tire tracks. He worked his way through the
dense windbreak of pines, aspens and large old cottonwoods that grew along the creek until he saw the house
in the distance.

The sun had set, leaving the sky a fiery orange. The
house was dark. Destry wouldn't be home yet. Closer,
something moved. A dark figure crept around the corner of the house.

Rylan tore after him, determined that this time he
wasn't letting the man get away.

As DESTRY DROVE UP INTO the yard, she saw Rylan. He
had someone down on the ground. She jumped out,
digging the pistol from her purse as she did, and raced
toward them.

"What in the world?"

Rylan looked up. "I caught your stalker."

"No, you've got the wrong guy," Hitch McCray

slurred. Destry could smell the alcohol from where she was standing. His gaze shifted to her. "Destry, you're the one who told me someone had been hanging around your house, spying on you. I was driving by when I saw a man trying to break into your house. I was only trying to catch him. I swear it."

"I've already called the sheriff," Rylan said to Destry, without letting Hitch up.

"The man took off through the trees," Hitch said to Rylan. "I would have caught him if you hadn't tackled me. I was trying to protect Destry."

"How was it again that you just happened to be driving by?" Rylan asked.

Hitch looked from her to Rylan and back again. "There's no law that says I can't come out here to see Destry."

"That's what I thought," Rylan said. "So much for you just driving by."

"This is just a misunderstanding," Hitch said, clearly drunk. "There's no reason to involve the sheriff in this."

"The dispatcher said the sheriff was in Beartooth, so he should be here soon," Rylan said. He sounded relieved, and when Destry looked at him, she could see it in his face. He'd been afraid for her, and now he'd caught her stalker red-handed. "He used a damned screwdriver to try to break into your house."

"It wasn't me, I'm telling you," Hitch said.

"Just shut up. You can tell it to the sheriff."

"I told you to call Deputy Billy Westfall," Hitch said. "He'll sort this out."

Billy Westfall? He'd see that Hitch never saw the inside of a jail cell, Destry thought, as she heard the sound of a siren in the distance.

"You're lucky I didn't shoot you the other night," she said, thinking that if she'd known it was Hitch she might have pelted him with a little buckshot.

"I don't know what you're talking about," Hitch mumbled.

By the time the sheriff arrived and took Hitch into custody, it was too late to go to Bethany's and ask about the locket.

"Are you going to be all right?" Rylan asked after everyone else had left. Hitch, it had turned out, along with trying to break into her house, had hit another vehicle when he was leaving the Range Rider bar. So it would be at least a day before he could get out on bail—that is if his mother paid it. The sheriff said that was doubtful, so Hitch would probably be spending some time behind bars, and Destry should be safe from him.

She wasn't worried, now that she knew it was Hitch. "I'll be fine," she told Rylan. Hitch had torn up the wood around the door, but he hadn't broken the lock.

"I'll feel better knowing your stalker is behind bars," Rylan said. "Once I find out what time Clete goes to work tomorrow, I'll give you a call." He stood in the doorway, hat in hand, looking at her in a way that made her melt inside.

"Thank you."

He nodded, as if trying to think of something more to say.

If he kept looking at her like that and didn't leave soon—

"Tomorrow then." He turned and walked to the back of the house where he'd left his horse.

"You sure you can find your way home in the dark?" she called after him.

He laughed, a wonderful sound that made the night feel magical. "The horse can. That's all that matters." And then he was in the saddle, tipping his hat and riding away.

CHAPTER NINETEEN

THE NEXT MORNING, DEPUTY Billy Westfall inspected his face in the bathroom mirror. "Damn, but you are one good-looking son of a bitch," he said and grinned at his image.

Behind him, his girlfriend, Trish, leaned against the doorjamb and rolled her eyes. "As my grandmother always said, 'that would sound a lot better coming from someone else.'"

He mugged a face at her before she turned back to whatever she'd been doing. He watched her go, a little crestfallen that it appeared the magic might have gone out of their relationship.

When they'd first gotten together, she would have laughed and agreed with him, and the two of them would have ended up in the shower lathering each other up.

Billy looked in the mirror again, his confidence lagging. It wasn't just Trish's recent indifference to him. He'd thought by this age, he would be sheriff. The fact that he was still a deputy at thirty nagged at him.

All he needed was one good case to solve by his lonesome, he thought and nodded to himself in the bathroom mirror. He'd already envisioned the headline that would appear in the local newspaper.

Billy "The Kid" Westfall Singlehandedly Solves Case

of the Century. The newspaper in Big Timber would put the story on the front page, along with his picture. People would be talking about it for years. Come election time, he'd run against Frank Curry and beat him by a landslide.

And then he'd be the one sitting behind that big desk. He'd be the one who everyone tipped their hats to when they passed him. He'd be *somebody.*

His hand went to the sidearm holstered at his hip. He ran his fingers over the grip, palming it as he stared down his image in the mirror. On the count of three, he drew the .45 from the holster with lightning speed, a move he'd practiced in front of a mirror for hours.

He'd show Frank Curry, he told himself as he re-holstered the .45. "Trigger-happy, my ass," he whispered, recalling how Curry had threatened to fire him for being a hothead.

All that would change once he made a name for himself. And Billy had a good feeling that time was coming soon.

"Where are you off to?" Trish asked, checking the clock on the wall. "You're not due into work for a couple of hours."

"WT Grant called and wants me to come up to his place for a little talk," Billy said puffing out his chest.

"Why would he want to talk to *you?*"

Yep, the shine had definitely come off this love affair.

"Maybe he doesn't like the way the sheriff is handling the Ginny West murder investigation."

She still looked skeptical. "Don't go getting yourself fired, Billy. Your job is hanging by a thread as it is."

Billy glanced around the apartment, sizing up how

long it would take him to pack up his stuff and move out. Not long at all, he thought.

WT GRANT STUDIED the tall, lanky deputy, hoping he hadn't made a mistake.

"Have a seat," he said as he steered Billy Westfall into the expansive living room. "What can I get you to drink?"

Billy looked around the room, big-eyed, before settling his gaze on the fully stocked bar. He licked his lips as he took in all the pretty bottles filled with alcohol. WT could see the internal battle waging.

"I'm going to have to pass this time," Billy finally said. "I'm scheduled to work this afternoon."

WT nodded. "I'll just pour you a short one then." He rolled over to the bar and poured them both a shot of bourbon.

Billy settled into one of the deep leather chairs and looked pleased as WT handed him the crystal glass.

"I'm sure you were curious after my call," WT said, turning his own glass in his fingers as he studied the deputy over the rim.

Billy was trying hard not to look too eager. WT liked that. Just as he liked the good-looking deputy's cockiness and that burning ambition that shone in his dark eyes. Billy was perfect.

"I'm sure you've heard that my son, Carson, has returned to the ranch," WT said.

Billy nodded and took a sip of the bourbon. He leaned back, crossed his legs and took in the room again.

"I need to know if I can count on you if there's any trouble," WT said and held the young man's gaze.

"Yes, sir," Billy said, sitting up straighter. "There's trouble, you just call me."

"Of course, you might need some help…."

It took Billy a moment. "I know someone who could back me up."

"Another deputy?" WT asked, afraid the man wasn't getting it.

"No, sir. Is that a problem?"

WT smiled. "No, actually that was what I was hoping you would say. So we'll keep this to ourselves."

Billy nodded and smiled. "Just what I was thinking. I take it you're expecting trouble?" he asked, sounding hopeful.

"I'm always expecting trouble," WT said as he glanced out the window wondering when his son would be back from getting rid of his fiancée. Or if Carson would be back at all.

RYLAN PICKED UP DESTRY the next afternoon. As she slid into the passenger side of his pickup, he knew he couldn't keep being around her like this. Last night, it had been hell leaving her. As he'd ridden away, he'd glanced back to see her silhouetted in the doorway. Desire had spiked through him, hotter than a Montana summer day.

This afternoon she looked fresh from a shower. Her burnished auburn hair looked damp, her skin glowing. Not to mention she smelled citrusy and good enough to eat.

He moaned under his breath as he got the pickup going. Being with her and yet having this distance between them was killing him. He couldn't take much more of this.

She wore a pale orange cotton Western shirt with pearl snaps down the front, jeans and boots. He tried not to notice the way her jeans hugged her perfect behind.

Her hair was pulled up in a long ponytail today. He itched to free it and bury his fingers in the silky depths. The fall breeze stirred the loose tendrils around her face. The past eleven years had made her even more desirable than she'd been at seventeen.

"Is everything all right?" she asked.

He hadn't realized he was gripping the wheel, a pained expression on his face. "Sorry, I was just…" He waved off the rest since he suspected from her small knowing smile that she knew exactly what his problem was.

It reminded him of their last year in high school. They'd been determined to wait until they were married before they were intimate. After graduation and a long, hot summer, they'd both agreed they didn't need to wait. They were ready to commit to each other.

And they had, he thought as he drove toward Bethany Reynolds's house. That long-ago commitment still had a death grip on his heart.

"I'm glad you confided in me," he said, studying her out of the corner of his eye as he drove. She seemed stronger and more determined today. Having her stalker behind bars had to have given her some peace. But, like him, she seemed more upbeat. Both of them were hoping that Bethany held the key to Ginny's murder and this would finally be over.

"I was thinking about the older men Bethany would have come in contact with through her job at the Branding Iron," Destry said. "Pastor Tom always writes his sermons down there on Fridays or Saturdays, the days Bethany works. But a lot of men hang out at the café."

Rylan didn't want to talk about Ginny's murder. He wanted to talk about them but, he reminded himself, there was no *them*. Not yet anyway, he assured himself.

"I just want to say, I'm sorry about the situation with the ranch," he said.

She nodded, smiling over at him. "I know you don't want to believe that the man is Pastor Tom," she said, changing the subject.

He realized that Destry probably regretted confiding in him, especially about her brother. Remembering what his mother had said about what she'd witnessed between Ginny and Pastor Tom, he shared it with her.

"I have to admit that since Bethany didn't attend church, I thought there probably wasn't a connection between her and the pastor. I forgot about his sermon-writing at the café where she works. By the way, I told the sheriff about your suspicions."

She gave him a look that made his heart pound. "Thank you for taking me seriously."

"I always do."

Destry laughed at that.

He studied her profile for a moment, thinking just how serious he was about this woman. They were bound by the past and by their love as much as by his sister's death.

"I broke my promise to you," he said, concentrating on his driving. Even as he said it, he knew it was a lie. He'd promised that night with Destry naked in his arms that he would love her forever. Over the years he'd felt as if that promise was a curse since he hadn't been able to forget her—no matter how hard he'd tried.

He felt, rather than saw, her turn from the window to look at him again. "I'm sorry," he said, sorry, too, for letting her think he'd ever stopped loving her.

"We were young," she said and turned away again.

"Not *that* young."

"Do we have to talk about this?" she asked.

"No. But there is something we do need to talk about." He told her about his girl-next-door theory, how Ginny and Bethany had the same coloring. "And I thought of you and thought whoever had been coming around your house was the same man."

"It's a nice theory, but Hitch didn't offer me a silver heart-shaped locket. Nor do Ginny and Bethany and I look that much alike."

"It's that fresh innocence, and maybe the freckles."

She mugged a face at him.

He regretted teasing her about them when they were kids. "I love your freckles. I always have."

After that, they rode in silence southeast through rolling pastures and hay fields, the land falling away from the Crazy Mountains toward the river. He watched the summer-dried landscape blur by with a sense of nostalgia. This country that he loved was deeply connected to Destry, and his feelings for her were rooted in them both.

Rylan liked the contrast between the rolling farmland and the pine-covered steep mountains of the Crazies. The valley was fertile and settled; the mountains were still wild and uncivilized. He'd always felt that pull between the two.

A half mile up the road, the land changed. Ravines with rock outcroppings and stands of pines and juniper sprung up. As they drove over a rise, the Reynolds's house came into view. It sat back against a small bluff surrounded by pines and tall cottonwoods. He was relieved to see that Bethany's SUV was still parked out front. He'd checked earlier, before he'd called Destry. Clete was at the bar. Bethany should be home, but that didn't mean she would talk to them, let alone tell them the truth.

"This could be a wild-goose chase," he warned Destry, not wanting her to get her hopes up. It was too late for him.

"Carson thinks the same thing we do, that Ginny's secret lover gave her the locket," Destry said, an edge to her voice that reminded him of what still stood between them—that deep perilous chasm that neither dared cross as long as the killer remained at large.

"Did he know Ginny was pregnant?" Rylan asked, hearing a catch in his voice. He was treading carefully. He didn't want to fight with her today. Just being with her like this felt nice. He didn't want to spoil it. But he had to know.

"She told him it was the other man's baby."

Stubbornly, he still didn't want to believe there *had* been another man, a man who'd made Ginny keep secrets, a man who had killed her to keep her from having what he believed was his baby.

As he pulled off the county road and dropped down a narrow dirt track to the Reynolds's house, he told himself that if there had been a secret lover, he'd seduced Bethany Reynolds into the same deadly pact, and they were about to find him.

NETTIE FELT STRANGELY free after Bob left to go pack. Free and independent, as if she could do anything she darn well pleased. It felt good, she thought, as she went to stand at the front window, considering the rest of her life.

She could see Kate over there pouring coffee and chatting away. It galled her. It was high time she proved to the town—and Bob before he left for Arizona—exactly what that woman was up to.

Locking the front door of the store, she sneaked out the back and cut across the road to the empty stone shell of the old garage off to the right and a little behind the café. She figured if anyone had seen her, they'd think she was headed kitty-corner across the street to the post office.

Working her way to the opening of the garage, she kept an eye on the street and the back of the café. Kate LaFond was always busy with her large table of ranchers who were there every day at this same time. But Nettie wasn't taking any chances.

When she was sure the coast was clear, she stepped inside the garage and glanced around. The large wooden barn-style doors that had once hung at the front of the garage had rotted off years ago. All that was left was the remaining three sides of the stone structure.

The same sandstone had been used to build the store. But unlike the store, the garage had fallen into disrepair. Claude had been sick a lot over the years and hadn't kept things up, Nettie thought as she checked the street and the back of the café again.

Often the cook would come out back for a smoke. Lou Parmley had been doing that for as long as she could remember. Claude had hired him right out of high school, and Lou had stayed on when Kate took over the café after Claude had died.

Once she was sure there was no one watching, Nettie moved deeper into the dim structure. It didn't take long to find the spot where the earth along the edge of the stone wall had been dug up. The shovel Kate had used was still propped against the wall, soft damp dirt still stuck to the blade.

Nettie stared at the spot, wondering if Kate LaFond had dug up something—or buried something. She could hear Bob as if he was standing next to her.

"She probably buried a dead cat that got hit on the road. But if you need to dig it up, then be my guest. Serves you right for being so damned nosy."

She grabbed the shovel and told Bob's voice in her head to shut up. Digging was easy since the soil had already been turned. She kept glancing toward the street and café as she sunk the blade in the dirt and turned over several shovels full. At one point, the blade rang out, but it was only a rock she'd struck.

After she'd dug down a good six to eight inches, she hit more rocks and leaned on the shovel for a moment to catch her breath. There wasn't anything here.

"No dead cat," she said to Bob, who of course couldn't hear her. He wouldn't have listened anyway, she thought.

So Kate had dug something up. But what could have been buried there? And if something had, who buried it there? Claude? Or Kate herself?

Disappointed and yet still intrigued, she quickly shoveled the dirt back into the hole. She eyed it to make sure the soil looked as it had when she'd come into the garage, then, leaning the shovel against the wall where she'd found it, Nettie started out of the garage when she heard the back door of the café slam.

Moments later she heard the crunch of gravel. Someone was headed this way. Nettie looked around for a
way out and spotted a hole in the stones at the back of
the garage. She hurried to it and had just shimmied
through the opening into the tall weeds growing along
the back when she heard someone step into the garage.

She held her breath, which wasn't easy since she
had been breathing hard moments before. She listened
but heard no movement inside the garage. That didn't
mean someone wasn't still there, though. Probably Kate.
The woman must have eyes in the back of her head. Or
maybe she'd spotted her when she'd crossed the street.
Kate would have guessed where she was headed, especially if she had something to hide in this old garage.

She heard the sound of a box opening and closing.
Nettie recalled seeing several wooden boxes along one
wall of the garage. Tool boxes. With a shudder, she realized that Kate could be arming herself.

She waited, taking shallow breaths, her back pressed
to the rough stonewall. Grasshoppers flew around her
in the weeds that were almost up to her neck. If she
squatted down, she was fairly sure no one would be
able to see her.

In the distance, she heard the back door of the café
open and slam shut. Finally she let herself breathe as
she made her way around the edge of the garage. There
was a pile of old junk among the weeds. She skinned
her shin on an rusted car chassis and, seeing that she
couldn't get through the junk, turned back. She had
no choice.

She'd have to get out the way she'd gone in—through
the garage. She crawled back through the hole, scrap-

ing her back on the rough stones but finally dropping into the cool darkness of the garage.

When she looked up, she saw the slim silhouette in the opening where the garage doors used to be. Nettie froze. At that moment, she half expected Kate to snatch up the shovel and come flying at her.

Instead, Kate let out a chuckle, then turned and walked back to the café. Nettie didn't move until she heard the back door of the café slam again. Then she took off like a bullet back to the store, fearing Bob had been right.

Kate LaFond *was* fooling with her. Just as Bob had said.

BETHANY JUMPED AT THE sound of a vehicle coming up the road. Her heart had been hammering since she'd come home and found another note on her door. It was the third one she'd found; the other two had been on her SUV when she'd gotten off work at the café.

At first she'd thought they were from Clete, that he knew. But they weren't in his handwriting and they sure as heck didn't sound like something he would write. The notes scared her and, worse, now that she was no longer sinning, she resented getting another one.

That's why she'd called him the moment she found the note. When a female voice answered at his end, though, she'd quickly hung up. If he'd been home, he would know it was her who'd called. It wasn't the first time she'd called and had to hang up.

Now, at the sound of the approaching vehicle, she rushed to the window, afraid it might be him coming up the road. Surely he wouldn't do something so dangerous. Clete might be watching the house even now, and if he caught him here…

At first she felt a rush of relief when she saw that it wasn't her lover's or her husband's vehicle. Then she recognized the man and woman who pulled in and got out. Her hand went to her throat, but of course she wasn't wearing the locket. It was hidden.

She let Rylan knock a couple of times before she went to the door. By then, she told herself she was calm enough and could handle this.

"Hey," she said, pretending their stopping by was a pleasant surprise. "What are you two doing out this way?"

"We came to see you," Rylan said. "Mind if we come in?"

She couldn't really object, now, could she? "Of course not. Come on in. I'll put on some coffee. I don't think Clete ate all the chocolate chip cookies I baked. I'll check."

"We don't need coffee or cookies," Destry said. "We need to ask you about the locket, the one Rylan saw you wearing at the bar."

Bethany stopped in midstep. "The locket? I told you—"

"We need to know where you really got it," Destry said. "It's important."

"I can't see why it would be," she said and saw Rylan and Destry exchange a look.

"I found one exactly like it hidden in my sister Ginny's jewelry box," Rylan said.

Bethany frowned.

"We suspect that the man who gave it to her was someone she'd been seeing in secret," Destry said.

What were they getting at? "I thought she was dating your brother."

"She'd broken up with him. Carson believed she was seeing a married man."

"What does any of this have to do with my locket?" Bethany asked.

"If the man who gave Ginny the locket killed her, then I think you can see what we're getting at," Destry said.

"Why would you think *he* killed her?" Bethany heard her voice break.

"To keep his secret," Destry said.

"And you think the same man gave me my locket?" she asked.

"Did he?" Rylan asked.

"No, I told you. It's just a piece of jewelry I hadn't worn in a while."

"Here's the thing," Destry said. "If you are seeing someone in secret, then you need to know there is a good chance that he's done this before. Ginny ended up dead, and we think it was because he felt threatened. If he feels threatened again, he might kill again."

"That's a lot of ifs, and none of them have anything to do with me," Bethany said, getting upset. "Are you sure you aren't just trying to find someone else to blame for Ginny's murder other than your brother?"

What they were telling Bethany was making her more than uneasy, and she didn't like the feeling. They were wrong, of course, but that still didn't make her feel any better.

"I told you I don't remember where I got the locket. It isn't like it is a one-of-a-kind piece of jewelry. There must be thousands of them around." When she was being honest, she admitted it was a fairly cheap piece of silver. Its value to her wasn't in dollars and cents, though.

"Even so, doesn't it seem odd that two lockets exactly alike turn up in Beartooth?" Rylan asked. "I wonder what the odds are of that happening, unless the same man bought them?"

"We'd like to see the locket," Destry said.

Bethany felt trapped, but she had no choice. It would be even more suspicious if she said she'd lost it or thrown it away.

She went in the bedroom and came back with the locket. Rylan held out his hand, and she dropped it into his large palm. Her own hands were shaking, so she hid them in the rear pockets of her jeans.

After a few minutes, Rylan handed the locket to Destry. "It's identical, isn't it?" Destry looked at it for a moment, then nodded.

Bethany reached for the locket, but Rylan took it back from Destry and pocketed it.

"I'm sorry," he said, "But I have to give this to the sheriff. If we're right, then your boyfriend could be a killer, in which case, you're in danger. Bethany, you need to tell us who gave you this locket."

"You're making a mistake protecting this man," Destry said.

She couldn't believe this was happening. "I already told you. It's just some old thing I've had, and I resent you suggesting that I might be cheating on Clete. If that's all, I have wash to do."

Destry looked as if she wanted to say more but changed her mind.

"Take care of yourself," Rylan said as they left. "I'm sure you'll be hearing from the sheriff."

Bethany waited until she heard them drive away before she dropped into the nearest chair. He legs felt like water, and she was shaking all over. She thought about the age difference between herself and her lover, the secrecy, his anger when she'd told him about forgetting to take off the locket.

"You remind me of my first love." That's the first thing he'd told her the day at the café. He'd been so sweet. She'd felt his gaze on her as she'd poured him a cup of coffee so he could warm up before he had to go back out into the cold. It had been winter and snowing. The café had been empty except for the two of them. Lou had gone out back for a smoke. It had felt cozy joining him in the booth to talk. She'd basked in his gaze, feeling the heat of his desire, reveling in it.

Bethany pulled out her phone to call him but quickly changed her mind. He'd said he would call. She hated to think what his reaction would be when she told him Rylan was taking the locket to the sheriff.

She was still sitting there, trying to get her fear under control, when the phone began to ring. It rang twice, then stopped. She held her breath as it began to ring again. Their secret ring. It was him.

CHAPTER TWENTY

RYLAN COULDN'T HELP the uneasy feeling he had as he drove away from Bethany's house. "What do you think?"

"She was lying through her teeth and scared. But now I'm worried about what she will do. If we're right, then she'll be scared enough that she'll contact him so he can reassure her."

Rylan shot her a look. "She couldn't possibly believe him over us."

Destry laughed. He'd forgotten how much he loved her laugh or how it affected him. "She's in love with him. She desperately wants to believe him. But as scared as she is, it will probably take more than him just telling her to trust him. I was thinking that she'll insist on seeing him."

"You think she'll go to him."

Destry nodded.

Was it possible Bethany would lead them to Ginny's lover—and killer? Anxious, he couldn't believe they could be this close to finding out the truth.

"Or he might come to her. Either way, she's in danger."

"I'd hoped she would tell us the truth, especially with you along," he said.

Destry seemed amused by that. "Clearly you don't know how strong a secret bond like hers can be."

"Love or lying?" Love, he got. The secrets, the lying, that was all alien to him. "I know a spot where we should be able to see her house, but she won't know we're watching. You up for waiting a while and seeing what happens?"

"Definitely. I don't like leaving her alone right now."

He turned the pickup around and drove back to a side road that wound up a ravine. Shifting into four-wheel drive, he climbed up out of a ravine onto a rocky, tree-lined ridge.

Through the pines, he could make out her house below—and had a good view of her SUV. He shut off the engine to wait. The pickup cab suddenly felt too intimate. Turning the key, he put down his window. Destry did the same, as if she, too, felt the closeness.

Sitting there with her reminded him of the old days. When they were teens, she used to come deer hunting with him. They'd spent many hours driving back roads, hiking through the woods, riding horses or sometimes just sitting in a pickup together. They'd always ended up making out. Did she remember steaming up the windows on his old pickup all those nights parked on some old logging road?

A warm breeze stirred the tendrils of hair that had escaped her ponytail. The air smelled of dried leaves and golden stubble and Destry's faint, sweet scent.

"Do you remember us?" he asked before he could stop himself.

She looked over at him. "Rylan—"

"I never stopped thinking about you. I tried my damnedest, too."

"So I heard," she said with a smile.

"I missed you. So many times when I was on the road driving late at night, I wished you were there with me." He shook his head. He knew he shouldn't be doing this. But if they found Ginny's killer, then maybe they could find their way back to each other. He was filled with hope that they still had a future. If her brother hadn't killed Ginny, if it was the mystery lover, then there was hope.

"I'm sorry I left the way I did. Destry, I'm so sorry."

DESTRY TRIED TO FIGHT the tears that welled in her eyes at his words since these were words she'd only dreamed of hearing. Just the way he was looking at her stirred up all those feelings she'd fought for so long.

She didn't know what to say, even if she'd been able to speak. Rylan never gave her the chance. He reached for her, dragging her into his arms. She breathed him in, his masculine scent and the great outdoors. It had been so long since he'd wrapped her in his arms like this in the cab of his pickup. Her arms went around his neck as he dropped his mouth to hers.

She felt herself melt into him and the kiss. He drew her even closer. His body felt solid against hers and so familiar she ached with need for this man, the only man who'd ever made her feel like this.

"I never broke my promise, Destry," Rylan said as he drew back to meet her gaze. "I never stopping loving you."

And then he was kissing her again, deepening the kiss, their bodies molding together as the fall breeze brought the scents of the season through the open window.

Suddenly Rylan let out a curse and drew back. "Bethany, she's on the move." He hurriedly started the truck and dropped off the ridge into the ravine as they both lost sight of Bethany's SUV.

Destry was so shaken by the kiss and Rylan's words all she could do was hang on as they headed down the two-track, the tall weeds in the center brushing the bottom of the pickup.

She looked over at Rylan, saw him breathe in the scene even as he raced down the road, fulfilled by it as she was. She hadn't been wrong about him. He loved this land the way she did. And he loved her.

"Listen, tomorrow let's ride up into the high country one last time before the snow gets too deep. I need to check a few things up there at the camp. You know that place we used to go?"

She nodded.

"Come with me. Let's get away from all this. Just for a while."

The thought of Rylan in the small camp up in the mountains, the two of them sitting around the campfire or snuggled together in a sleeping bag, made her heart leap. She knew he was counting on them finding Ginny's killer and finally putting an end to this rift between them. He was that sure that if they found Ginny's secret lover that they would have found the murderer?

She knew that was what they both were counting on, for Carson to be cleared so it would clear the way for them to find again the love that had connected them for so long.

What would it hurt to be gone for a couple of days? She had Carson's check. She could drop that off, then pack for the horseback trip up in the mountains. A couple of days in the mountains with Rylan would be a dream come true.

"We need this," he said as he drove. "Come with me no matter what happens today." He reached across the seat for a moment to squeeze her hand.

She touched her tongue to her lower lip, relishing the memory of the kisses. The passion was still there. So was the love. She almost told him then how she felt and that she would go with him, follow him anywhere because she'd never stopped loving him, either.

But something held her back as he drove as fast as he could down through the ravine. Bethany had a good head start because they hadn't been paying attention. Destry could see that Rylan was worried they might have already lost her.

As they hit the county road, there was no sign of Bethany.

"She had to come this way, right?" he said.

There were only a few side roads, most of them going into the rocky foothills or rolling fields now planted with winter wheat.

He turned onto the road they'd driven in on and roared down it toward the Crossroads.

Why was Destry hesitating? She'd loved being back in his arms, loved kissing him again. She felt her heart soar at the thought of putting all the bad feelings behind them and finding their way back to each other.

As the pickup came over a rise, she saw Bethany's SUV turn east toward Highway 191. "There she is."

"I see her." He gunned the pickup, and they flew down the unpaved road, gravel pinging off the under-carriage, the engine roaring.

Destry watched the SUV getting smaller and smaller.

"I think you're right about her running to her lover," Rylan said as he kept his foot on the gas pedal.

By the time they reached the Crossroads, Bethany had disappeared again.

Rylan swore as he turned east and floored the gas. "I'm not sorry I kissed you. Just in case you're sitting over there wondering." He shot her a look but quickly went back to driving. "I'm not sorry that I told you I never quit loving you, either."

She knew what he wanted her to say. She might have, too, if they hadn't come flying over a rise and seen Bethany's SUV pulled off the side of the road ahead.

Next to it was a bright red sports car—Carson's. Bethany was sitting in the passenger seat.

Rylan started to slow but then gunned the engine, flying past them in a blur. But not before they'd both seen Bethany in her brother's arms.

Rylan didn't slow the truck until they were out of sight of the sports car. He pulled over to the side of the road and sat for a moment before he looked over at Destry, as if waiting for an explanation. As if she had one. His face was flushed with anger.

"Carson didn't give Bethany the locket," she cried. "He isn't the other man."

"Quite the coincidence since he was involved with Ginny and apparently now Bethany."

"Carson swore to me he didn't give Ginny that locket."

Rylan raised a brow. "Destry, he lied about you being at the ranch that night eleven years ago."

She couldn't argue that. She knew now why her brother had dragged her in as his second alibi—just as Rylan had always suspected.

"When are you going to see what is right in front of your eyes? Your brother is guilty as sin. He always has been."

"Carson couldn't have given that locket to Bethany. He hasn't been in town long enough to start an affair." She knew she was clutching at straws, still defending her brother out of fear that Rylan was right about him.

"How do you explain what we both just saw back there?" he demanded.

"I can't. Not right now anyway."

"You mean not until you ask your brother and believe whatever lie he tells you." He slammed the pickup into gear and made a U-turn back the way they'd come. "Your brother is taking the ranch from you. That should have told you everything you needed to know about him. It's high time we got the truth out of him."

But by the time they reached the spot where they'd seen Bethany and Carson, the red sports car was gone. Bethany's SUV was still parked beside the road. It was empty.

Destry felt confused and worried. Why did it keep coming back to Carson? Because he was guilty?

Rylan dropped her off at her house, leaving without a word. By the time she reached the big house, Carson still hadn't come back. She thought about waiting for him, but WT was in a snit and Margaret was busy cleaning, so she cleared out.

Back at her own house, she paced the floor, too stirred up to sit. She couldn't wait to speak with her brother, but like Rylan had said, she feared Carson would lie to her.

Her heart ached. She didn't want to believe Carson was guilty. But the true heartbreak was Rylan. Hadn't she warned herself not to get too close? Once they'd seen Carson with Bethany, she and Rylan were back where they'd been all these years—apart—with Ginny's murder between them.

As THE POKER GAME BROKE UP, Carson couldn't believe he'd lost three thousand of what he'd gotten from WT and another five grand in credit before Lucky Larson cut him off.

"You're done," the ranch hand said. "Leave your IOU." Carson scribbled his name and the amount he owed. "You'd better be good for this."

"I am. I'll have the money soon, trust me."

"I don't trust you. But I know where to find your old man. Something tells me the last person you want to know about this is WT Grant."

Carson grabbed the ranch hand by his shirt collar with both hands. "You say a word to my father—"

"I won't as long as you don't take another powder. You disappeared eleven years ago. How do I know you won't again?"

Carson let the man go. "Because I'm not going anywhere until I get what I came home for."

"Just make sure you pay off your IOU soon," Lucky said. "Otherwise, maybe we'll have to talk about you putting up your sister as collateral. I haven't forgotten that Destry and your ranch manager fired me. She owes me."

"Leave my sister out of this," he said. The cowboy had never hidden his interest in Destry.

Once outside, Carson stood in the shadows of the pines a little disoriented. He could hear the creek nearby. It took him a moment to remember where he was. It was like that when he gambled. Lost time, lost money, lost memory.

The cold air seemed to bring him out of it. He'd planned to call Destry and tell her he wasn't going to need her money. That's when he'd felt lucky and thought he could make back enough that he could hold off his creditors until he got ranch money. He'd given Cherry a couple grand of the five he'd gotten from his father and left her at the Bozeman airport, three grand burning a hole in his pocket. Unfortunately when he'd called Lucky Larson, this afternoon was the soonest he could get into a game. He'd been a little late because of Bethany.

As he started toward his sports car, he heard someone call his name. A man came out of the pines, moving fast.

Carson didn't have time to react before a fist connected with his jaw.

CHAPTER TWENTY-ONE

DESTRY THOUGHT OF THE certified check she had yet to give to her brother. Her hope was that it would take the pressure off, give Carson time to reconsider selling the ranch. She knew she was probably just kidding herself, but she couldn't sit back and do nothing.

But Rylan was wrong. She was no longer blind when it came to her brother.

Unable to sit still any longer, Destry headed up to the big house to wait for Carson. She was glad to see his red sports car parked out front. But when she entered the house, she found WT alone in the living room.

She had just stepped into the room and was about to ask him if he'd seen Carson when her brother stormed in. She gasped in shock. "What happened to you?"

"I ran into your boyfriend's fist," Carson said as he came into the room. He pushed past her and WT to get to the bar where he took a towel and some ice and applied it to his bruised jaw. His left eye was almost swollen shut and the color of a thunderhead. His lip was cut, his cheek red and his knuckles on both hands skinned.

"I hope you held your own," WT said.

Destry ignored him. "Rylan did this to you?" she cried. Rylan had been furious, but she'd hoped he'd taken off for the mountains instead of taking out his anger on Carson. This was Rylan's way of resolving things?

"Didn't I just say that?" Carson said, dropping into a chair with his ice pack in one hand and a drink in the other. He closed his eyes as if his pain was worse, thanks to her.

"Someone tell me what the hell is going on," WT demanded. "Last time I talked to you, Carson, you were taking Cherry to the bus station and coming right back. That was two days ago."

"You took Cherry to the bus station?" Destry asked.

"The airport." He shot WT a scowl. "I wasn't putting her on a *bus*."

"Rylan was at the airport?" WT's tone was disbelieving.

"I took her yesterday. Today I went for a ride. I stopped for a drink, all right?" Carson snapped.

"I thought you weren't going back to the Range Rider?" Destry said, unable to keep the fury out of her voice. She was just as angry with Rylan, but this wouldn't have happened if Carson had stayed on the ranch. She knew that was unreasonable, but she couldn't help feeling that her brother just asked for trouble, bringing it on himself.

"What were you doing at the Range Rider?" WT wanted to know.

"I wasn't," Carson said impatiently and took another gulp of his drink. "I was at a friend's." He shifted his gaze away from Destry's.

"A *friend's?*" Destry said. "So you have been seeing Bethany Reynolds?"

"*What?*" Carson cried.

"I saw you with her this afternoon. Did you give her a heart-shaped locket just like you did Ginny?"

Her brother glared at her. "I told you I didn't give

Ginny a locket. As for Bethany, I just happened to see her as I was driving by. Her car had broken down beside the road. She was upset. All I did was calm her down and give her a ride into Big Timber."

"Big Timber? Not Beartooth?"

Carson let out a curse. "That's where she wanted to go. You think I've got something going with *Bethany?*"

"Do you?" WT asked, as if he, too, didn't trust that his son was telling the truth any more than Destry did. "She's married to *Clete Reynolds*. You think Rylan can throw a punch, wait until Clete gets his hands on you."

"Are you both crazy?" Carson demanded.

She shoved the certified check at him. "Make sure that gets where it's supposed to go or you'll have to deal with me."

"Is that a check you just gave him?" WT bellowed.

"Both of you, get off my ass," Carson said, throwing down his drink and the bar towel. The half-melted ice cubes careened across the hardwood floor as he stalked out with the check gripped in his hand. A moment later they heard the rev of the sports car engine, then the sound of flying gravel as he sped away.

"What the hell was that about?" WT wanted to know as Destry started to leave, as well.

"Don't you know?" she asked him, meeting his gaze.

"Would I have asked if I knew?" he snapped.

"Maybe if you took the time to get to know your son, you'd *know* what was going on," she said and headed for the door.

"WANT TO TALK ABOUT IT?"

Rylan glanced over his shoulder as his father walked

into the barn. He continued to saddle his horse. "Not particularly."

"That's quite a shiner you got there. Run in to a door, did you?"

"I honestly tried not to get into it with Carson Grant," he said with a sigh. "I'm not proud of what I did, but it's been a long time coming."

"And Destry?"

Rylan stopped clinching the saddle for a moment, recalling the feel of her in his arms, her lips on his. "I love her, but as long as her brother is walking free, there's no hope in hell for the two of us."

Taylor West sighed. "You're that sure Carson killed Ginny?"

"I don't know and I can't stand around waiting for the sheriff to arrest someone."

"So you're heading for the hills this late in the evening?"

Rylan turned then to look at his father. "I keep messing things up. I can't stay here right now. I know you're disappointed in me."

"No, son. I'm not sure I wouldn't have done the same. I talked to the sheriff again today. He says he's making progress."

Rylan shook his head. "I'll believe it when I see it."

"You sure you want to leave now?"

"I can't face Destry right now, and I know the woman. She'll come looking for a fight of her own once her brother tells her what happened. There's enough animosity between us."

He wouldn't have left now if her stalker was still on the loose, but with Hitch behind bars for a while, Destry would be safe.

"You could hit some weather up there."

Rylan nodded. "I'm packing for snow. I just need to get my head on straight, and I can't do that here. I think best on the back of a horse. You know that."

His father chuckled. "I feel the same way. But this might not be a problem you can ride away from, son."

"I know. I'll be back in a couple of days. You can do without me that long?"

"Your mother and I are flying down to Denver. There's a bull down there I want to take a look at. Your brothers will be handling things here on the ranch. They've almost got the rest of the hay brought in for winter."

"I haven't been much help lately. I'm sorry about that. I've been worried about Destry, but after today it appears that the only person to worry about is her brother, so she should be all right. Add to that, the woman is stubborn as a damned mule and she's capable of taking care of herself."

His father placed a hand on his shoulder. "This is going to resolve itself."

"Yeah? Unfortunately it looks like it will be too late for Destry and me by the time it does."

"Be careful up there," his father said, glancing toward the mountains.

THE CALL CAME IN THE wee hours of the morning. Destry sat up in bed with a jolt. It took her a few moments to realize what had awakened her.

She'd come straight home after her encounter with her brother. She'd been worried but even more disgusted with Carson and his lying. While she was worried he'd get in more trouble after taking off the way he had, she'd known, though, that if she went into town looking for him, she would have been tempted to pay Rylan a visit—one that would make matters even worse.

The phone rang—and apparently not for the first time, she realized. She snatched it up, aware of the hour, fear instantly growing in her chest. No one called this time of the night unless it was bad news. Her first thought was Rylan. Then her brother. "Hello?"

"Destry, it's Margaret. Carson's been shot."

"Shot?" The words made no sense. Destry sat up and tried to catch her breath. "Is he all right?"

"The doctor said the bullet caught him in the shoulder. They're rushing him into surgery. That's all I know. WT and I are headed for the hospital now."

"I'll meet you there."

"Destry?"

She had turned on the lamp and had been looking around for clothes to wear but stopped as she heard something else in Margaret's voice.

"WT told the sheriff about Rylan beating up his son. He's convinced that Rylan shot Carson."

"No, Rylan wouldn't do that."

Thirty minutes later, after trying Rylan's number and leaving him several messages, Destry rushed into the hospital. She hurried down the hall toward the sound of raised voices, recognizing WT's and the sheriff's.

"Have you lost your mind?" Sheriff Frank Curry demanded. He was standing in the waiting room beside WT's wheelchair. There was no sign of Margaret.

"Rylan West shot my boy!" WT bellowed.

"So you decided to take the law into your own hands by offering a fifty-thousand-dollar reward for Rylan West? Dead or alive?"

Destry gasped, but neither man heard her. Nor had either looked in her direction when she'd come into the room.

"That would be against the law," WT said.

"You sent Billy Westfall after him, knowing he'd bring Rylan West in draped over his horse. Damn you, WT. You've signed that cowboy's death warrant," Frank yelled.

"It's your deputy just doing his job, something I fear you are no longer capable of doing, Frank."

"You know Billy Westfall is a hothead. Hell, WT, if word gets out about this fifty-thousand-dollar reward you've offered, every other gun-crazy son of a bitch in the county will be after Rylan. Do you have any idea what you've done?"

"I'm just trying to get justice for my son."

A nurse stuck her head into the room and cautioned them to hold down their voices.

"When have you given a damn about justice?" the sheriff asked, lowering his voice. "You sure that's what you want, WT? Because if your son lives, there is more than a good chance I'm going to arrest him for Ginny West's murder. And if those vigilantes you sent out kill Rylan West, I'll be back with a warrant for your arrest, as well."

"On what charge? You can't prove I sent anyone after him. Nothing wrong with offering a reward for the arrest of whoever shot my son."

"I'll find some charge to lock up your sorry ass," the sheriff said.

"Excuse me."

Destry turned as a doctor appeared in the doorway behind her. WT and the sheriff also turned. Both seemed surprised to find her standing there. The sheriff looked embarrassed that she'd overheard them.

"You asked me to let you know when Carson Grant was conscious?" the doctor said. "He is asking to see the sheriff."

"To tell you that Rylan West shot him," WT said.

"Actually, he said Amos Thompson shot him," the doctor said. "Apparently he and Mr. Thompson got into an altercation outside the bar in Beartooth before the shooting. But I'll let him tell you himself."

Frank arrowed WT a withering look and swore as his radio squawked. He stepped away but came back a moment later. "Bethany Reynolds is missing. Clete found her SUV abandoned beside the road."

"You just get the man who shot my son," WT ordered. "I'm sure Bethany Reynolds is fine. Carson said he gave her a ride to Big Timber earlier."

"Carson gave her a ride?" The sheriff swore. "Call your vigilantes off, WT, and pray that you aren't too late. You do remember how to pray, don't you?"

"Have you forgotten I saved your life?" WT called after him. "You wouldn't be here right now if it wasn't for me."

Frank stopped and turned. "No, WT, I haven't forgotten. You've just gone too far this time."

"Call those men you sent after Rylan right now and tell them he didn't shoot my brother," Destry demanded.

But WT only shook his head. "It's too late. Lucky saw Rylan headed into the mountains. He and Westfall have already gone after him."

CHAPTER TWENTY-TWO

THE SUN WAS JUST CRESTING the horizon when Destry reached the ranch. She glanced toward the Crazies, golden in the cold fall morning light. Rylan had gone up into the mountains just as he'd said he was going to, and now he had a bounty on his head and two men hunting him, probably more.

The only edge she had was that she knew where Rylan was headed. All she could do was pray that Billy Westfall and Lucky Larson didn't.

She was in the barn when she heard the creak of the wheelchair. She didn't turn, couldn't bear to look at WT right now.

"Where do you think you're going?" he demanded behind her.

"I'm going after Rylan before you get him killed."

"The hell you are."

She continued to saddle her horse. Life was a choice, she saw that now, and she was making hers. Since her brother's return, she'd been fighting to save him and the ranch. Now she knew that she couldn't save either. But she might be able to save Rylan.

"After everything that saddle tramp's done to hurt you, you'd risk your life for him?" WT asked.

"What about what you've done to me?" she snapped, turning on him.

WT had the good grace to lower his gaze but said in his defense, "Whatever I did, it was for your own good."

She glared at him as she turned to slap her saddlebag closed and reached for the reins. "Don't try to stop me."

"How could I?" he said, indicating the wheelchair.

"You couldn't, even if you weren't in that chair. Maybe it's time you quit using it as an excuse."

"Just like your mother," he said in disgust.

She swung around again, all her anger, frustration and pain coming out as she looked into the face of the man who, for twenty-eight years, had been her father. "You couldn't possibly understand what it's like to really love someone, to forgive them for hurting you, to be willing to give up everything for them. I love Rylan, and someone has to stop this."

"You'll get yourself killed if you go up there."

She shook her head sadly. "Then I will die trying." She led her horse out of the barn and swung up into the saddle.

"You might need this," she heard WT say behind her.

She turned, and he wheeled over to hand her the rifle and scabbard she'd overlooked in her anger.

Their eyes met for a moment. She thought she glimpsed something akin to regret in his eyes. She took the rifle, and as she spurred her horse, she heard him say, "Good luck."

WT GRANT WATCHED HER ride off, surprised he was fighting back tears. She'd always been a natural on the back of a horse. Her back was straight, her head high. She'd also been as stubborn as any woman he'd ever known. Damn if she *wouldn't* die trying to save the man she loved.

"Fool woman," he muttered even as he felt a surge of pride that threatened to close his throat. Sometimes she was so much like her mother and enough like him, that she really could have been his daughter.

"She's gone after Rylan, hasn't she?" Margaret said next to him. He hadn't heard her join him. He ignored her, not wanting her to see his moment of weakness.

"I've never told you what to do," she continued.

He snorted at that, but it didn't shut her up.

"This time, though, I can't sit back and see you make the biggest mistake of your life, and for a man like you, who has made so many…"

"I tried to stop her from going," he said in his defense, although he hated defending himself to her. Probably because he knew soul deep that he had no defense for the things he'd done.

"I'm not talking about her riding off to find Rylan. I'm talking about this ranch that you've spent your life building."

"I'm doing the only thing I can."

"Oh, stop being such an old fool and treating me like one, as well," Margaret shot back. "You're leaving the ranch to that louse of a son of yours to get back at Lila for hurting you. The only way you can get even with her is by punishing her daughter, who just happens to be the only person in your life, besides me, who gives a damn about you."

He didn't answer. Couldn't since he knew what she was saying was probably true.

"Destry is *your* daughter, Waylon, in every way that matters. She's never been anyone else's. She's a hell of a lot more like you than Carson is, and she loves this ranch. She still loves you, even as difficult as you have made it. You die and leave this mess the way it is, and I will never forgive you."

"Butt out of my business, old woman."

He could feel her still standing there, but he couldn't look at her. He couldn't bear to.

"Just remember. You brought this on yourself." She dropped an envelope on his lap. With that, she turned and stormed off muttering "old man" and a few choice words he wished he hadn't heard.

He didn't need to open the envelope to know what was inside, but he did anyway. Margaret had quit him. He balled up the short note and threw it as far as he could. He'd never felt more alone sitting there in the dim light of the barn as the sun rose over the land he'd fought so hard for. Dust motes danced in the air like the remnants of failure.

The damned woman was right about one thing. He was an old fool who'd already made way too many mistakes in his life, and he feared he was about to make another one. But that had never stopped him before.

SHERIFF FRANK CURRY had his hands full. His trigger-happy deputy Billy Westfall hadn't just taken off in the mountains after Rylan and the reward. He'd left word at the office that he'd deputized Lucky Larson, one of WT's former ranch hands, to go with him.

Frank swore that no matter what pull Billy had with his grandfather, he was sacking him—if Billy lived long enough. He couldn't help worrying about Billy and Lucky armed and dangerous up there in the Crazies. Rylan had no idea what was coming after him. Frank just hoped to hell Rylan West saw them before they saw him.

His radio squawked. It had been doing that all morning with one problem to solve after another. Clete had been calling him repeatedly for updates on his missing wife. So far, Frank hadn't located her. Where he wanted to be was in the Crazies looking for Rylan West, but that wasn't possible with everything that was going on down here in the valley and him one deputy shy.

"It's Bethany Reynolds," the dispatcher said. "You want me to patch her through?"

He breathed a sigh of relief as he took her call. He'd been trying to contact her. "Bethany, where are you?"

"I need to talk to you."

He needed to talk to her as well about the locket. "Okay, just tell me where you are."

"You won't tell Clete?" she asked, sounding scared.

"Not until we talk." He took down the address. "I'm on my way."

Bethany was staying at an out-of-the-way motel in Big Timber. She'd registered under an assumed name after telling the clerk that her husband was after her and trying to kill her.

"Is that true?" Frank asked once they were settled in her motel room. He took the chair by the window, while Bethany said she was too nervous to sit.

"Clete killing me?" she asked. "It's possible once he finds out…." She started to cry. "I've done something awful."

Through tears and nose-blowing, she told the story.

"He used to come into the Branding Iron Café after the regulars had left and we would sit in a back booth and talk. He seemed so lonely. I felt sorry for him at first."

Frank heard the catch in her throat. He knew what

was coming. As impatient as he was, he didn't interrupt Bethany's story. He let her tell it the way she seemed to need to.

"I would make him laugh and smile, and he said that seeing me helped him get through the day," Bethany continued, her gaze shying away. "Then one day he came out to the house to drop something off for Clete. After that, we started meeting. At first we would just talk, and then…"

"One thing led to another?" Frank offered.

She nodded. "I knew it was wrong, but he was so sweet and he needed me and I guess I needed him. He listened. Clete doesn't listen. And Grayson does little romantic things."

"Grayson?" Frank hadn't been able to keep the shock out of his voice. "Grayson Brooks, the local contractor?"

Bethany nodded through her tears.

"He gave me the locket, the one Rylan took from me and gave to you."

Rylan had suspected the man who'd given his sister the locket was Tom Armstrong, but when Frank had talked to Tom, the pastor had denied not only having an affair with Ginny, but also giving her a locket. Not that even pastors weren't apt to lie about something like this.

"Grayson gave you the locket?" His tone must have given him away because she started to cry harder. When Frank had compared them, he'd seen that the lockets appeared to be identical.

But Grayson Brooks? He'd known Grayson all his life. The entire community wanted to make him a saint because of how he doted on his sick wife. Anytime anyone needed something done, Grayson would show up with his tools and fix whatever it was.

Frank had been in law enforcement long enough that he knew people often had secret lives. But this was one he couldn't get his head around.

"Is it true he gave a locket just like it to Ginny?" Bethany asked.

"It appears so."

She hugged herself, eyes wide with fear. "Is he going to kill me, too?"

THE COTTONWOODS ALONG the creek were like a golden thread woven into the pale fabric of the land as Destry rode into the Crazy Mountains. The land changed with the altitude, going from the rich grasslands to the stands of shimmering aspens still clinging to their leaves, to a sprinkling of pines and finally into the heavy timber. The wildflowers that had blanketed the ground all summer had dried, their heads now bobbing in the breeze as she passed.

Ahead the land rose in sheer rock bluffs. She wound her way along the granite faces and through the dark green of the pines, watching for any sign of Rylan's tracks—or the men after him. Mottled sunlight fingered its way down through the branches.

Clouds obscured the peaks, sending down a cold biting wind that moaned through the boughs of the trees and bent the buckskin-colored grasses under its will. The mountains were dark, a deep blue, the color deepening as the day wore on. The tops of the pines swayed and sighed with the wind, the cold deepening the higher she rode up the mountain.

Destry looked back only once at the ranch she loved. She'd made her choice.

She found the first fresh tracks a few miles from the ranch. One horse and rider headed back in. Rylan. With relief she saw that no one else had crossed his tracks. At least not yet. The hours passed, the October sun doing little to warm the air here in the mountains.

As she crossed the creek, the water rushing clear over the rocks, a buck came bounding out of the brush, startling her and her horse. Instinctively she reached for the rifle in her scabbard, only to relax as the deer crashed through the brush and disappeared.

Destry knew she was jumpy. Ahead, a stand of aspen blazed orange, the leaves fluttering in the wind. Over the roar of the creek and the wind in the trees, she knew she wouldn't be able to hear any other riders until she was almost on top of them—and they wouldn't be able to hear her.

She told herself that Billy Westfall didn't know where Rylan had gone. More than likely he would head for the Forest Service cabin over on the North Fork. That would cost Billy hours.

In the distance, a coyote howled. The eerie sound made her flesh crawl. She felt alone and vulnerable. It was a new feeling, one she resented. She'd never been afraid here.

But then she'd never had anything to fear other than a grizzly or bad weather. Now she had at least two men up here in the high country with her, both armed and determined to find Rylan West and collect the reward. She doubted they would let anything or anyone stop them—especially up here where there was no law. Up here, it was every man for himself.

GRAYSON BROOKS studied his wife. Anna's eyes were closed, her thin lashes fluttering like tiny bird wings against her pale cheeks. Her color was fairly good today, compared to what it had been just a few days ago.

The hand he held was so thin, just skin and bones, and yet so delicate, just like Anna. He'd fallen for her the moment he'd seen her. People joked about love at first sight, but it had been exactly that.

She'd stepped into a ray of sunshine. Her strawberry blond hair had seemed to catch fire, lighting up her delicate features. Her wide blue eyes were bright as the freckles that had dusted her cheeks and nose. She'd looked so innocent, so pure, as if she'd been saving herself for only him.

Grayson looked from Anna to Dr. Flaggler, who was slowly packing up his medical bag. Neither spoke as the doctor headed for the door. Grayson watched Anna's chest rise and fall before he let go of her limp hand and followed the doctor out.

"She's better," Grayson said, practically challenging the doctor to disagree.

Dr. Flaggler nodded, his keen old eyes the palest of grays. Grayson saw compassion brimming there. "Cancer patients often seem to bounce back some during the final stages."

Grayson shook his head angrily and turned away to hide the burn of tears. "She's only forty-two." But she'd been sick for the past fifteen of those years.

"I'm sorry." The doctor had said this each time the cancer had returned. But each time, Anna had been able to fight it. Each time, though, the fight had taken a toll on her body. Now she was frail, little fight left in her.

"What about chemo or some new drug?" Grayson asked as he walked the doctor out to his car.

Dr. Flaggler shook his head as he opened his door and tossed in his medical bag. They'd had this discussion already. He could see the finality in the doctor's expression.

"A month at the most. A couple of weeks are probably more realistic." The doctor met Grayson's gaze. "She should get her affairs in order."

With that, the doctor climbed into his car and left.

Grayson stared after him for a moment before going back to the house. Anna's *affairs?* The word ate at him the way her cancer had eaten away inside her body.

When she'd first been diagnosed, he'd told himself that it was his penance. He'd prayed for forgiveness and the cancer had gone into remission.

Each time he'd strayed, the cancer had come back. This time, it was going to kill the only woman he'd ever truly loved.

He'd never been strong. Not like Anna. Nor was he as forgiving. She knew of his needs, the hunger in him that was not unlike cancer. It ate away inside him. He'd prayed not to feel this need. He knew it had nothing to do with sex and everything to do with finding that old Anna, the one he'd lost. He'd filled that need with a young body and pretended.

But Anna had known. He'd seen the pain in her eyes each time. As careful as he'd been, she always knew. His infidelity had sickened her. It had been no surprise when it had appeared as cancer in the breast over her heart.

"Grayson?" Her voice was a whisper. She reached for his hand.

"I'm here, sweetheart."

He closed her hand in his, and she drew him closer. He had to bend down, putting his ear practically against her lips to hear her.

As he listened, tears welled and spilled. He brushed at them with his free hand. Drawing back, he met her gaze.

"How can you forgive me?" he whispered.

She shook her head, but the movement seemed to have exhausted her. She closed her eyes, her hand went limp in his.

He gently placed it on the bed next to her. At the sound of a vehicle coming up the road, he left her, closing the door to her room.

SHERIFF FRANK CURRY sat in front of the house for a few moments before he climbed out of his patrol pickup. For too many years, he'd been the one who brought the bad news.

"I'm sorry but your son has been killed in a bar fight."

"I'm sorry but your daughter was in a car accident tonight on the way home. There was nothing the doctors could do."

He hated that part of his job. He was fine with arresting bad guys or even questioning those he suspected were guilty. But this was the first time his investigation had brought him to the door of a person he would never have suspected.

"Afternoon, Sheriff," Grayson Brooks said as he opened his front door. "Why don't we talk out here on the porch so we don't disturb Anna? She's resting."

Frank nodded and took one of the chairs at the end

of the long porch. The sun slanted down to coat the floorboards in warmth. A light breeze stirred the tall pale grass in the field. In the distance, a dozen Angus cattle stood, red as blood in the sunlight.

"I think you know why I'm here," the sheriff said as Grayson took a seat and stretched out his long legs. He had a kind, open face. Today he looked older than his forty-five years. Usually he could pass for much younger. Frank could see how both Ginny and Bethany would have felt safe with this man.

"I need to ask you about Ginny West and Bethany Reynolds," Frank said.

Grayson nodded but didn't look at him.

Frank pulled a tape recorder out of his jacket pocket, set it on the porch railing, turned it on and, after the preliminaries, said, "You gave both Ginny West and Bethany Reynolds a heart-shaped locket, is that right?"

"I gave it to Anna on the day we were married."

"And you gave one to Ginny West and later Bethany?"

He nodded, tears welling in his eyes. "I gave them a locket like Anna's so they could wear it when we…" He took a deep breath and let it out. "When we were together."

"Was Ginny West carrying your baby?"

Grayson swallowed, his face a mask of pain. "Anna always wanted a baby, but she couldn't have one. How is it that often the women who so desperately want a baby can't have one and the others…"

"I have to ask you, Grayson, what happened the night Ginny West died?"

He shook his head.

"You didn't meet Ginny that night in town?"

"I met her." For a long moment, he seemed lost in the past. "She'd called upset because she'd gotten another note, a Bible quote. I didn't know what to do. It seemed so unfair that she was pregnant. I wanted a baby with Anna, not Ginny. I should never have gotten involved with her. She was so young, so…innocent."

Frank waited for him to continue.

"That night, I told her I would pay for an abortion. Or if she was determined to have the baby, I would pay her to leave town and continue to support her as long as she kept my part a secret."

Frank could well imagine how that had gone over. He thought of Ginny, how pretty and sweet she'd been. He tried to imagine what she'd seen in Grayson, who would have been thirty-four to her twenty. What Frank saw was a lonely, sad man with a sick wife. Whatever Ginny had seen that attracted her, it must have been the same thing Bethany had seen.

"We met at the Royale."

That would explain why she'd left the ranch pickup behind the bar that night. It would have been easy to walk down to her old abandoned theater without being seen. It would also explain why the hair clip was found there.

"She cried and then she got mad because she didn't want to hear that I wasn't going to leave Anna. We argued. I heard someone coming and left, promising that we would talk again when we were both calmer."

"She was alive when you left?"

He didn't answer, again seeming lost in the past. "I just left her there. I went out the back way and drove home to Anna. I told her everything." He broke down, his next words barely audible. "She forgave me. She always forgives me, no matter what I do."

Frank allowed him time to pull himself together before he asked, "Do you have any idea who left the Bible quotes for her?"

"No. Anna didn't just forgive me. She insisted that I help Ginny, that I be a father to my child." He looked as if he might break down again. Grayson Brooks had always seemed like such a strong man. Frank saw now how his weakness had been slowly eroding him over the years.

"Grayson, I have to ask you. Did you kill Ginny?"

"Kill Ginny?" He seemed shocked by the question.

"You said yourself you wanted her to either get rid of the baby or leave town. You had the most to lose."

He shook his head. "I had everything to gain. Anna and I wanted the child Ginny was carrying to be part of our lives. You should be talking to Carson. He went into the theater as I left. I thought maybe he and Ginny would get back together. I knew she still cared about him. That was until I heard she'd been murdered."

"If that's the case, then, Grayson, why didn't you come forward with this information?" Frank demanded.

"By then, it was clear that Carson had killed her. I figured it was just a matter of time before he was arrested."

"You also didn't want anyone to know about you and Ginny."

Grayson hung his head as if in shame. "It was bad enough what I'd done. I didn't see what the point was in having the whole county talking. If Ginny had lived, then it would have been different. But with her and the baby gone, I had to think of Anna." His voice broke. "I couldn't do that to her. Anyway, I had good reason to assume that Carson Grant would be arrested for what he'd done, since I wasn't the only one who saw him go into the theater that night."

"Who else saw him?"

"Bob Benton. He was coming back from one of his nightly walks and I saw him cut between the buildings and stop. There's a window where he was standing that looks down into the room where I left Ginny. I saw him glance in. He would have seen Ginny and Carson together. He might have even seen Carson kill her before getting rid of her body on the road out of town."

"What was Bob Benton doing between the buildings?"

Grayson shrugged. "He didn't come forward, either?" Frank shook his head. "I wonder why?"

Frank was wondering the same thing as he shut off the digital recorder. "Did you love Ginny?" he asked.

He looked confused by the question. "I love *Anna*. She's the only woman I've ever loved."

"Then why the affairs?"

Grayson again looked surprised. "They reminded me of Anna when Anna and I first met. They had this sweet innocence about them. For a few stolen hours I could pretend they were her—before the cancer."

CHAPTER TWENTY-THREE

A BLUE GROUSE ROSE FROM the deep grass in a thunder of wings. The mare reared, almost unseating Destry. But she hung tight as the grouse flew off into the fading light. A quiet dropped like a shroud over the mountains.

She settled the horse and fastened her gaze again on the dense timber ahead. The mare's ears prickled, and Destry thought she caught the scent of a campfire on the wind.

On the ride up, she'd crossed elk and deer tracks but no horseshoe tracks other than the single ones she'd been following. She'd stopped long enough to let the mare eat some grass and get a drink from the creek while she scanned the mountainside with her binoculars.

She ate some jerky, sniffed the air for the scent of a campfire again but found none. Nor could she see anything in the darkness of the heavy timber ahead. The sunlight was now obscured by low clouds. The day had become bleak and the wind stung. A pewter-gray sky hung over the top of the snow-capped peaks.

As she rode through a tight canyon between the peaks, she spotted a patch of burnt earth where someone had recently made a fire. Climbing down off her horse, she inspected the tracks around the small fire ring. Two men. She'd stumbled onto Billy the Kid's camp. But she wasn't the only one, she saw. Someone else had been here. Rylan? Or was someone else tracking them, hoping to collect on the reward?

The cold dampness seemed to soak through her duster all the way to her bones. She could see tiny crystallized snowflakes dancing in the air. A snowstorm was imminent. It wouldn't be hard to get snowed-in up here in the high country this time of year. She'd brought what food she could pack, but not enough if she couldn't get out of the mountains in a few days.

Destry looked toward the mountain peaks ahead of her. Rylan was up there. She could feel his presence. Just a little farther. The clouds hung heavy and damp with the promise of a snowstorm, but there was no turning back now. She couldn't leave Rylan up here with killers on the hunt.

She climbed back on her horse, urging the mare forward.

THE VALLEY WAS BATHED in the warm rays of the sunset, but a bank of dark clouds had settled in the Crazies, Sheriff Frank Curry noticed as he drove toward Beartooth.

He was wondering when the first snow would blanket the lower ground and stay for the rest of the winter, when he spotted Bob Benton's pickup coming down the road toward him. He hit his siren and lights. Bob drove on past and didn't appear to be slowing down.

Flipping a U-turn in the middle of the two-lane, Frank went after him, noticing that Bob had his camper shell on the back of his truck, and it appeared to be full of boxes. After talking to Grayson Brooks, the sheriff had left Bob a message asking that he call him. He hadn't heard a word, and now Bob seemed to be leaving town.

Frank got right up behind the pickup, flashed his headlights and started to pull alongside, when Bob finally slowed and pulled over to the edge of the road. There wasn't any traffic, but then there seldom was on this stretch.

Getting out of his patrol pickup, Frank walked up to the driver's side of Bob's truck.

"I know I wasn't going over the speed limit," Bob said after rolling down his window. "I got a taillight out or somethin'?"

It was just getting dark enough that the glow of the dash lights inside the pickup cast an eerie light over Bob's face. Frank could see that the man was sweating, even though the night was cold, a chill wind blowing through the truck window.

"You didn't get my message?"

"Your message?" Bob echoed.

Frank pulled off his flashlight and shone it into the windows of the camper shell. "That's quite a load. You moving?"

Bob hesitated. "It's a private matter, Frank."

"I'm going to need to see your license, registration and proof of insurance."

"You have to be kidding." He let out an impatient sigh and began digging the documentation out with obvious irritation. "If this is about me and Nettie—"

"Actually, it's about Ginny West."

Bob froze in midmotion of pulling his registration from his glove box. When he did move, it was slowly. "Ginny West?" he repeated.

"I have a witness who saw you standing by the theater that night."

He handed Frank his license and papers. "A witness?"

"I think I'd better follow you to the sheriff's department," Frank said after giving all three pieces of information a cursory glance.

"Is that really necessary?" Bob asked. He'd paled in
the pickup's dash lights.

"I need your statement. The quicker I get it, the
sooner you can be on your way."

Bob started to whir up his window.

"Uh, Bob. You can't outrun me in this pickup of
yours, so I hope you won't try."

Bob looked sick and scared, like a man with a horrible secret.

NETTIE DIDN'T GO UP TO THE house until she knew Bob
was gone. She'd seen his pickup go by in front of the
store. He'd had the camper shell on the back but she
could tell he hadn't taken all that much.

No man could pack up all his belongings in such a
short period of time. And yet she knew he was gone.
As he'd driven past the store, he'd turned, as if knowing she would be looking out.

She'd seen his expression and known he wouldn't
be back for anything he'd left. It depressed her that the
sum of his life with her could be loaded in the bed of
a small pickup.

Nettie finally had to go up to the house after he'd
left just to see. She opened the door and stepped in, listening. It didn't seem any different. She half expected

to see Bob in his chair, asleep, a book lying open on his lap.

His chair was empty, but the book he'd just finished on the small table next to it. She made a note to herself to get rid of the chair. Then she turned and walked back down the mountain to the store.

As she started into the back, she glanced into the woods at the bear trap the FWP had dropped off. It was still empty.

Nettie shot a look over her shoulder, the skin prickling on her neck. She'd be glad when they caught that damned grizzly.

Putting Bob and the bear out of her mind, she walked through the store to the front window. Kate LaFond was serving a table of ranchers and their wives who'd come in for dinner.

Past her, Nettie could see the old garage where she'd seen the café owner digging. Had the woman being playing with her?

Nettie shook her head. Kate LaFond was hiding something, and if it took until her last dying breath, Nettie intended to find out what it was.

"HOW ABOUT YOU START by telling me the truth?" Sheriff Frank Curry suggested.

Bob Benton sat across from him in the interrogation room, looking as nervous as a heifer in a bullpen. They'd been going at this for some time.

"Did. You. Kill. Ginny West?"

"No," Bob cried. "I told you. I had nothing to do with it." He was sweating profusely, his face red and blotchy.

"But you were there that night and you're obviously hiding something."

"Maybe I should call a lawyer."

"Do you need one?" Frank asked.

Bob swallowed.

"Listen, if you didn't kill her, but you saw something that will help in this investigation, then you have to tell me. Bob, what are you afraid of?"

"That what I tell you will incriminate me."

Frank chewed on that for a moment. "Short of murder, you have nothing to worry about. What did you see?"

Bob looked like a man in physical pain. "Can't you turn off the tape recorder?"

Hesitating only a moment, Frank shut off the recorder and waited.

"I go for walks at night." He couldn't meet Frank's gaze. The sheriff watched Bob swallow and felt his stomach roil. What secret was Bob Benton about to reveal?

"The witness saw you between the buildings by the theater," Frank prodded. "The witness said there's a window that looks down on the room where Ginny West was and that you were seen looking into it. What did you see?"

Bob began to cry in huge silent body-racking sobs. "I saw them making love."

Frank felt a chill settle deep in his bones. "You saw Ginny and *Carson* making love?"

Bob nodded but kept his head down, his body jerking with the sobs.

It was the same room where he and Lynette had both lost their virginity and probably a lot of other girls in town, Frank realized. Did Bob know that?

He suddenly felt sick to his stomach as he realized

why Bob had been beside that building that night and no doubt many other nights.

The man was a Peeping Tom. It was all Frank could do not to lose his temper and do something he would regret. He swallowed back the bitter taste in his mouth, the revulsion, the fury, and asked, "Did you see him kill her?"

"No," Bob said, wiping his face as he glanced up with red-rimmed eyes and quickly looked away. "I left."

Frank studied him for a long moment. There was more. He could feel it. "But you went back."

The room fell silent.

Bob stilled, then nodded and began to cry again. "It was horrible. The blood." He began to cough as if he was going to be sick.

Frank kicked the trash can over to him, but Bob managed to pull himself together after a moment.

"Did you see the killer?"

"Carson. He was mopping up the blood. He had blood on him."

"Did you see Ginny or the weapon in his hand?"

"No. I ran." He lowered his head further, a broken man.

Frank would have loved to have thrown Bob in a cell down the hall, but the Peeping Tom law was weak at best. In a case like this, the only thing he could hold him on was withholding information in a criminal investigation. "Where were you headed when I pulled you over?"

It took Bob a moment before he raised his head. "Arizona. Quartzite."

"I'll need you to sign a statement. You might as well get yourself a motel, because I can't let you leave town.

Not yet. And Bob, if and when you get to Arizona, get some help."

"I will. I promise."

As soon as he had Bob Benton's signed statement, the sheriff headed for the hospital to arrest Carson Grant.

IT BEGAN TO SNOW, HUGE flakes that whirled on the wind and pelted Destry as she rode through a narrow gap between two rock cliffs. She shivered against the cold. Her body ached from the long ride, from the fear that had settled in as painful as the snowy cold. The country opened a little, but between the trees and the snow, she couldn't see five feet in front of her face.

She climbed off the mare to walk the last part, praying Rylan hadn't changed his mind and turned back. Or worse, that Billy and Lucky had already found him. An eerie quiet blanketed the mountainside that not even the wind in the pines could chase away.

Destry suddenly felt entirely alone, as if she was the only one on this mountain. It was a strange, alien feeling because it came with a fear that this time her headstrong determination was going to get her killed, and Billy Westfall might be the least of her worries.

Being trapped in the mountains in a late fall storm was deadly. Even if she changed her mind and headed back now, she wouldn't make it. Not with the snow falling so hard, not with the temperature dropping so quickly.

Her mare needed rest. So did she. The horse stumbled, as if bringing home just how dire the situation had become.

The snow swirled around her on a gust of wind. Her head came up, her heart pounding as she caught a whiff of campfire smoke. But at the same time, the mare snorted and pulled back on the reins, ears up, sensing something on the wind.

Destry patted the horse as she drew her rifle from the scabbard. She tried to see ahead through the trees but the blowing snow was blinding. Stumbling forward, leading her horse, she followed the scent of the campfire as she cradled her rifle. She'd always been a better shot than her brother, especially with a rifle. She just hoped she wouldn't have to use it.

As she was almost out of the dense pines, she came up short. The small fire she'd smelled had burned down to only coals. She could see where someone had made a camp against the cliffs and a fallen pine, but there was no one there.

Her heart and hopes plummeted. Rylan had been here, but he was gone.

A limb snapped off to her left. She swung the rifle. A dark shape came out of the pines. Her finger trembled on the trigger for an instant before the man took shape, and she saw his face.

"Could you please lower that rifle?" Rylan said. "You're making me nervous."

CHAPTER TWENTY-FOUR

Rylan shook his head as if he couldn't believe she was here. His gaze locked with hers.

She lowered the rifle, but she didn't dare move, didn't dare breathe, as he took a step toward her. The look in his eyes held her motionless as he closed the distance until they were merely inches apart.

He lifted his hand slowly as if gentling a skittish horse. His fingers brushed back a tendril of her wet hair, his rough fingertips skimmed over the tender skin of her cheek, sending a shiver through her.

"I'm glad you don't try to cover your freckles," he whispered hoarsely.

His warm brown eyes were dark with a desire she knew well. His touch, the way he was looking at her, it sent her pulse into a full gallop.

His hand slipped beneath her braid to cup the nape of her neck. He slowly drew her to him. His gaze locked with hers as his mouth dropped to hers.

Her breath escaped in a rush, a soft moan that spilled from her. He drew back to look into her eyes again. "Destry." The word came out half plea, half curse. "What the hell are you doing here in the middle of a snowstorm?"

"Looking for you."

"Well, you found me," he said, his voice as rough as his fingertips.

The words tumbled out in a rush as she told him about Carson being shot, WT offering a fifty-thousand-dollar reward for Rylan and Billy Westfall teaming up with Lucky Larson to come after him.

Rylan nodded. "I suspected *something* was up. I saw a campfire down the mountain and checked it out. I gathered Westfall and Larson were looking for me, so I gave them a couple of trails to follow. I just assumed it was over the dustup between me and your brother."

"Dustup? Is that what you call it?" She noticed that his right eye was turning a little black-and-blue and his cut lip was in the process of healing.

"It's been coming for a long time. You know that. But I never would have shot him."

"I know that. It's another reason I'm here."

"So you trust me?" His grin was crooked, but his gaze was intent.

Did she? She loved him, but she wasn't sure she could trust him with her heart. She heard his horse whinny somewhere in the distance. "You heard me coming."

He nodded and smiled. "I thought the deputy and your ranch hand might be smarter than I figured them." He sobered. "I'm sorry about your brother. Is he going to be all right?"

"The bullet missed anything of importance. Amos Thompson was the one who shot him, but by the time Carson was conscious and told the sheriff…"

"Your father had put a reward out for me. Fifty thousand?" He let out a low whistle. "I'm impressed. I didn't know I was worth that much."

"That's not funny. They're probably tracking you as we speak."

He shook his head. "They were traveling light. I'm sure by now they have been forced to turn back. They clearly weren't as determined as you. Nor as well prepared for the weather," he said, taking in her duster.

He still had his hand cupped around the nape of her neck. His fingers gently caressing her warm skin, making it feel hot under his touch.

"Come on, let's get out of this weather. I moved the camp when the storm came in." He led her and her horse around the cliff face to where fallen rocks had made a windbreak. Rylan's camp was back under an overhang of rock that had formed a cave of sorts. "I was just about to get another fire going."

She took care of her horse, hobbling the mare with his in the pines. By the time she returned with her saddlebags, Rylan had a warm fire blazing at the edge of the entrance into the rocks. She piled her gear with his out of the falling snow back under the rocks. When she turned, she saw that he was watching her, his eyes dark again.

He shrugged out of his slicker and dropped it on a rock nearby. "You came all this way to warn me, huh? Even after I got in a fight with your brother?"

She removed her slicker, as well. Water ran from it in rivulets of melted snow. "Why does that surprise you?"

He laughed. "Everything about you continues to surprise me." Their eyes locked as the smoke from the campfire curled up and out into the falling snow. Past it, thick, lacy snowflakes fell in a silent shroud, blanketing the country below them.

Destry felt the warmth of the fire heat her face. Or

was it Rylan's gaze? It was hot enough to melt away the last of her misgivings. She felt herself go liquid inside. It didn't matter what was happening down in the valley. She and Rylan couldn't change any of it. All of that would play itself out, one way or another. She had given up on saving her brother or the ranch.

But she hadn't given up on Rylan. Couldn't. She'd had to make a choice. She'd chosen the man she loved.

"I came after you because I've never stopped loving you. Never will. No matter what happens up here or below these mountains," she said. "You can either take me on those terms or not."

He grinned. "That's laying it right out there." His grin faded, his gaze smoldering coals. "It won't be easy," he said, shoving back his Stetson.

She smiled. "When has it ever been easy for us?"

His gaze blazed hotter than the fire burning behind him as he took two long strides and pulled her roughly to him. Her heart took off like a shot. This time the kiss was pure passion, his mouth taking possession of hers the way he'd taken possession of her heart years ago.

He hooked an arm around her waist and pulled her against the solid sinew of his body as his other hand brushed across her cheek, sending shivers ricocheting through her. Her chest crushed against his, and she swore she could feel the thunderous beat of his strong, resilient heart.

She slipped her arms around his neck as he swept her up and carried her over to his sleeping bag stretched out on soft earth.

"I've always wished that our first time had been in a proper bed," he said as he lowered her, his face inches from her own. "Not happening this time, either. Maybe someday, huh?"

His words ignited the fire that she'd kept banked for eleven long years as she watched him toss aside his coat. As he leaned down to kiss her again, she grabbed each side of his Western shirt and jerked, hearing the snaps sing. Her palms pressed the warm sun-browned flesh over the hard contours of his broad chest, desperately needing to feel him pressed against her.

She traced along a familiar scar, then ran her fingers over several new ones. Her gaze lifted to his and she felt tears burn her eyes. "You've been hurt," she said in a choked whisper.

"We've both been hurt," he said as he lowered himself onto the sleeping bag beside her and took her in his arms.

RYLAN FELT HER FACE pressed against his bare chest, felt the hot tears and pulled her closer. "I'm so sorry, Destry, for leaving."

"All that matters is that you came back."

His lips found hers again. He pulled her on top of him, the crush of her lush rounded breasts firing a passion in him he'd never felt with any other woman.

"Destry," he breathed as she sat up and shrugged out of her coat, then her Western shirt, exposing a pretty pink bra. He could see the dark of her nipples beneath it. He felt a jolt of desire fire his body.

His gaze met hers as she unhooked the bra, releasing her full breasts. He drew her down, his mouth finding the hard tip of her nipples, his tongue caressing a moan from her lips.

Later he wouldn't remember taking off her jeans

or his either. But he recalled the feel of her bare flesh against his, the heat of her skin and fire in her pale blue eyes like a flame that never died out.

He entered her, stealing her breath and his. She arched against him, her hair fanned out across the sleeping bag. He cupped her buttock, lifting her into him until there was nothing between them, no breath of air, nothing but their passion and need and, yes, love, he thought as she shuddered against him, her face beautiful in the pleasured glow that heightened her freckles.

He loved this woman. Had never stopped loving her. He knew then that he couldn't live without her. As she'd said, whatever happened, he wasn't letting her go. Not again.

He looked into her eyes, saw to his amazement not just love but forgiveness lighting them. A moment later she let out another cry of pleasure as she arched against him. He finally let himself go, releasing all the pain, regret and guilt of the past eleven years.

Destry Grant loved him and he loved her, he thought holding her to him, their bodies glistening with sweat in the firelight as they tried to catch their breaths. Loving her was one thing, he realized as he looked into her eyes. Saving her was another. It was one thing to say she'd let go of everything. But he couldn't shake the fear that she was still dangerously involved in what was happening in the valley below these mountains—whether she wanted to be or not.

THE SHERIFF HAD CALLED ahead. He knew Carson was being released from the hospital. He planned to be there.

"What are *you* doing here?" WT demanded when Frank walked into the hospital.

He'd hoped Margaret would be here. Unfortunately he didn't see her. "How is Carson?"

"He's going to live. They're releasing him. I'll be taking him home." WT gave him a challenging look, daring him to say different.

Frank shook his head. "I can't let you do that. I'm going to have to take him in. Given the evidence and the eyewitness—"

WT let out a curse. "*Eyewitness?* Where the hell has this eyewitness been the past eleven years?"

The sheriff didn't answer. It would come out soon enough that Bob Benton had been there that night. Carson had admitted having intercourse with Ginny before her death.

Grayson had been her lover and met her that night at the theater. The pastor's wife had found her beside the road and had apparently attempted CPR. Because of all that, all of their DNA had been found on Ginny West's body or at the murder scene.

With Bob's testimony about seeing Carson with Ginny and later seeing blood on Carson, Frank thought he had a case that would stand up in court.

"I suspect you've seen this coming for eleven years," Frank said when WT quit swearing long enough for him to interrupt. "I don't think you would have sent Carson away unless you knew he was the one who'd killed that girl."

WT shook his head, but a lot of the fight seemed to have gone out of him. "He's my son. I was just protecting him." Beads of sweat had broken out on his forehead. He wiped at them with a shaky hand. "He has to take over the ranch. I've been waiting for that since the day he was born."

"I'm sorry."

"Are you?" WT looked pale and small in the wheelchair. "You think Carson is like me." He let out a humorless laugh. "But you're wrong. He's just like his mother. And Destry...."

Frank held his gaze. "Destry is just like you."

WT scoffed at that. "I suspect you know better than that."

"Lila and I were just friends. Never anything more. She loved you till her dying day."

WT swore again. "I know you think I killed her," WT said. "I wanted to, true enough. But I couldn't have hurt her..." His voice broke and he looked away. "Now you're going to put my son in prison to get back at me."

"That's not true, WT."

"Lila's horse spooked." He shook his head. "I know I should have left her where she fell. I knew you would never believe me. But I couldn't leave her there. I carried her down to the house and called you."

That had been WT's story, and there had been no way to prove otherwise, although Frank had always suspected there was more to it.

"This isn't about Lila," the sherrif said quietly.

"The hell is isn't." WT met his gaze with anger burning like a bonfire. "You think you were the only man to fall for my wife? Everyone loved Lila. *Everyone,*" he said with a sneer.

"You're wrong about Lila, just as you're wrong about me." There was only one woman Frank had ever loved. Lynette.

WT shook his head, still fuming with a fury that encompassed the world around him. There was no reasoning with him.

"The best way you can help Carson is to get him a good lawyer," Frank said. "It will be up to a jury to decide if he's guilty. Everything else is in the past. Dragging it out won't stop your son from being arrested."

"Like hell. You do what I say or—" He broke off and grabbed his chest.

At first Frank thought he might be faking it. But all the color had drained from WT's face. An instant later, he slumped over in the wheelchair.

"WT? Nurse! Nurse!" Frank called until he saw one running toward them. "My friend. I think he's having a heart attack."

"Does WT know where you are?" Rylan asked as they lay together in the sleeping bag listening to the crackle of the fire. The flames licked with tongues of hot orange at the wood, shooting sparks up into the night like fireflies that drifted on the wind with snowflakes.

"We said our goodbyes in the barn," she said.

Rylan chuckled. "Let me guess. He wasn't happy about you riding up into the mountains to warn me."

She smiled. "You could say that."

"I'm sorry."

"Don't be. As people say about WT, it's complicated. He was my father for all these years, good or bad. Everyone said I was like him in temperament and like my mother in looks."

"You have never been like WT in temperament," Rylan said with a chuckle as he slowly ran his hand from her waist down the curve of her hip. "You said you didn't know who you were. But you do now, don't you?"

She looked into his eyes and smiled. "Destry Grant."

He laughed. "Well, Destry Grant, I hope to change that. How do you like the sound of Destry West?"

She blinked.

"I didn't mean to do it this way. But nothing about our relationship has been what you'd call usual. The thing is, I don't want to wait another day to make you my wife. Say yes, woman."

She laughed, tears pooling in her beautiful blue eyes. "Yes."

"Someday our children are going to ask us where we were when daddy proposed," he warned her. "What are you going to tell them?"

Destry laughed. "That we were in the Crazies in a snowstorm beside a crackling fire, and that it was the most romantic moment your father could have ever chosen."

SOMETIME DURING THE NIGHT, the storm broke. Destry woke to see blue sky and sunshine. The snow glittered like billions of diamonds, so bright that it hurt her eyes.

Rylan stirred beside her. They lay in each other's arms like that for a long while. As she stared out at the beautiful day, she wished they could stay here forever. The snow had turned everything a silken virginal white. It was dazzling.

Just as being here in Rylan's arms felt amazing. But she knew they couldn't stay here forever. They would have to go back, and she feared what was waiting for them.

"There's something I need to tell you," she said, her words coming out on a white cloud in the cold morning air. "WT's not well." She could tell Rylan didn't know what to say. "He apparently doesn't have much time left."

"Like you said, he's your father, the only one you've ever had."

She nodded. "I can't help the way I feel, no matter how he's behaved toward me or what he's done."

Rylan hugged her. "You have to go back."

She nodded against him. "I do."

"We'll go together."

Just then, she heard the *whomp whomp* of helicopter blades. The horses whinnied, and Rylan was out of the sleeping bag and pulling on his jeans and boots as he rushed to the opening of the rocks.

Destry wasn't far behind him. She watched the helicopter hover over the open snowfield twenty yards away, then slowly set down in a shower of snow. It wasn't until she saw Sheriff Frank Curry waving to her that she knew that the fear she'd awakened with this morning was real.

"It's WT," the sheriff said when he'd made his way through eight inches of fresh powder to reach them. "He's had a heart attack. He wanted me to find you."

She nodded. "I need to see him."

"We'll have to hurry," Frank said.

Rylan promised to bring her horse out as soon as he could break camp. "I'll see you at the hospital later." He hugged her tightly before letting her go. She clung to him for a moment. Frank assured her that Billy Westfall and Lucky Larson were no longer a problem. They had come out of the mountains last night, both suffering from hypothermia and half dead. WT had retracted his reward for Rylan.

She hurried to the helicopter, telling herself it didn't

matter that she and WT didn't share the same blood. They'd shared their love for the ranch and Montana. WT was her father and he was dying.

Rylan waved, standing in the snow in front of the rock cliff. As the chopper lifted and turned toward Big Timber, she lost sight of him. Out the window, the day shone like a jewel as they flew along the edge of the mountains, Crazy Peak rising over eleven thousand feet in a cone of crystal white.

When they dropped out of the mountains, the land below bare and dry, Destry saw the W Bar G spread before her and began to cry. She wasn't going to make it in time. She felt it heart deep. Just as she'd told Rylan, she and WT had said their goodbyes yesterday in the barn.

CARSON PUSHED OPEN the door to his father's hospital room with his free hand. His left arm was still in a sling, his shoulder where the doctor had dug out the bullet was bandaged and hurting like hell.

Getting shot had more than wounded him. He'd lain in the front seat of the sports car unable to move, praying that someone would come along and help him. He'd had a lot of time to think as he'd lain there on the verge of bleeding to death. Fortunately a rancher had come along and, it being Montana where everyone stopped to help when they saw a vehicle beside the road, he'd been saved in more ways than one.

He'd heard about people seeing a white light right before they died. That they glimpsed their entire lives passing in front of their eyes. Neither had happened. In fact he couldn't be sure what had happened to him was even real. No doubt it was nothing more than loss of blood that made him think Ginny had come to him.

"Only a few minutes," the nurse warned as she looked up from the end of WT's bed when Carson stepped into the room. Putting back his father's chart, she left.

Carson went to his father's bedside. WT Grant had shrunk down to the pale old man lying there. Carson thought of how much of his life he'd spent being afraid of his father, the rest hating him. All that anger seemed to have bled out of him after being shot.

WT opened his eyes. "Son." He looked surprised to see him.

Carson pulled up a chair and sat down. When his father reached for his hand, he clasped it, startled that there was still a lot of strength there.

When WT spoke, his voice was a whisper. "There's so much I need to say."

"Don't try to talk. Let me." He cleared his throat. "You don't have to say anything. I know you hate me."

Carson couldn't deny that he had for years. He'd blamed everything on his father. "I want you to know. She loved you. Mother. I used to hear her crying herself to sleep at night. There wasn't anyone else until you moved out of her room, until you stopped being her husband."

WT's old eyes filled. He shook his head. "I don't want to talk about her. The ranch. I had to—"

"I only wanted the ranch for the money, but a part of me wanted to destroy the ranch to get back at you for hurting my mother." His father didn't look surprised. "I'm sorry I'm not the son you wanted."

WT squeezed his hand and tried to say something, but Carson interrupted him, needing to get this out.

"I didn't kill Ginny." WT didn't seem to be listening. "Dad, I'm telling you the truth. I know you think I did, but I didn't. I could never have done that to her. I *loved* her." But WT had closed his eyes. His hand suddenly went slack.

Carson saw that he was gone even before he heard the monitors go off. He felt the change in air pressure in the room, heard a nurse rush in. A moment later, the sheriff and his sister burst through the door.

He didn't realize he was crying until his sister knelt down beside him. He leaned into her, her arm around him, and they both cried for their father, the meanest man in Sweetgrass County, as Nettie Benton was fond of saying.

DESTRY FELT NUMB AS they gathered in the hall outside WT's room a while later. Margaret, who'd been waiting in the hall for them, put her arm around her.

"I'm sorry," Sheriff Frank Curry said. "But I have to take Carson in. I only let him come say goodbye to his father."

"It's all right," her brother said before Destry could argue. "Get me a good lawyer, will you?"

She nodded as the sheriff led him away.

"Come on, I'll take you home," Margaret said. "Why don't you come stay in one of the bedrooms up at the house with me?"

Destry shook her head. "Rylan is bringing down my horse later. I need to go home."

"I understand."

"Will *you* be all right?" Destry asked. Margaret was dry-eyed when they'd found her waiting in the hall, but it was clear she'd already done her share of crying for WT.

"I'll be fine," the older woman assured her. "Do you mind if I make the arrangements for the funeral? WT and I discussed it earlier."

Destry was relieved and said as much. "I wish I could have gotten here before… The sheriff said he was asking for me?"

"Yes, but you mustn't feel badly about that. He said the two of you had already said your goodbyes before you rode up into the mountains."

She smiled at that, remembering that she'd thought that same thing in the helicopter.

"He *did* love you," Margaret said. "Against his stubborn will."

Destry nodded, her throat constricting with emotion. "I know how you felt about him. I'm sorry."

"Don't be. I'm thankful I was able to spend all these years with him."

"But you deserved so much more."

Margaret shook her head. "I always knew that the only woman he would ever love was your mother. Waylon and I, well, we understood each other. He cared about me. I was the only woman in his life other than your mother. That was enough."

They drove in silence for the rest of the way home. Destry had never been so happy to see the homestead house.

"We'll talk later," Margaret said as she pulled up in front. "But there's something I have for you." She reached into her purse and drew out a small buckskin bag. "It's a few of your mother's things I was able to save for you. I didn't want to give them to you until—"

"Until he was gone."

"I knew how much it would hurt him if he saw you wearing anything of hers."

Destry nodded as she took the bag but didn't open it. "Thank you." She put it into her jacket pocket, gave Margaret a quick hug and climbed out before she began to cry again.

"Let me know if you need anything. I'll be at the house for now."

"I'll be fine," Destry said. "Rylan will be here soon. He's asked me to marry him."

"About time," Margaret said and smiled. "I knew the two of you would find your way back to each other."

Once in the house, Destry stood under the hot shower letting the heat seep into her. She felt chilled as if in shock. WT was gone. Carson was in jail facing a murder conviction.

She thought of Rylan and hugged herself, praying he would make it safely out of the Crazies. The sheriff had assured her that word was out that Rylan hadn't shot her brother, and WT had canceled the reward.

She knew by now that news of WT's death would be making the grapevine rounds—as well as Carson's arrest. She thought of the check she'd given him to pay his gambling debts. He'd need more money for a good lawyer.

As she came out of the shower and dressed, she remembered the small buckskin pouch Margaret had given her. She dug it out of her jacket pocket and, taking it over to the bed, carefully poured out its contents.

Her breath caught. There were diamond earrings, an agate ring, a turquoise necklace and several silver bracelets. But that wasn't what had stolen her breath and had her pulse pounding.

Lying on the bed was a thin silver chain with a mis-shapen heart locket—exactly like the one Bethany had showed them yesterday. Exactly like the one Rylan's sister had hidden in her jewelry box. Like it, this one was also tarnished.

CHAPTER TWENTY-FIVE

AFTER THE SHERIFF TOOK Carson to county lockup, he drove to Beartooth to check on Nettie. He'd been worried about her for years. But now with Bob gone, he had to make sure she was going to be all right.

As he pushed open the door to the Beartooth General Store, the bell tinkled. He noticed that it was almost closing time. After the day he'd had, he'd lost track of the time.

"Lynette?" he called.

She came out of the back. He studied her as she moved behind the counter, trying to discern how she was taking Bob leaving her.

Good riddance, he'd thought, but he needed to make sure Lynette wasn't hurting from it.

"What?" she said as he made his way to the counter.

"Just needed a bottle of orange soda," he said, walking past her to the cooler. He could feel her gaze on him. Was he that transparent? Probably.

"I'm fine," she said.

"Who said you weren't?" he asked as he set the soda on the counter and dug out his cash.

"I don't need you checking up on me."

"Is that what you think I'm doing?"

"I know you're here for more than a bottle of orange

soda," she said, hands going to her hips. "If this is about Bob leaving—"

"It isn't. But if you need anything…"

She mugged a face at him but then seemed to have a thought. "There is something you can do for me that you should have already done," she said. "I need you to find out everything you can about Kate LaFond."

He wondered if every man felt this way about his first love. Grayson Brooks apparently had. He'd kept trying to find his Anna in other women.

For years Frank had been forced to hide the way he felt. But no more. He was still crazy about this woman, he thought, as he opened the soda and took a drink. The years hadn't diminished it in the least. Lynette was still that redheaded, feisty woman who'd made his blood run geyser hot.

"Kate LaFond's hiding something," Lynette continued. "I saw her digging in that old garage of hers in the middle of the night. Bob said she's just messing with me because she knows I've been watching her. But she couldn't have known I was watching that night. Nope. It's more than that." She took a breath. "Frank?"

He nodded and smiled.

"Have you even heard a word I've said?"

"Yep. I'll see what I can find out about Kate LaFond. I trust your instincts, Lynette."

She opened her mouth to argue but quickly snapped it shut. "Seriously, you'd do that for me?"

"I'd do anything for you, Lynette. Don't you know that?"

"You're not just doing it to appease me? Or because you think I'm an addled old woman or that you feel sorry for me?"

He grinned. "You can't be sure, can you?"

She started to stomp off mad, but he touched her arm and stopped her.

"Feel sorry for you?" he said. "Why would I do that? I think you are the strongest, most determined and, by far, the most interesting woman I've ever met, and you've only improved with age. Addled? Not hardly. Sure, you're a terrible gossip, but," he said, quickly raising a hand to keep her from flying off the handle, "that's only because you have a keen sense of people and you like to share it and because we're all flawed and you find that interesting, the same way I find watching crows interesting."

She cocked a brow at him. "Is this your idea of sweet talk?"

"Is it working?"

She scoffed at that but gave him a weak smile. "This is because Bob left me, isn't it?"

"Nope, I've been wanting to say this to you for years. I'm not sorry to see Bob go. I've been hoping he would." Bob would have to testify but the Peeping Tom aspect wouldn't come out if Frank could help it. Not to protect the bastard but to protect Lynette. "With him gone, there is nothing stopping you from becoming the woman you've always wanted to be."

"And who exactly do you think that woman is?"

He shrugged. "I have no idea. But I can't wait to get to know her."

She smiled. He hadn't seen that particular smile in a very long time. It held no sarcasm, no sharp edges, no cynicism, and it lit up her eyes with a light that burned bright. For a moment, in the last of the sunlight coming through the front window of the store, she was seventeen again, back when the two of them were crazy about each other. Back before they'd both tried to find happiness with someone else, no matter how fleeting.

DESTRY JUMPED AT THE sound of a vehicle pulling up outside, and moments later there was a loud knock at the front door. She was too shocked over what she'd found in her mother's jewelry to move at first.

Peering out finally, she saw Grayson Brooks. She stared down, confused. What was he doing here? If this was about the barn stalls—

She wasn't up to company right now, but Grayson's knock was insistent.

Leaving the jewelry on the bed, she hurried downstairs to open the door. "Grayson? If this is about the barn stalls—"

"I heard about your father and also about your brother being arrested," he said. "I just stopped by to tell you how sorry I am."

"Thank you. I appreciate that." She was distracted, her mind still racing after seeing the silver locket. It had to be just a coincidence, and yet she knew better. She thought about what Rylan had said about the women the man had given the lockets to all resembling each other—and she was the spitting image of her mother, wasn't she?

"Do you mind if I come in for a few minutes?" Grayson asked, his Western hat in his hand. "I don't want to bother you at a time like this."

She did mind. But Montana ranching hospitality was legendary. Most households always had a pot of coffee on. "No, of course not, come in. I could put on some coffee…" She was glad when he shook his head.

"I just wanted to apologize. I feel responsible."

"Responsible?" What was he talking about?

"The sheriff didn't tell you?"

"We only spoke for a minute at the hospital."

Grayson looked around the room nervously. "My timing leaves something to be desired." His gaze settled on Destry and he smiled. "Has anyone told you that you look just like your mother?"

"Yes, as a matter of fact." He was making her uncomfortable the way he was staring at her. Why would he feel responsible? Certainly not for WT's death, but for Carson being arrested?

"Your mother and I... Well, I always admired her. Used to see her in church all the time. What a beautiful woman she was. She was a bit older than me, but didn't look it. I was seventeen when she died." He moved farther into the room, smiling as he looked around. "You haven't changed a thing in this room."

She stared at his back, realizing two things simultaneously. He'd known her mother and had been in this house.

"She was so young and innocent-looking," Grayson said, turning to face her again. "Just like you are now."

Destry fought to make sense of what he was saying. She couldn't help the shudder that moved through her. Or the fear.

"Anna and I married young. She was seventeen. She'd just had another miscarriage and had gone up to Great Falls to spend some time with her folks, when I happened to run into your mother at the post office. She reminded me of Anna. I used to watch her in church. But I guess I already told you that."

Destry tried to take a breath, her heart a drum in

her chest. He'd watched her mother? Is that what he was saying? Or was he trying to tell her— Her stomach dropped.

It hadn't been Hitch. Just like he'd argued. There'd been someone else sneaking around her place.

"Everyone loved your mother. We were all devastated when she died and in such a freak accident," Grayson said as he moved around the room.

"Horseback riding can be dangerous," Destry said, edging toward the back door and the loaded shotgun. He was making her nervous. She wished he would just leave. She didn't want to use the shotgun. She prayed he wouldn't make her.

She was almost to the shotgun when he said, "But I didn't come out here to talk about your mother. I have something for you." She turned to see he was holding up a silver locket. "I gave one to your mother years ago. I bought this one for you."

SINCE HE WAS ALREADY in town, Frank walked down to the small, hole-in-the-wall post office to pick up his mail after he left Lynette. There'd been talk of closing these small post offices lately, but townsfolk like those in Beartooth had fought it.

"The post office is what makes us a town," Lynette had argued. "It's where everyone comes to get more than their mail. They stop and visit. You take it away and you take away the heart of these small communities."

Frank could hear faint music playing in the back of the post office and the voices of several locals visiting with the postmistress, asking her about her new grandbaby.

Lynette was right, of course. It would be a real shame if post offices like this were to close. But that didn't mean she was going to be able to save this one or the others on the chopping block. It would come down to money, he thought, with no small regret.

He dug out the stack of mail, realizing that he hadn't been in for a few days. As he was sorting through the bills and junk mail, he saw that one of the letters had been returned because it needed more postage, but it had been put in the wrong box by mistake.

As he started to take it to the window to give it to the postmistress, he realized there was something familiar about the handwriting. For a moment, he couldn't put his finger on it. When he did, he stumbled to a stop, heart racing.

The handwriting. It was the same hurried scrawl as that of the notes Ginny West had received before she'd been murdered.

DESTRY'S BLOOD TURNED to ice. She was only inches from the shotgun. *"You and my mother?"* She thought of the chain and locket lying on the bed upstairs. "Are you telling me you had an affair with my mother?"

Grayson quickly shook his head. "It wasn't like that. I'm not sure she ever even wore the locket. At least never when I saw her. But she was nice enough to take it and thank me. I could tell she thought I was too young for her and she was in love with someone else."

Destry felt a moment of relief. Then Grayson took a step toward her, holding out the silver locket. "I don't want that," she said.

He frowned and stopped. "But I bought it for you. I thought... Well, it doesn't matter what I thought. Everything has changed. I'm going to lose my Anna soon." Sadness filled his eyes. "Once that happens, I won't have anything left." He looked at the silver chain, the locket dangling from his thick fingers. "I won't need this or want it."

"You're the one who's been watching me from the woods," Destry said, backing up until she could feel the cold steel of the shotgun.

Grayson nodded. "I wanted to know everything about you before I gave you this."

A jolt of fear shot like a lightning bolt through her.

"You reminded me so much of your mother. But like your mother, you're in love with someone else, aren't you? I'd hoped you might like me."

She snatched up the shotgun and pointed both barrels at him.

He took a step back. "Please, I don't mean to scare you. I just had to—" He raised a hand and took another step back. "That's not necessary."

She moved toward the phone. "We'll see what the sheriff has to say about that."

"The sheriff already knows," Grayson said. "I told him everything. Except for how I felt about you. I'm sorry. I didn't mean to upset you." He moved toward the door.

"You're not going anywhere until the sheriff—"

Grayson stopped and smiled. "You won't shoot me. You could have the other night and you didn't. Don't worry, I won't bother you again."

She was tapping in 911 when she heard another vehicle approaching. Grayson turned and left quickly, leaving the front door open. He was right. She couldn't very well force him to stay since they both knew she wasn't going to shoot him.

Destry put the phone back and hurried to the door, the shotgun in hand, as a vehicle she didn't recognize pulled into the drive. As Grayson sped away, Linda Armstrong stepped out of the other vehicle.

Destry never thought she'd be glad to see the pastor's wife. Her hands were shaking as she leaned the shotgun against the wall by the front door and said, "I can't tell you how glad I am to see *you*."

Linda frowned. "Was there a problem?" she asked, looking after Grayson's pickup as he sped away.

"Not now," Destry said with a shake of her head.

"I came out to give you my condolences," Linda said. She'd brought a box of candy from the general store. Destry recognized the brand Nettie carried. There appeared to be a card taped to the top of the box.

Destry was just thankful for the company right now. She still felt shaken by what Grayson had told her. "Come in. I'll put on a pot of coffee. Please make yourself at home. I just need to make a quick call."

She hurried upstairs and called the sheriff's department. The sheriff was on a call, so she left a message for him to return her call as soon as possible.

"Was that Grayson Brooks who just left here in such a hurry?" Linda asked as Destry came back downstairs.

"He dropped by to give his condolences," Destry said as she went into the kitchen to make coffee. No way was she telling Linda what Grayson had said, since the pastor's wife was good friends with Grayson's wife, Anna.

"You have some wonderful artwork," Linda called from the living room. "I was just admiring it."

Destry had the coffee going before Linda finally ap-

peared in the kitchen doorway. "It should be just a minute. Have a seat," she said as she dug out some cookies
Margaret had baked a few days earlier.

"Doesn't it get lonely out here by yourself?" Linda
asked as Destry put a plate of cookies and two cups on
the table. "It's more remote than the parsonage. At least
I can walk down to the store or the café."

"I like peace and quiet," Destry said as she noticed
the card the pastor's wife had brought. It was addressed
as if she'd planned to mail it and had changed her mind.

"I miss the ocean," Linda said and took a bite of
cookie. She'd never made her feelings about Montana
a secret, which hadn't exactly enamored the locals over
the years. Fortunately, everyone liked Pastor Tom.

Destry felt for her, being forced to live somewhere
she didn't like. Wasn't that what WT had been trying
to do with Carson?

"It gets dark here so early in the day, especially in
the winter." Linda shivered, even though it was quite
warm in the house.

Destry didn't know what to say. Fortunately, she
heard the coffeepot shut off and hurried to get them
each a cup. When she turned back, Linda was staring
at her. Even when Destry poured the woman her coffee, she didn't stop staring.

Destry felt uneasy, still spooked from Grayson's
visit. "Do you like sugar or cream in your coffee, Mrs.
Armstrong? I'm sorry, I should have asked."

"Please call me Linda. Mrs. Armstrong makes me
sound so old," she said. "Black is fine." She picked up
her coffee cup, but was watching Destry over the rim
as she took a sip and put it down. "I remember the first
time I really noticed you. You were wearing a yellow

dress. Tom commented on how lovely you looked in it. Every time you wear it, Tom always says how pretty you look in it."

Destry smiled uncomfortably. "He says that to everyone in church."

"Does he? I guess I haven't noticed."

She felt goose bumps skitter across her flesh at the look Linda was giving her.

"I saw you and Tom with your heads together after church," the woman said. "Your discussion looked rather intense."

Like Linda's discussion with Grayson, Destry thought with a sudden chill. Did Linda know about the lockets? About Grayson's relationship, not only with Bethany, but with Ginny?

"Mrs. Armstrong, I have no interest in your husband," Destry said, getting to her feet under the pretense of refilling both their cups. Neither of them had hardly touched their coffee.

She topped off Linda's cup and her own, then returned the pot but didn't sit back down. "The few times we've even talked, Tom was merely offering his help if I needed any," she said, leaning against the kitchen counter.

"That's the way it always begins, isn't it with men? Tom used to offer your mother help and that West girl when she came to him crying because she was carrying his baby—"

"Ginny?" Destry didn't realize she'd let the word out until she saw Linda's expression.

"Yes, Ginny. Sunday you asked my husband about the notes, didn't you? You said a friend of yours had gotten one. You made that up."

"No, I—"

"Don't lie to me," Linda snapped.

The card Linda had brought her suddenly caught her eye again. It lay on top of the box of chocolates on the table. Even from where she stood, she could see the familiar scrawl of the angry handwriting—

With a start, Destry knew where she'd seen it before. Linda had written the threatening notes to Ginny before she was murdered, and now Destry knew why.

SHERIFF FRANK CURRY stepped into the church and removed his hat as he headed for the office. The door stood open. "Where is your wife?" he asked the moment he saw the pastor behind his desk.

"Linda? She'd running some errands."

"I need to ask you if you've seen this before." He took the bagged copies of the notes Ginny had received and laid them on the desk.

Tom Armstrong's reaction was immediate.

"That's your wife's handwriting, isn't it?"

"Yes." He looked sick. "She promised me she would stop. I'm sorry. Who was it this time?"

"Ginny West."

All the color drained from the pastor's face.

"Ginny West confided in you, didn't she? Did you tell your wife?"

"No, of course not," he cried. "She overheard and misunderstood."

"She thought Ginny was pregnant with *your* baby?"

Tom nodded. "Yes, but once I explained…"

"You're sure she believed you?"

The pastor looked away, and Frank sighed as he

picked up the evidence from the pastor's desk. "I need to talk to your wife."

"It's not her fault. It's mine. I broke our vows years ago, and she has never been able to forgive me. She gets insanely jealous sometimes if she even sees me talking to a woman."

Frank felt his heart drop. "Who is your wife jealous of now?"

Tom frowned, then his eyes widened in alarm. *"Who?"*

"She's been talking about Destry Grant after seeing us together at church Sunday. That was one of the stops she was going to make today. But she wouldn't hurt Destry." Tom wrung his hands, fear making him sweat. "No, she wouldn't hurt Destry."

"What aren't you telling me?" Frank demanded.

"The guilt must have been killing her. I've seen it eating away at her, but I didn't understand what was causing it until I found the jacket. Don't you see? She's been doing penance all these years. Why else would she have kept Ginny's letterman jacket other than to remind her of what she did?"

"What *she* did?" That stopped Frank in his tracks. "*You* put the letterman jacket in the church clothing bin?" He let out a curse. "You're afraid she'll do it again."

THE PHONE RANG, MAKING Destry jump. She snatched up the receiver from the kitchen wall. "Hello." Her brain was racing. Linda had written the notes. Linda thought the baby Ginny had been carrying was Tom's. And now Ginny's letterman jacket had been found in an old clothing bin at the church.

"Destry, it's Sheriff Curry. Don't say anything. But if Linda Armstrong is there—"

"Yes."

"She is?"

"That's right," Destry said, turning her back to Linda.

"Tom and I are on our way. Are you going to be all right until we get there?"

"I'll certainly try." She hung up the phone, pulse pounding in her ears. She glanced toward the back door, belatedly remembering that she'd left the shotgun by the front door. When she turned back to the kitchen, she saw that Linda had gotten up from the table.

"Who was that?" Linda asked.

"Just a friend of mine."

"Liar. That was Tom, wasn't it?"

"No, it wasn't Tom."

Linda let out a laugh as sharp as barbed wire. "What is it about Tom? Women just can't seem to resist him. I heard Ginny crying and telling my husband that she didn't know what she was going to do if he didn't leave his wife and marry her. I thought Ginny was determined to have him and that's why she got herself pregnant. When she caught me putting another warning note on her car, she threatened to tell Tom. I promised to stop, but I knew I couldn't trust her. I thought she was lying about the baby not being Tom's."

Destry took a step back. "Did Tom tell you Ginny was carrying his baby?"

"Of course not, I knew he would lie, too, just like he always has," Linda said, moving slowly toward her. "Ironic, isn't it?" Her laugh died on her lips. "Grayson thought the baby was *his*."

In a flash, Destry recalled Sunday and the intense conversation Linda had been having with the contractor. "Grayson confided in you."

"His wife is my best friend," Linda said indignantly. "He confessed everything, even how he felt about your mother—and now you."

Linda took another step toward her. Destry noticed that the woman had one hand behind her back. Destry's gaze shifted to the kitchen counter behind the pastor's wife. With heart-stopping fear, she saw that one of the knives was missing from the wooden block where she kept them.

Her pulse began to pound as she backed out of the kitchen. "Is Grayson the one who hurt Ginny?" Destry asked. She could hear the sound of a siren in the distance. The sheriff would be here soon. Grayson and his silly lockets, his romantic gestures. He hadn't killed Ginny. Who was she kidding?

Linda's eyes glittered with hatred. "Ginny cried and swore on her Bible that Tom wasn't the baby's father. I didn't know it was Grayson fooling around with her. Even when she swore it wasn't Tom…" Her voice died off into a low moan. "I didn't mean to kill her. I just wanted to talk to her, to tell her she wasn't having Tom. I knew about that sinful place in the old theater. I wasn't surprised to find her there after your brother left, her smelling of sex." She made a disgusted face. "She grabbed up a piece of old pipe that was lying on the floor and threatened me. I…I tried to take it away from her." Linda touched the underside of her left wrist.

Destry saw the thin, white line of a scar and remembered what Bessie had said about Linda's arm bleeding.

Not, though, from a fall later beside the road, but at the old theater during a struggle with Ginny.

"Ginny was telling the truth," Destry said. "It wasn't Tom's baby. It was Carson's. That's who she'd been with just moments before you found her in the theater. You killed her for nothing. Tom had never been involved with her and Grayson had broken it off."

Linda didn't seem to hear her. "I panicked. At first I thought she was dead. I knew I couldn't leave her there. It would lead the sheriff to Grayson. I had to protect him for Anna's sake. Ginny's letterman jacket was lying there. I wrapped her in it and carried her out the back way to my SUV. She wasn't all that heavy. Just a child." Her voice caught. "Then I realized she was still alive."

A chill snaked up Destry's spine. She didn't want to hear any more of this, but she didn't dare stop her from talking. The sheriff and Tom would be here any moment.

"I realized what I had to do. I would take her to the hospital," Linda was saying, a dazed look in her eyes. "I never planned to kill her. I hadn't gone far when she woke up. I'd put her in the passenger seat so I could keep an eye on her. I told her not to be afraid, I was taking her to the hospital. But when she looked out the window, she realized I wasn't on the right road. I hadn't realized I'd taken a wrong turn until that moment. She started screaming, thinking I was taking her out in the woods to kill her. She…" Her voice broke with emotion.

"It was an accident," Destry said.

"She opened the door, and before I could stop her, she threw herself out." Linda stopped moving, stopped talking. When she spoke again, her voice was low, controlled. "I saw it in the side mirror. I was shocked. I started to stop, but she wasn't moving. She was just lying there. I panicked."

"But you went back," Destry said. "You went back with Bessie."

Linda nodded. "Yes."

Destry saw her worst horror in the woman's eyes. "Ginny wasn't dead."

"She would have told the sheriff. No one would believe me that it had been an accident. I had no choice. I put my hand over her mouth and nose as I pretended to give her CPR."

Destry couldn't help the gasp that escaped her lips.

Linda's gaze seemed to clear. "I know that was Tom on the phone a few minutes ago. He found Ginny's letterman jacket where I'd hidden it. I couldn't get rid of it. I needed to keep it where I could look at it. I needed to beg for forgiveness every day for what I did."

"Tom knew?" Destry asked, shocked.

"Tom?" Linda shook her head with a smirk. "I wanted to bare my soul to him, but I knew he wouldn't keep my secret. I knew I couldn't trust him. And I was right. When I found the jacket missing, I knew what he would do with it. He would betray me and now he has."

She took another step, and as she did, she brought her hand out from behind her back. The blade of the knife flashed in the light coming through the kitchen window. "I'm already going to spend the rest of my life in prison, so *I* have nothing to lose. I won't let you have Tom. Or Grayson."

Destry broke then and ran to the shotgun, grabbed it up and swung around to point it at the woman's heart. "Put down the knife. I don't want to shoot you."

"Grayson told me you fired a shotgun at him the last

time he was out here. He said he'd seen it by the back door when he'd looked in your window. He is enchanted by you. That's why he came out here, wasn't it? To tell you. I saw the silver locket he left on the shelf by your front door."

Destry hadn't realized Grayson had dropped it there before he left. "I have no interest in Grayson or Tom."

Linda took another step toward her. "He'll still want you, though. He can't help himself. Your type are like nectar to bees for men like Tom and Grayson."

"Please don't make me pull this trigger," Destry said, remembering that she'd replaced the buckshot with heavy load steel. At this distance, even buckshot would kill the woman.

Linda took another step. "Tom will blame himself for your death, just as I'm sure he blames himself for Ginny's. Let him live with that guilt. He deserves it. Him and his holier-than-thou attitude. I saw the sheriff's car down at the church. I knew he'd given him Ginny's jacket. Which meant it was just a matter of time before my blood was found on it. My husband has committed the ultimate betrayal, don't you see?"

Destry knew she had no choice. As Linda took another step toward her, she pulled one trigger and flinched. The gun made only a dull click.

Linda smiled.

Destry pulled the second trigger, but even before she heard the empty click, she knew. While she had been making coffee, Linda had emptied the shotgun.

AFTER RYLAN PUT DESTRY'S horse in the barn and hung up her tack, he rode toward her house, anxious to get to the hospital. He feared he would be too late. He just hoped Destry hadn't been too late.

But as he rode past her place, he heard a siren in the distance. The sound seemed to grow as if headed this way. A bad feeling settled in his belly. He'd seen Russell when he returned Destry's horse. Russell had told him that WT had died and Margaret had taken Destry home. As he neared her old homestead house now, he saw that the fence was still down from the other day when he'd caught Hitch McCray sneaking around her house. Was it possible Hitch was out of jail already?

Thinking he was probably on a fool's errand, he rode through the open gate and galloped toward Destry's house. He couldn't shake the feeling that she was alone and in trouble.

He had just crossed the creek, when he heard the scream. He swung down from his horse, dropping the reins as he raced across the grass to her back door.

It wasn't until he was almost there that he heard a loud sermonizing female voice. The loud chant of words sent his pulse racing.

"I will rescue you from a forbidden woman, from a stranger with her flattering talk, who abandons the companion of her youth and forgets the covenant of her God; for her house sinks down to death and her ways to the land of the departed spirits."

By then he'd reached the back door, and what he saw through the window made his heart drop. Linda Armstrong had a knife in her hand and Destry backed into a corner.

Destry had the shotgun in her hands, but the barrel wasn't pointed at Linda. He didn't have time to make sense of that when the blade of Linda's knife caught the light as she lunged forward, righteous fury blazing on her lips. Destry swung the shotgun.

The gun stock grazed the pastor's wife's head, but she didn't go down. She stumbled back, readying herself to charge again. As she swung the knife, the blade missed Destry's shoulder by a hairbreadth.

It happened in the instant Rylan was reaching for the doorknob. He grabbed it, expecting to find the door locked. He should have known better. It was still daylight. Destry was determined not to spend her life locked in.

The door swung open with him right behind it. Linda heard him and turned, brandishing the knife. He held up both hands. "I don't know what's going on, but you don't want to use that," he said to her.

As Linda charged him, her scream pierced the air.

He dodged to the side as she thrust the knife at him. She turned back, quicker than he'd expected, though. He saw the blade, felt it burn as it cut through his shirt and into his arm.

Linda came at him again, the knife blade gleaming in her hand, blind fury blazing in her eyes. Like a startled grizzly, she charged him.

Linda was almost on him.

He tried to step away, but Linda was too close.

A loud crack filled the air as the stock of the shotgun connected with Linda's head. She stood for a moment looking stunned, the knife still gripped in her fist. Then her eyes rolled back in her head, and she crumpled to the floor at his feet.

Rylan kicked the knife away and, stepping past her,

dragged Destry into his arms. They both stared down
at Linda unconscious on the floor as the sound of a
siren filled the air.

EPILOGUE

IT RAINED THE DAY OF WT Grant's funeral, but quickly turned to snow before the service was over. To Destry's astonishment, the whole county turned out to pay their respects.

Carson had been released from jail and cleared of all charges after Linda Armstrong finally confessed to the murder of Ginny West eleven years ago and the attempted murder of Destry Grant and Rylan West. The crime lab found Linda's blood on Ginny's letterman jacket, just as she'd feared.

Carson stood next to Destry at the gravesite as Russell Murdock, her father's long-time ranch foreman, said a few words over the coffin before it was lowered into the ground. Russell had been surprised when Destry and Margaret had asked him.

"You knew WT as well as anyone," Margaret had said. "We all know how he felt about religion. He would have wanted you to say something over his grave."

"I'm not sure I'm the right person to do this," he'd said.

"You might be one of the few people around who can think of something good to say about him," Destry had told him.

Russell had chuckled at that. "In that case, I'd be honored."

The service broke up with everyone invited back to the big house. They came with casseroles and condolences. Margaret played hostess from the kitchen while Destry moved through the throng of people, thanking them for coming. There was a crowd because few of them had ever seen the inside of WT's folly.

Carson disappeared shortly after they arrived at the house. At one point, Destry saw him outside, standing at the edge of the pool, looking off toward the Yellowstone River as if surveying his kingdom—much like WT used to do when he was alive.

"How are you holding up?" Rylan asked, as the crowd began to thin.

"Okay," she said. "I appreciate your family coming."

"I don't know what happened between WT and my father years ago, but at one time they'd been friends. I know that my mother and father think the world of you." He grinned. "And my brothers are jealous as all get out."

She couldn't help but smile.

"Can I see you later?"

"You know where I live."

"Still going to stay at the homestead until our wedding?"

"Until Carson makes me move."

Rylan's jaw tightened, and she regretted her words. Rylan and Carson had given each other wide berths all day.

Russell was one of the last to leave. Now he seemed downright shy as he approached Destry, hat in hand. He kneaded the brim of his hat and studied his boots.

"I can't tell you how sorry I am about everything," he said, not for the first time.

"I'm just glad Ginny's killer has been caught."

"And that it wasn't your brother," he said.

"I saw you talking to the sheriff. Did he mention what will happen to Linda?"

"Frank said the state will require a mental evaluation to see if she's competent to stand trial." He shrugged. "Either way, she'll be locked up for a long time."

"I wonder how Tom is doing."

"I'm sure he blames himself."

She nodded. "Linda was counting on that. It's too bad. He isn't leaving, is he?"

"Everyone is trying to convince him to stay. I think he will."

"Destry, there's something I need to tell you." Russell looked down at his boots for a moment, before he met her gaze again. "I know about the paternity test. Your brother told me, but I knew already. WT wasn't your birth father. I am. I would have told you sooner—"

"But you knew how WT would take it."

He nodded and studied her for a moment. "You knew?"

"I found a photograph of you and my mother." She couldn't hide her relief as she looked at the big man and smiled.

"It wasn't an affair. Your mother was having her issues with WT. We just happened to be in the same place, so to speak. It was only once. We both regretted it. Your mother loved WT." He smiled shyly. "I was hoping that maybe you and I could get to know each other better. That is, if—"

"I'd like that and I suspect my mother would have liked it, too."

He smiled then. "I know she would have."

CARSON STOOD AT THE edge of his father's swimming pool and looked out across the W Bar G. What was it about land that drew some people as if they felt a need to take root like a tree and grow there? He'd never understood it, still didn't.

He let his thoughts drift on the breeze. They took him back to something that had been nagging at him. At his father's funeral a few weeks ago, he'd seen a woman who'd looked familiar, but he hadn't been able to place her. He couldn't shake it because he felt that remembering her was somehow important.

Hearing a door open behind him, he turned, figuring it would be Destry. The two of them hadn't said much to each other since he'd gotten out of jail. He'd never forget that she was the only one who'd believed him innocent. But even she had begun to doubt him. Not that he could blame her. He'd certainly given her reason. He thought about what she'd done, trying to help him, and felt so much love for her that it nearly dropped him to his knees.

"WT's lawyer is here. It's about his will," she said, joining him at the edge of the pool.

"Remember when we were kids and I taught you to swim?" he asked. "I think about those days a lot." He took a breath and let it out. "Here. It's the check you gave me. I don't need it now. The casino wrote me off as a bad debt when they realized I was probably going to prison. I suspect Cherry had something to do with it."

Destry took the check and folded it before putting it into her pocket, then she turned, and he followed her back into the house. "Once they hear that you were cleared—"

"I'll make sure they get paid, don't worry."

The lawyer was waiting for them in WT's den. "If you'd both like to take a seat."

"I think I'll stand," Carson said. "Can I offer you drink?" he asked the lawyer, who shook his head. "Well, if you don't mind, I think I'll have one. Destry?" She, too, shook her head as she sat down, her hands clasped in her lap.

He poured himself a drink, the lawyer waiting patiently. Carson watched his sister's face as WT's will was read. He smiled when he saw her astonished expression and heard her gasp. Her gaze flew to him.

"It's pretty cut-and-dried," the lawyer was saying as he handed Destry the papers to sign. "Your father made provisions for Margaret and for Carson but left the ranch to you as sole owner," he said to Destry.

"Carson, was this your doing?" she asked him.

He had to laugh. "In a roundabout way. I'd say it was more my bad behavior and the fact that, ultimately, he knew you were the one who loved this place and would see that his legacy lived on."

"You knew he'd changed his will?"

"I'd hoped he did the right thing, but I couldn't be sure. I think he was trying to tell me at the end, but I didn't let him."

"He can't have left everything to me," she said. "It's not right." Destry ignored the lawyer to go to her brother. "I can't agree to this."

"He only left you the ranch," Carson said. "As his attorney said, WT made a provision for me. He knew you would never live in this house, so he left it to me. Of course he knew me well enough that unless I live in the house and get a paying job, it reverts to charity if Margaret doesn't want it."

"He was trying to control you right till the end."

"Or maybe he just didn't want Margaret to live here alone," Carson said. "I can walk away and make a life for myself. Maybe I will. I don't know yet. Now that Ginny can finally rest in peace…"

"Carson—"

"I love you, little sis." He pulled her to him and gave her an awkward hug. He'd be glad when his shoulder healed, but he knew some wounds never would. "Dad did the right thing in the end. Be happy. *I'm* happy for you. I really wouldn't have wanted it any other way."

As he started to leave the room, he remembered the woman he'd seen at the cemetery. "Hey, I saw a woman at the funeral." He described her to his sister. "You know who she is?"

Destry smiled as if she thought he was going to be all right if he was already interested in some woman he'd seen at the funeral. "Sounds like Kate LaFond. She recently bought the Branding Iron Café in Beartooth."

"Kate LaFond?" He nodded, thinking how strange it was because he knew that that hadn't been her name when he'd crossed paths with her years back.

RYLAN WEST AND DESTRY Grant's engagement party was held just before Christmas at the community center. There was a country band and lots of food and dancing.

Everyone was there, including friends and family. Destry's best friend, Lisa Anne Clausen, was finally back from Wyoming where she'd been taking care of her young nieces and nephews while her sister recovered from a car accident.

"I am so glad you're here," Destry said, hugging her. "I can't tell you how much I've missed you."

"Nothing ever happens around here and then I leave and all hell breaks loose," Lisa Anne complained. "It will give those women on the grapevine enough fodder to last till spring." Her gaze went to Carson, who was standing over by the door. "I'm going to have to go dance with your brother. He looks so alone over there."

Lisa Anne had always had a crush on Carson, dreaming that he'd come back one day, sweep her off her feet and they'd get married and have a bunch of kids who'd grow up with Destry's bunch of kids here in the shadow of the Crazies.

Destry had once dreamed the same thing, all of them getting together for Sunday barbecues, their children playing together in the creek just as they had as kids.

She shoved away the thought since it wasn't going to happen. Carson had made it perfectly clear this life wasn't for him. After WT's affairs were all wrapped up, she figured he'd pull up stakes and be gone any day.

But he was still here, she thought, as she watched Lisa Anne go over to him and strike up a conversation. A few moments later, she was dragging him out onto the dance floor as the band broke into a slow country song.

Bethany and Clete Reynolds joined them. Destry watched, glad to see they seemed to be working out their problems. And there was Hitch McCray doing his best to get one of the Hamilton girls to dance with him. His mother had gotten him out of jail and paid his fines. Some things never changed.

Destry's gaze settled on an older couple on the dance floor, and she had to smile as the sheriff twirled Nettie Benton around, both of them laughing.

Russell smiled at her from across the room. It was

good to talk to him, to learn about her mother from a man who had loved Lila and loved talking about her.

"I've been looking all over for you," Rylan said, coming up behind her. He nuzzled her neck as he looped his arms around her. "I think they're playing our song," he said, turning her to face him.

She looked into his eyes and felt that wonderful tug at her heartstrings. She loved this man, would always love him and couldn't wait to become his wife. There was nothing standing between them, and, as problems arose, which they were bound to, they would face them together. Their love for each other was the lasting kind.

She smiled at her future husband. "Wait a minute. We have a song?"

He laughed and, taking her hand, led her out on the dance floor. "We do now."

* * * * *

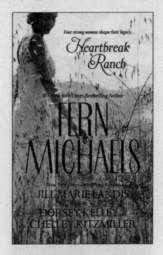

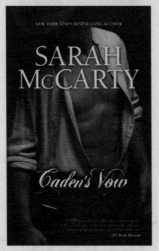

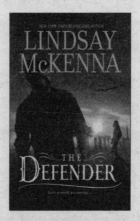

REQUEST YOUR
FREE BOOKS!

2 FREE NOVELS
FROM THE SUSPENSE COLLECTION
PLUS 2 FREE GIFTS!

YES! Please send me 2 FREE novels from the Suspense Collection and my 2 FREE gifts (gifts are worth about $10). After receiving them, if I don't wish to receive any more books, I can return the shipping statement marked "cancel." If I don't cancel, I will receive 4 brand-new novels every month and be billed just $5.99 per book in the U.S. or $6.49 per book in Canada. That's a saving of at least 25% off the cover price. It's quite a bargain! Shipping and handling is just 50¢ per book in the U.S. and 75¢ per book in Canada.* I understand that accepting the 2 free books and gifts places me under no obligation to buy anything. I can always return a shipment and cancel at any time. Even if I never buy another book, the two free books and gifts are mine to keep forever.

191/391 MDN FEME

Name _____ (PLEASE PRINT) _____

Address _____ Apt. # _____

City _____ State/Prov. _____ Zip/Postal Code _____

Signature (if under 18, a parent or guardian must sign)

Mail to the **Reader Service:**
IN U.S.A.: P.O. Box 1867, Buffalo, NY 14240-1867
IN CANADA: P.O. Box 609, Fort Erie, Ontario L2A 5X3

Not valid for current subscribers to the Suspense Collection
or the Romance/Suspense Collection.

Want to try two free books from another line?
Call 1-800-873-8635 or visit www.ReaderService.com.

* Terms and prices subject to change without notice. Prices do not include applicable taxes. Sales tax applicable in N.Y. Canadian residents will be charged applicable taxes. Offer not valid in Quebec. This offer is limited to one order per household. All orders subject to credit approval. Credit or debit balances in a customer's account(s) may be offset by any other outstanding balance owed by or to the customer. Please allow 4 to 6 weeks for delivery. Offer available while quantities last.

Your Privacy—The Reader Service is committed to protecting your privacy. Our Privacy Policy is available online at www.ReaderService.com or upon request from the Reader Service.

We make a portion of our mailing list available to reputable third parties that offer products we believe may interest you. If you prefer that we not exchange your name with third parties, or if you wish to clarify or modify your communication preferences, please visit us at www.ReaderService.com/consumerschoice or write to us at Reader Service Preference Service, P.O. Box 9062, Buffalo, NY 14269. Include your complete name and address.

SUS11

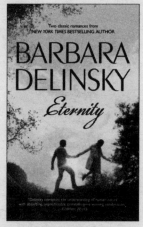

Two timeless stories of love and intrigue
from *New York Times* bestselling author

Catherine Anderson

endless
night

Available now!

www.Harlequin.com

A grand old English estate where no one cares
overmuch for propriety....

Top historical romance authors

CAROLE MORTIMER
and HELEN DICKSON

welcome you to Castonbury Park, where all's fair in love,
whether in the lord's drawing room or in the servants' quarters!

Scandalous

Pick up your copy today!